She wasn't sure what to do anymore, but she knew that sooner or later, she had to tell him the truth...

How Flynn wanted to have this man hold her close. "There's something I need to tell you."

Marshall's look was speculative as he waited for her to continue.

An innate caution stopped her confession. "Have you heard from Suzy since the last time she called?"

"No, I haven't." The muscle in his jaw clenched as anger lit his brown eyes, turning them obsidian. "I hope never to hear her voice again."

Any last doubts of him still loving her cousin were demolished by his expression and clenched fists. "What do you mean?"

"It's not important. What did you want to tell me? We got off track."

"Never mind. It will keep."

It definitely wasn't the time to confess her involvement. If she did and he told her to leave, she might never get to the bottom of Suzy's disappearance. The diary had become more than an annoying obsession now. It could be truly a matter of life and death.

Flynn Steven's cousin Suzy, once married to Marshall Beckett, reveals details of her awful marriage to a tyrant. She begs Flynn to see if the son she left behind is okay and locate her hidden diary, a "matter of life or death." Flynn is at a crossroads in her life where she can renew her contract as a world-traveling concert violinist or search for what she really longs for—a home, with a special person to love. She arrives at Marshall's horse ranch, Rainbow's End, under the pretense of answering his ad for a nanny. But Suzy had failed to tell Flynn that in the same ad he advertised for a wife. This rugged, coppery-haired rancher is burned out on love and wants a woman to bear him children, without investing any emotional commitments. When they decide a marriage of convenience is the only way to save Rainbow's End, sparks fly between them. But when he learns that she came under false pretenses, will he give her a chance to explain, or just send her packing?

KUDOS for *Romancing a Tasmanian Cowboy*

In *Romancing a Tasmanian Cowboy* by Pinkie Paranya, Flynn Stevens is convinced by her cousin, Suzi, to answer an ad for a nanny placed by Suzi's ex-husband Marshall Beckett and, while there, find a diary that Suzi left behind when she divorced him, one that could ruin her if it fell into her ex-husband's hands. But Flynn soon discovers that Marshall isn't the monster Suzi made him out to be, and Flynn's loyalties ae torn. Should she help her cousin or follow her heart that is falling for Marshall? Like most of Paranya's books, the story is heartwarming, fun, and suspenseful, weaving in lots of surprises. A great love story. ~ *Taylor Jones, The Review Team of Taylor Jones & Regan Murphy*

Romancing a Tasmanian Cowboy by Pinkie Paranya is set Down Under in Tasmania. Our heroine, Flynn Stevens, heads for Marshall Beckett's horse ranch, pretending to answer an ad for a nanny. But what she is really after is a diary that Marshall's ex-wife, Flynn's cousin Suzi, left behind when she divorced him. According to Suzi, Marshall was an abusive husband, and Suzi fears for her life if he finds the diary. But Flynn soon learns that Suzi has been less than truthful. Marshall is not a monster, just a lonely man, trying to raise his young son on his own. It doesn't take long before Flynn is head over heels for both of them. But what will Marshall do when he finds out why she is really there? *Romancing a Tasmanian Cowboy* is another jewel in the crown of this talented author. A heartbreaking, heartwarming love story, it will keep you entranced all the way through. ~ *Regan Murphy, The Review Team of Taylor Jones & Regan Murphy*

Romancing
a Tasmanian
Cowboy

Pinkie Paranya

A Black Opal Books Publication

GENRE: ROMANTIC SUSPENSE/WESTERN ROMANCE

This is a work of fiction. Names, places, characters and incidents are either the product of the author's imagination or are used fictitiously, and any resemblance to any actual persons, living or dead, businesses, organizations, events or locales is entirely coincidental. All trademarks, service marks, registered trademarks, and registered service marks are the property of their respective owners and are used herein for identification purposes only. The publisher does not have any control over or assume any responsibility for author or third-party websites or their contents.

Romancing a Tasmanian Cowboy

Chapter 1

Flynn needed to regain her life. Without her passport and money that was in her purse when it fell overboard on the ferry, she felt invisible. Coming from the mainland of Australia to the island of Tasmania should have been a breeze.

It was a relief to leave the ferry. Now, after getting off the bus, somewhere in the boondocks, she stopped on the little dirt road, set her backpack down for a rest, and breathed in the rain-promised air. She wore scruffy old jeans and walking boots bought at a surplus store in Melbourne, and now she deftly braided her hair into a long thick braid and removed her earrings. This was how she imagined a person a little down on her luck and looking for an adventure might dress. Who but an adventuress would answer an ad in the Melbourne paper for a job in Tasmania? When her cousin Suzy sent her the ad, she'd admitted it might be slightly old. But she assured Flynn that probably no one would stay and work for Marshall Beckett very long.

What had possessed her to leave her orderly life and charge off to champion her erratic cousin. A cousin who made the fantastic claim that she'd lost custody of her son and had left behind a diary that meant life or death to her.

So like Suzy to dramatize, but then Flynn fell for it.

She picked up the backpack again, catching a sound of pounding hooves that blended with a simultaneous crash of thunder, interrupting her daydreams. Before Flynn could connect the sound with the road beneath her feet, a huge black horse bore down on her. She stood frozen in terror, eyes closed tightly, unable to move as she waited for the impact.

A whoosh of air brushed past and the heavy smell of horse assaulted her. When she dared open her eyes, the dust had not yet settled. Someone held her in a tight grasp, high above the road and close to a warm hard body.

"Bloody hell, woman! What are you gawking at in the middle of the road?"

She took a deep breath. Raw anger replaced her fear. She'd been through enough for one day. "I don't take guff from some farmer with manure on his boots. Why don't you watch where you're going! You nearly ran me down. You don't own the road."

He let her down slowly, pulling her close against his body suggestively, as if to show his control.

She un-shouldered her backpack, letting it slide to the ground while she struggled to slow her heartbeat. Hands on hips, she glared up at the giant on horseback. He swung down from the saddle and faced her.

Flynn's impression was of lean strength. She was small, vertically challenged her mother used to say. He towered over her, his face in the shade of his hat. The man's shoulders were wide, his hips slim, and he moved with graceful agility. When he took his hat off, thumping it against his denim clad leg, his burnished-copper hair had streaks of sun-bleached lightness threaded through the crown.

His dark-brown eyes held a bold look of approval and admiration, mixed with indignation.

He glanced away across a field, plainly disconcerted by her glare. Seconds passed before he looked back at her. His eyes were wary. It was his mouth that caused her anger to dissolve into confusion. A sensual mouth, tilted at the edges for easy laughter. However, he was not laughing now.

Chapter 2

What the hell are you doing? Standing in the middle of the road, off with the fairies, isn't exactly bright, you know?"

Flynn was speechless. The man was blaming *her* for walking on the road! She shut her eyes in an attempt to gather her composure. That pause sometimes made her fellow musicians nervous. She had never been one to hold back her temper.

A smattering of raindrops added to her indignation. Tears of angry frustration welled up in her eyes. She raised her head impatiently to clear them away.

"I haven't the time to argue with you," she said. "It's starting to pour down rain."

A sprinkle of freckles across deeply tanned cheeks seemed to crinkle when he grinned. The oaf was laughing at her!

"'Tis a bit of a stretch, wouldn't you say? Of course if we stand here yabbering long enough, it could happen." He looked up at the sky. "I haven't seen you around these parts before. You're a yank, aren't you?"

She ignored his question. "I'm looking for a place with the absurd name of Rainbow's End and a man called Marshall Beckett. I suppose you know all about him.

Everyone else on this island seems to." When she'd lost her purse on the ferry, locals rushed to commiserate with her. She learned a lot about Marshall Beckett and his farm called Rainbow's End.

Silence stretched taut like a rubber band pulled tight.

Mirth again replaced the tight lines around his mouth. "Well, maybe I do know of the place. What do you want with him?"

He leaned back a little to look into her face—examining her as if she were a horse he was inspecting.

"It is none of your business. Are all Tasmanian cowboys so rude?" she countered.

Flynn knew she hadn't misjudged his look of undisguised admiration. The appraisal she saw in his brown eyes made her uncomfortable and yet stirred something deep inside her. She had learned from her mother to grasp and maintain control of situations, which he seemed determined to not allow.

"I 'spose you could call me a cowboy." He waved out toward the grazing cattle and horses in the meadow. "Although I doubt we're comparable to your wild west types."

"We don't have many of them left anymore, outside of movies and novels. But again, where is Rainbow's End? "

"It's not far from here." He waved his arm toward the pasture bordering the dirt road. "That's a part of it." He didn't offer more in the way of explanation.

Flynn sighed. "Do you work for Beckett?"

"Might say so," he said laconically.

The challenge in this man's eyes was more than she was up to meeting just now. "Point out the direction. I'd like to get there before the rain actually washes me off the road." The sprinkles did seem to come down a little thicker.

He swung a leg gracefully up over the saddle as he mounted. "There's room behind me. Sultan won't mind. I'll drop you off at the door." He reached down to take her hand.

She looked up at the enormous horse and then nervously sidestepped the tanned, muscled arm stretching toward her. Not for anything would she have subjected herself to riding on that horse. Just the thought of holding tight, bumping up and down against his broad back, wasn't her idea of a graceful entrance.

"Absolutely not!" She tilted her chin in the air. "I prefer to walk."

He looked surprised. "Why walk when you can ride?"

"I prefer not to arrive at my destination sitting behind someone like a sack of potatoes and smelling of horse."

"I'll not argue that. Though leaving you here alone goes against my gentlemanly instincts." He emphasized the last two words, making her wonder if he was still laughing at her or just being sarcastic. "You apparently know what you want. Follow the road as it twists around. Up there by that clump of eucalypts." He pointed ahead toward a steep rise in the road. "That will be Rainbow's End."

Humph. Rainbow's End, indeed.

He pointed up at the darkening sky. "I hope you get there before she lets loose."

When she didn't answer, he waved cheerfully, as he turned away, shouting "Cheerio" back at her. Instead of going up the road, he directed the horse over a fence and galloped off through the meadow.

Flynn took a deep breath. "Country clod!" She stuck her tongue out at his retreating back as she watched him ride away, and then laughed at herself.

Only when he disappeared behind a grove of trees

did she begin to walk up the road. She hoped he wasn't a close neighbor.

What has Suzy lured me into? There was no way her cousin could have fit into this provincial countryside. They had gradually lost touch after high school, when Flynn had gone on to train with the New York Symphony and begin her concert tours while Suzy went on her modeling gigs. Then one day Suzy had called, ecstatic with news of her marriage. Typical Suzy—last minute spontaneous decision with no time for wedding invitations. Had she not wanted anyone to meet her intended?

When Suzy's son was born, she sent Flynn a note. Timmy had been only a babe in arms when they finally met again. Suzy came to one of Flynn's concerts and they spent a few hours together afterwards. When Flynn had asked about her married life and husband, her cousin was uncharacteristically evasive.

Flynn understood this to mean she wasn't happy with her husband, and that was the last time they saw each other. Timmy should be about six now.

Feeling the breeze against her face brought her back to the present. The rain drifted down in fits and starts, pelting her with what felt like hard little balls and then letting up to an annoying drizzle. She pushed forward, her backpack pressing heavy on her shoulders. When she arrived at Rainbow's End, she wondered if she should tell Marshall Beckett about her lost possessions on the ferry ride. She had the letter from the ferry captain stating what had happened, but she preferred not to show it to him, especially if he was as uncompromising as Suzy claimed. It would be humiliating to give him the upper hand by letting him know she had nowhere else to go. However, there was always the risk he might not hire her without her first showing him Captain Dugan's letter.

She resisted the urge to call Dolores for help. Rivalry

between mother and daughter had always existed below the surface. Dolores was more of an older, fault-finding sister whom she could never please. Flynn wasn't even sure where her mother was right now. She could be anywhere.

Flynn brushed the tendrils of damp hair back from her face and felt a surge of relief when she saw the large grove of trees at the top of the road's incline.

A sense of urgency to see Suzy's son, to see how things were going with the boy, made her walk faster. *How could this Marshall Beckett get away with kicking Suzy out and taking the boy away from her, leaving her with nothing?*

At the top of the road she stopped. There stood the house Suzy's letters had described as the dreary prison she so despised.

It appeared to be an odd-shaped, rambling sort of two-story house, painted buttercup yellow and trimmed in apple green. Wild ferns, blooming hedges and a lush profusion of uncontrolled flower plots scattered here and there, like the graceful spreading of a full, colorful skirt. Toys littered the porch encircling the house.

Flynn was confused. From her cousin's description, she had expected to see forbidding gables and bars on the windows.

On the porch swing, sipping from a large, frosted glass in a leisurely manner, sat the man she had met on the road.

Damn! She wanted to shout and shake clenched fists up at the sky, but instead she approached the porch and set her backpack down against the step. Squaring her shoulders, she lifted her head to stare directly at him. Waiting for him to speak first.

"Did you enjoy your walk?" He smiled pleasantly.

She smiled sweetly back. It crossed her mind that her

face might suffer permanent damage with the strain.

"Oh, to be sure. A really delightful walk, although I am a bit soaked. Did you enjoy our conversation on the road where you nearly ran me over?"

Looking at his face, she felt drawn by the hint of laughter on his lips. In spite of the humor, there was something secretive in the depths of those dark eyes, something that warmed her and yet at the same time made her uneasy. The copper glints in his hair matched the hair on his arms, revealed by rolled-up sleeves. A matching curly nest of hair showed just above the open-collared shirt.

He had an air of authority—an assurance bordering on arrogance. His eyes watched her with the stealth of a hawk searching for a rabbit.

What kind of a mess would this turn out to be? She had nowhere to turn for help. Common sense rushed to her rescue. *I had better cool it until I replace my belongings. And there is still Timmy to check on and the diary to look for.*

He rose from his position on the swing. His easy grace seemed calculated. "Let me introduce myself. I'm Marshall Beckett." He reached down to give her a hand up the stairs. "The farmer with manure on my boots."

Marshall Beckett? She flushed at his jibe, ignoring the proffered hand as she fought to retain her composure, while at the same time furiously trying to think what her next move should be.

"Is this part of your farm? The bus driver said it was at least a mile to your house." She forced herself to look up into his ruggedly handsome face again and somehow her smile became real. Nothing Suzy had said about this man had prepared her for meeting him. Belatedly, she wondered why Suzy had never sent pictures.

She couldn't have gotten off to a worse start. This

could work to her advantage, posing as an adventuress. *Dumb idea. Why would an adventuress take a job as a nanny? For the lark of it? The most likely scenario was to earn a bit of money to continue traveling.*

"I'd like—I'd like to discuss some business with you." She despised the hesitation in her voice. The clouds settled, lower and darker. Thunder rolled across the sky and out of the corner of her eye she saw lightning strike into the fields.

"Business?" Once again his eyes crinkled at the corners. It was becoming an infuriating habit. She wasn't here for his amusement.

How could Suzy have put up with this unmannerly, arrogant man for even a few years? It was easy to see how she might have been attracted at first. Impetuous, restless Suzy was a magnet for macho men. Flynn usually attracted the more cerebral types.

Had she imagined that fleeting, wary look in his eyes? Suzy never could abide enigmas. So far, Flynn had mentally listed numerous reasons why Suzy might have succumbed to this man's magnetism and then not have wanted to stay with him. And yet...there was something compelling about his smile. Was that hiding something, too? This was not going to be easy.

Chapter 3

Marshall Beckett reached for her backpack where she'd left it on the steps and set it down on the porch, out of the rain. "Pretty heavy for a slip of a girl," he commented, opening the screen door for her.

Flynn bristled at his use of the word *girl*. She suppressed her retort—somehow the word didn't seem inappropriate, coming from him. Maybe Tasmanians regarded feminism differently.

A woman who looked to be in her seventies stood barring the way. She was ribbon-thin, with a frown that creased her severe expression. Curiously, her pale blue eyes held kindness.

"Hoppy, let me introduce Miss..." Marshall raised a questioning eyebrow.

Flynn hesitated, wondering if Suzy had ever mentioned her. It could get complicated, using another name. "Flynn Stevens," she said truthfully.

"Mrs. Hopkins, Miss Flynn Stevens."

"I'm pleased to meet you, Mrs. Hopkins."

"No need to be. I'm only the housekeeper," the older woman said stiffly, ignoring Flynn's proffered hand.

"Don't be taken in by that note of virtuous humility."

Marshall put his arm around the housekeeper's shoulder. "She jolly well runs the place, and us along with it."

Mrs. Hopkins' face softened at his teasing but her countenance stayed disapproving. *Why? Didn't they ever get visitors here at Rainbow's End?*

"Be a dear and bring some cider into the library, Hoppy. The young lady looks frazzled."

Oh boy, just the description a woman wants to hear about herself. It took Flynn by surprise and she turned away to hide her smile.

The moment Flynn stepped into the library, an eerie feeling of coming home washed over her. She stopped in her tracks, bewildered. Once again she found herself struggling to regain her composure as she looked at the high ceiling and spacious shelves, a rich mahogany polished to a mirror finish. Shelves of books, along with leather couches and large chairs filled the room. The roll top desk across one corner had to be an antique, but held a computer and printer on one side. At the sound of a throat being cleared, she turned to face her cousin's nemesis.

"So, you made it on your own before the rain caught you." His eyes were alight with amusement.

Almost, with no thanks to you. She plucked a tissue from a box on the desk and wiped her face with exaggerated care. She was barely wet. In all fairness, it was she who had insisted on walking rather than ride behind him. The thought of clinging for dear life to this man, bouncing up and down on a horse's rear end while leaping over fences, made her want to smile.

Had she always been so conscious of her dignity? Her mother was, but she hadn't imagined it to be true for herself. Patterning her personality after her mother was not a pleasant thought.

"Would you mind if I sat down?" Light sarcasm tinged her words.

Marshall had the grace to look embarrassed for a moment. "Of course." He motioned toward a comfortable-looking leather chair that appeared big enough to eat her alive.

Flynn chose another, hard-backed and very uncomfortable, just to be contrary.

Marshall's mouth twitched slightly at the corners. "You must be dry and dusty after your little walk."

"Not really. The rain took care of that. I'm just slightly frazzled as you so courteously pointed out to your housekeeper."

He grinned at her, his expression not the least apologetic. Marshall's cinnamon hair, crisply curled on top, was cut shorter in the back than she was used to seeing. Male musicians in the orchestra fancied long hair, pulled back in a ponytail or tied with string at the nape of their necks.

She couldn't imagine Beckett with hair like that or wearing an earring, either.

Sitting was a mistake. He appeared twenty feet tall when he stood close to her chair. Her heart beat faster and she hoped it didn't show in her throat at the opening of her shirt.

Her mind raced, thinking of possibilities. Of course he would want references—if she asked for the position of nanny. She hadn't any to offer him, even if her purse hadn't fallen overboard.

"I—I came in answer to your ad in the Melbourne paper." The half-truth did not come easy with his steady gaze appraising her, but she had to get on with it if she wanted to stay long enough to see Timmy.

"My ad?" He looked skeptical. "It's been a while since I ran that ad, and I definitely regret doing it in the first place. You're not Australian—how would you know about it?"

It was easier to answer with a bigger kernel of truth this time. "I was traveling through and someone in Melbourne told me about it. I'd always wanted to visit Tasmania and was at a loose end." She turned up her palms. "So here I am."

His eyes were thoughtful.

"Loose end, eh? Well, at least that's an original approach. None of the other applicants used it."

"Yes, well, I realize the ad was an old one, but perhaps the position has been hard to fill?" *More like impossible to fill, with your attitude.*

Flynn looked around for pictures. She and Suzy hadn't had many taken together. By the time they were teenagers, she would have been an idiot to let herself be photographed next to Suzy. While other girls, including herself, went through awkward adolescence with the usual skin problems and uncontrollable hair, Suzy had always looked gorgeous.

Just then the housekeeper intruded by plunking an icy drink on the desk, and then left as quickly as she'd arrived, her slim body bristling with disapproval.

Marshall grinned. "Hoppy can be a dragon at times, but she's more a part of Rainbow's End than I am. She was here from the first, taking care of the three of us." Flynn liked the softened look that came into his expression when he spoke of the elderly woman.

"Three of you?"

He motioned for her to pour the tea. "My younger brother, me and the old man."

Flynn waited for him to continue. Suzy had mentioned Marshall's mother had died of a fever when he was very young, right after his younger brother Damon's birth.

"I've interviewed a mob of women for the position and I'm jack of it. Young, old, interesting and dull—none of them worked out."

Could it be you're probably impossible to please? Relieved those words hadn't slipped out, she smiled.

"Maybe you didn't give them a chance. Sometimes it takes a while to fit into a strange place."

It was as far as she dared go. No need to antagonize him.

She wasn't used to biting her tongue. Her reputation for saying just what she thought when she wanted was something she was proud of. It was a type of artistic freedom to show temperament. Her mother had instilled that into her as soon as she spoke her first words.

When Marshall sat down behind the oak desk, she felt more at ease.

"Flynn. Odd name. It suits you."

This wasn't the time to explain how her mother, impatient to be through with the untidiness of giving birth, chose the last name of the doctor taking care of her.

"Funny, you don't look the sort to answer that ad, or go traipsing all over the country alone. However, I still need someone to watch my son," he admitted. "Hoppy's getting too old for that sort of thing."

"There's nothing mysterious about me. I was traveling around and ran short of funds. When someone told me about your ad, I thought why not?"

One dark eyebrow curved upward, his eyes narrowed in speculation. "Do you have a working visa?"

She shook her head, still reluctant to tell him about her lost purse. It was easy to imagine what he'd think about that bit of carelessness.

"No. I was in Europe already and applied for an ETA, an electronic travel authority."

"We can go over that later. You look like a kid play-

ing dress-up. You can't seriously tell me you're comfortable in that getup?"

He came uncomfortably close to the truth. She
wasn't the blue jeans type at all. This pair was the first
she'd ever owned.

"If you're referring to my size—I wasn't aware you
also needed a groundskeeper or stable hand."

He frowned. In several long strides he was at her
side, lifting her out of the chair by her elbows. He took
her hands in his and turned her palms upward, moving a
hard finger gently over her skin. The contact warmed her
palm and made it hard to breathe. Intermingled smells of
horse, hay and aftershave assailed her nostrils.

Could he hear her heart pounding? How absurd that a
stranger could make her tingle in every part of her body
by stroking her palm with one finger. The strange warmth
was no doubt indignation at his effrontery. She knew she
probably should jerk her hands away, but curiosity won
out. What was he up to?

"Mmm…" He sounded puzzled. "Your hands are
somewhat as I expected. You've seldom washed a dish in
your life, have you? Yet you have calluses on the tips of
your fingers of your left hand."

She pulled her hands out of his grip and moved away
from him. Did he recognize the calluses of a musician?
At some point Suzy might have offhandedly mentioned
her professional violinist cousin. He could put two and
two together and toss her out on the spot.

"I play guitar once in a while. Do you wish to examine my teeth also?"

He laughed. "No, I don't think so. You're a Yank.
With that black hair, I guess you're part Mick."

"Mick?"

"Irish."

She nodded. "My father."

He shook his head. "I have to admit you are a spunky looking sheila. I am assuming you have no references or you would have presented them by now."

She blushed at his compliment. He probably didn't realize she understood his meaning, knowing spunky meant sexy or good looking. "Not really. I've worked various jobs since leaving school." She needed to take the offensive and get away from his mention of references. The glint of amusement in his eyes did nothing to soothe her.

"Merely an observation," he said dryly. "Timothy is a puzzling little boy. He can be quite a handful. You look young for this responsibility,"

"I'm old enough, in the remote possibility that age has anything to do with my being here." She cautioned herself belatedly. *Temper, temper.*

They stood toe to toe, and though she had to lean back to look at him, she gave him glare for glare. This job was necessary, even if Timmy weren't involved. She had no option but to stay long enough to get her passport replaced and wire the bank for money.

Besides, Suzy swore they would meet soon, one Tuesday afternoon in the village churchyard. Flynn had to stay here at least a couple of Tuesdays to see if her cousin showed up.

Marshall ran his hand through his thick crop of hair. "Well, you might do. If we can get along."

Hah! Fat chance. Poor Suzy, how did she tolerate this condescending, dominating man?

"I've yet to decide whether to send Timothy to boarding school on the mainland. It might be the best place for my son. Make a man out of him."

"That seems a shame. He's a little boy. How can you make a man out of a little boy?"

"Our ideas here may be a little old-fashioned and

outdated by your standards. We still demand that our off-spring behave like human beings."

"You mean miniature adults?"

"Timothy is beyond that. I don't know if he's six-going-on-twenty or it's just me." He looked down at his hands. "I wanted—want us to be a family, but we don't get on."

"Do you love him?" That was totally inappropriate of her. She saw him flinch and the stark pain in his eyes.

"Love him? He's my life! He's the future for Rainbow's End."

She felt awkward witnessing his sudden struggle for self-control.

"I suspect it's part my fault. The old man was a strict disciplinarian. He raised my brother and me without our mum, and I figure I didn't turn out too badly. It's the only way I know."

"Does Timmy have a mother?"

Marshall's eyes narrowed and he held up a hand toward her. "I do not have a wife, and Timothy does not have a mother. We do not speak of her."

So why did you kick Suzy out, if Timmy needed a mother? Giving voice to that question would likely end the conversation immediately, and she'd be walking down the road again.

"Every child is different,." Flynn conceded. Suzy's parents had died in a car accident when her cousin was only five. She had flourished under her aunt's courteous disregard, but Flynn had always felt deprived, more like an orphan than Suzy.

She reached into her backpack and retrieved the letter from the ferry captain. It went against her grain to let this man see the consequences of her carelessness on board ship, but as a father, his protective attitude was understandable.

Marshall sat behind the desk and spread the folded paper out to read.

It was easy to see why Suzy might have been captivated by Marshall Beckett. Damp hair curled on the back of his neck, a neck bronzed by the sun. She hastily pushed that thought aside, feeling particularly vulnerable, separated from her normal routine and the people she knew on a daily basis. She had to keep her perspective, for Timmy and for Suzy.

"Ah, I'm acquainted with Captain Dugan." He gave her a speculative look, as if he guessed her thoughts.

She waited for his ridicule. It was almost anticlimactic when he handed back the letter. "I doubt you would want to venture out without your passport and money," he commented.

He had her there.

The silence stretched between them. Never before had any man regarded her in such a bold, appraising way. Was he going to tell her to leave?

"I pride myself on judging character. I'm sure you'll do fine." His manner was carefully polite. As if he needed to keep a proper distance between them.

"Although you do look about fifteen." He leaned back in his chair. "Do you always travel in foreign countries so…so informally?"

She flushed, but refrained from saying anything.

"Ah, but you are an American." Marshall pushed back the chair and strode to the doorway, calling out for the housekeeper.

Flynn tried not to watch, but found it impossible to stop staring at the way his wide shoulders moved, the graceful slope of his back and his slightly bowlegged stance. It was as if the world belonged to him and him alone. Very disconcerting.

"Hoppy, please show Miss Stevens upstairs to the room next to Timothy's."

The woman glared at Flynn, her mouth set tight, and she turned on her heel without a word.

Flynn followed her, feeling Marshall's eyes on her backside just as she'd watched his only moments before.

The stairway was free hanging, a graceful swoop that turned and circled to a landing at the top. She liked what she saw as she entered the bedroom. Had Suzy had a hand in the decorating? It definitely wasn't her cousin's style, but maybe she had changed.

The housekeeper's grim expression softened in the face of Flynn's obvious delight.

"It's one of the nicest rooms in the house, miss. Full of sunlight in the mornings, with the smell of heather coming in through the windows."

Pale blue walls reflected the subdued sunshine that sifted through white organdy curtains. The furniture was white wicker, the bed covered with a blue-and-white crocheted spread. The room lifted Flynn's spirits. Maybe things might work out.

She could stay here long enough to see if Timmy was okay, look for the diary Suzy insisted was so important to find, and contact a bank for money and identification so she could apply for another passport. How long would that take? She had some vacation time coming anyway. She'd never bothered to take any time off in all the years she worked with the orchestra.

So many decisions. She still had to decide if she wanted to renew her contract for the next five years. If she did, that would push her over the edge of thirty. Her successful career didn't seem quite so bright and shiny lately. She needed a rest.

Yet the tingle when he looked at her with those dark, appraising eyes, the touch of his hands when he held hers and opened her palms, told her living in the same house with Marshall Beckett would be anything but restful.

Chapter 4

"You and Timmy will have to share a bathroom, but the connecting doors lock from either side. The little nipper is a quiet one, he is." The housekeeper's brisk speech broke the silence.

Flynn tried to lighten the tension in the room by asking, "Do you not call it a loo?"

"Gracious no. That is a slang word and we prefer Timmy not use them."

"I stand corrected. So much for my Australian dictionary."

That got a chuckle out of the housekeeper.

"You've been here a long time."

Mrs. Hopkins folded her thin arms across her chest. "I came here as a housekeeper for the first Mr. Beckett. Mrs. Beckett seemed to be always ailing. No one expected her to have children, let alone two sons. Mr. Beckett asked me to stay when the missus passed on after Mr. Damon's birth."

"Damon? That's Marshall's brother?" She didn't want them to suspect how much she already knew. Mrs. Hopkins' lips tightened in disapproval. "You are an employee, Miss Stevens. You are not to refer to them by their first names until they give you leave. Although the

Becketts have always been informal about the division with their help, However, I don't presume, and neither should you."

A warm flush crept up Flynn's neck and she felt properly chastised.

"The brothers have never been close. When Mr. Damon moved to the next farm, he wanted me to go with him. I'm partial to Rainbow's End. 'Tis my home and will be till I die. I couldn't leave."

Mrs. Hopkins' attitude about her future made Flynn uneasy. Did she want to know that far ahead about her own future? The idea was at once beguiling and intimidating.

"Since I raised the boys, you might say I'm allowed certain privileges," Mrs. Hopkins continued. "One privilege is I always speak my mind."

So do I. She waited politely for Mrs. Hopkins to say what was on her mind, biting on the inside of her lip at her unaccustomed restraint.

"I don't hold with sheilas traipsing all over God's green earth, alone and dressed in daks like—like some ragamuffin." She sniffed, twitching her long, narrow nose. She took a deep breath and continued. "I also don't approve of them answering such rubbish as that ad of Mr. Beckett's. I warned him about it. It's brought nothing but trouble."

Flynn looked down at her scuffed boots. On one hand, she didn't blame Mrs. Hopkins for looking askance at a strange woman popping into her life, but on the other, she was not used to being treated in such a condescending manner.

"Then Timothy doesn't need a nanny?" she asked quietly.

Mrs. Hopkins hesitated. "Yes. He does. I do what I can, but timid as he is, the little mite's still too much for me. It isn't fair to him, either. He needs someone closer to his age, to treat him like a little boy."

"And his father doesn't?"

The elder woman frowned. "He loves Timmy. He just doesn't know what to do with him. I'm worried he'll send the lad away. T'would be a disaster for both of them."

"Well then, what would it hurt if I give it a try? I promise to do my best."

A guilty twinge of conscience stabbed her. She wasn't going to stay long enough to do any good at all, even if she could have managed it.

The housekeeper gave her a long, searching look. "One so-called nanny knew about computers. Mr. Beckett has one in the library. She set up lessons for Timothy and they work fairly well, but I am often busy with running the house and don't care for the silly things anyway."

"I know a little of computers so I should be able to pick up the slack on that and help with Timmy's lessons," Flynn offered.

Seemingly satisfied by what she saw in Flynn's expression, Mrs. Hopkins sighed. "He's been so lost without—" She didn't finish the sentence.

Beckett already informed her they didn't allow Suzy's name to be mentioned.

How could Suzy have been taken in by such an insufferable man? Never mind Marshall Beckett's looks, what did he have inside for blood, ice water?

"When can I see Timmy?"

Mrs. Hopkins' mouth actually arranged itself in a smile. "At dinner. Promptly at six."

"Thanks."

"We don't dress for dinner, but…"

"I understand," Flynn said, "I do have a few dresses." She spoke to the ramrod-stiff back as the housekeeper left the room.

She dropped her knapsack on the bathroom floor and locked both doors. What she needed more than anything else right now was a long soak in a tub and a shampoo. She turned the water on and let it run.

What exactly was a nanny supposed to do? Her mother had hired many during their childhood, but it was hard to remember what they did. They were there, that's all. The only nanny who came to mind was the one in *The Sound of Music*, and Flynn was damned if she wanted eight or nine kids clinging to her skirt as they ran up and down the mountains, singing at the tops of their voices. She laughed out loud at the image.

After she crawled out of her clothing, she eased herself down into the steaming water and raised her foot to look at the blister on her heel, gained from wearing the rough boots. Surplus military footwear was not at all like the soft, velvety-suede high tops she usually wore. It had been Suzy's crazy idea to dress according to someone a trifle down on her luck and on an adventure.

Before she turned into a prune, she climbed out of the tub and dried herself on a thick towel. She looked critically at her mirrored image as she turned sideways. *Not too shabby for almost thirty.*

The first thing she had noticed, once Mrs. Hopkins left the bedroom, was that there was no lock on the bedroom door. So she dressed in the bathroom, fishing through the backpack to retrieve a pair of walking shorts and a sleeveless blouse.

Once dressed, she unlocked the adjoining bathroom door and emptied the contents of the backpack onto the center of the bed. The first object that caught her eye was the photo of the three of them, herself with Suzy and her son. So much time had gone by since then. If Marshall

Beckett ever laid eyes on this picture, he'd kick her out
without a moment's hesitation.

*How could a father keep a son away from his moth-
er?* Flynn held the picture for a moment. Why had Suzy
never invited her to visit? It was a bit late to think about
that now. She was tempted to tear up the photo and hide
the pieces until she could throw them away.

But she hated to do that. It was the only picture she
had of Suzy. She buried the picture way down inside her
backpack.

Flynn lay down on the bed to rest. It seemed only
minutes until she awoke to glance at the clock on the
dresser, alarmed that the time had passed so quickly.
Leaping up, she rummaged through her pack to drag out a
fairly serviceable dress. She'd brought two dresses, a pale
yellow and the green. She hadn't planned on staying
long.

One glance at the pull-down ironing board in the
closet and she decided against trying it. She'd never
ironed a piece of clothing in her life and now wasn't the
time to start.

She brushed her long hair until it gleamed and gathered it at the nape of her neck. With accustomed ease, she
twisted a strand as thick as a finger around the bulk of it,
fastening it with several hairpins underneath. The shorter
hair on each side of her cheeks escaped and curled forward with the humidity and heat.

Don't they know about air conditioning here?

Voices filtered upward as she made her way down
the stairway to the dining room. Marshall broke off
speaking to Mrs. Hopkins when he looked up at Flynn,
his look approving as his gaze swept over her. He nodded
a greeting and moved to the table to hold out a chair for
her.

"Where's your son?" she said when they were seated.

He shrugged. "I usually eat in the library while Timothy eats with Hoppy. Tonight I told him as a special treat we would eat together in the big room, like a proper family. He's probably off with the fairies somewhere and has forgotten all about it."

"I'll go fetch him," Mrs. Hopkins offered before bustling off.

"You look—charming." It was clear he was unused to making small talk or offering compliments.

"Thank you." *So do you.* Flynn had a most consuming urge to flirt with him, something she'd rarely done in her life. Yet the thought of Suzy was a continual refrain running through every place in the house and touching everyone.

When she looked across the polished table at Marshall, she understood the instant fascination that must have flared up between him and Suzy. In spite of the obvious physical attraction, she couldn't begin to imagine her volatile cousin coexisting, even for a few years, with the forceful personality of Marshall Beckett.

"Mind telling me why you're inspecting me, Miss Stevens?" He sipped the chilled wine, regarding her over the rim of his glass.

"Sorry. I hadn't realized I was staring. I'm a great woolgatherer."

"You've come to the right place then. We've plenty of sheep around here."

She looked startled for a moment and then laughed. Aussie humor—dry and literal.

"You've quite a place here. I never expected to find anything so elaborate. When I imagine an apple orchard I think of a farm, and this goes beyond that idea."

He grinned. "I agree. Rainbow's End is special. Do you like horses?"

She tilted her chin. Was she supposed to? Was that in a nanny's résumé? She decided to stay as close to honesty as possible. The network of truth-stretching she had begun made her uneasy. No need to add more to it when it wasn't absolutely necessary. She wouldn't have wanted to chance her hands, even wearing gloves, with handling anything like a horse's reins. Accidents happened.

"I like horses, but only from a distance," she answered. "The horses I saw in the meadow are beautiful, but I'm city bred and never even owned a cat."

"At least you're honest. Some of the other nannies weren't quite so forthright. Maybe I can teach you to ride—if you stay long enough. You can add another page to your education."

Flynn felt uneasy at the direction his conversation was headed. She didn't want to dig herself in too deep with fabrications. She would leave as soon as she could.

"It must be interesting, being on the road so much, traveling here and there, willy-nilly. Do you have a family, rellies who worry about you. You're welcome to use the phone. Call anywhere you like."

"Thanks, that's very kind of you." She didn't much care for his subtle probing, but he did have the right. She was, for all intentions, becoming a part of his household. "My father passed away several years ago, but we weren't close. He left when I was a child. My mother and I lead separate lives, both going our own way. No one needs to worry about me. I'm an adult."

"I keep forgetting that. You look fresh out of school."

At any other time she would have accepted those words graciously, as a compliment. Somehow, coming from him, they sounded patronizing.

"Has Tasmania always been your home?" She switched the subject over to him, a tactic that usually worked with her fellow musicians whenever the conversation turned personal.

Marshall shook his head. "I was born here, but I've lived and worked all over Oz, and a lot of other places to boot. Done everything from mining to hunting 'roos in the outback. When my old man was dying, he called me home, and I've been here since."

There was that complacent certainty of place again. Was everyone here rooted to the earth like trees? Didn't he miss traveling?

Mrs. Hopkins came into the room with the boy in tow.

Flynn felt the tension crackle between father and son. Timmy was small and slender, with a shock of hair the color of soft butter hanging across his forehead. Like Suzy's.

The laughing baby in the photo she'd brought with her was gone. In its place was a drawn, tight little face with his father's remote brown eyes staring back at her.

"This is Miss Flynn Stevens, Timothy. She'll be taking care of you."

"Don't need taking care of," the boy muttered, a whispery sound as he stuttered over the words.

"I have to go to Hobart and Melbourne sometimes." Marshall's voice was coaxing with a streak of iron beneath it that said the boy wasn't to argue.

"Is Hoppy leaving?" Timmy's chin took a defiant tilt as he stared into his father's face.

" Hoppy isn't going anywhere. She has other duties, she can't be running after you all day. You do need someone to take care of you and help you with your lessons."

Flynn frowned. Marshall could have explained that

Mrs. Hopkins was elderly and couldn't run after Timmy anymore, which was true. The way he explained it was hurtful, as if his son wasn't worth running after.

A frustrated look came over Marshall's expression and Flynn sensed the conversation wasn't going the way he'd intended.

Timmy put his hands on either side of his hips and glared at his father. "You want to send both of us away, don't you?"

Marshall's brows crashed together and his lips tightened. Flynn waited for the explosion, bearing out Suzy's complaint about his terrible temper.

"Son, that's not true."

Marshall's voice didn't sound convincing, even to Flynn.

"Timmy, do you like to go for walks?" Flynn interjected, to give the boy breathing space. "We could do that. Or ride? I could learn so we could ride together." She would be careful with her hands.

Marshall snorted. "He's afraid of horses."

It looked like he was about to add something but stopped short. *What was he going to say?* Afraid like his mother?

Of course Suzy would probably have feared falling off a horse. She had always been paranoid about harming her body, including damage to a fingernail. How did this man talk her into having a child?

"That's okay. I'm afraid of horses, too. Knowing my luck, I'd probably get on the wrong way and wind up facing his tail, but I'm willing to learn."

Timmy hid a giggle behind his hand and pulled a heavy chair up to sit down in front of the food he looked at with distaste.

Silence stretched interminably. Only the loud, hollow, tick-tock of the grandfather clock intruded. Flynn looked up from her plate to catch Marshall's eyes, narrowed with speculation.

"Where are some of the places you've traveled, Miss Stevens?" The husky timbre of his voice broke into the quiet.

Both Flynn and Timmy flinched. She was pleased to see the tiniest of smiles tug at the corners of the boy's mouth as he noticed her start.

"Oh, heavens. I've been to a lot of places." She kept her approach airy and light, like she imagined a world-traveled adventurer would sound. For once she didn't have to lie as she began ticking the European countries off her fingers. She'd performed in all those places.

"My, that's impressive." He didn't sound impressed at all.

She tightened her self-control to keep from being childishly defensive.

" Have you been to America?" she asked.

"No. Don't want to travel anymore. Had enough."

He seemed to be holding back a smile. "Might I inquire how you usually travel? Bus? Plane? Hitchhiking?"

She waved a hand breezily as if it weren't important. "There are lots of ways to get about. I wound up here, didn't I?" To her own ears, she sounded flippant, her words brash, hopefully fitting the personality she was trying to create on the spot.

Was she overdoing it? Judging from the thoughtful look in his eyes, he didn't seem convinced about something.

"You say you saw my ad in the Melbourne paper?"

"No, I didn't say that," she corrected him. "I said someone told me about it. She wasn't sure of the exact wording, but something caused her to remember the name of your farm and that it was in Tasmania."

Damn Suzy, why didn't she warn me the ad was old

and outdated? Because her cousin could overlook any obstacle when she needed help.

"How long did you stay in Australia?"

"I was only in Melbourne a short time. I wanted to take a trip out to the Barrier Reef and then back to the States."

"I know—knew someone in Melbourne," Timmy stammered.

Marshall scowled. "You haven't had a bite of your dinner, young man. No wonder you're so thin. Eating bread and jam isn't enough for a growing boy."

The first time the boy ventured to speak during the entire meal and his father cut him off at the knees. Flynn looked toward Mrs. Hopkins, but the older woman seemed to take no offense at Marshall's heavy-handed treatment of his son. The housekeeper probably brought the boy cookies and milk later in the evening to make up for it.

"May I be excused, sir?" Timothy asked.

His father glared at the barely touched plate. "Go ahead."

"I'll go up with you," Flynn offered. "I can start my duties now." She rose hastily, nearly upsetting her chair.

She caught a puzzling look of regret in Marshall's expression when he watched his son leave the room. It was as if he wanted to get through to the boy, but didn't know how. Any fool could see he was going about it all wrong.

"Hoppy can go up with him. You don't have to begin work on your first day here."

The vulnerable look had disappeared from his eyes, only to be replaced by a sardonic twist to his lips. He must have sensed she didn't want to be alone with him. His eyes raked over her boldly as she stood next to her chair. His look sent shivers through her body so that she turned away to hide her discomfort.

Flynn followed Mrs. Hopkins and the boy upstairs, too weary to invent any more layers to the new Flynn she was building.

If it was true her life had always been easy, as her mother was fond of pointing out, this would be a good test of her mettle. She wasn't leaving until she found the diary and discovered what had happened between Marshall and Suzy. Somehow there had to be a way to fix the void between Timmy and Marshall. *If* she stayed that long.

Chapter 5

Flynn woke early, eager to see Rainbow's End without filtering her first impressions through Suzy's eyes. One of the few things Dolores taught her that had stuck was the importance of forming her own opinions. Everyone seemed to be still asleep when she opened the front door and closed it quietly behind her.

Morning smells filled her. She stood for a moment looking out over the garden, inhaling deep, reveling in the humid heaviness of dew-laden vegetation. She stopped in her tracks, seeing Beckett seated on a bench just outside the white lattice gazebo. She felt like an intruder spying.

Bent over, elbows on his thighs, he rubbed his fingers and thumb across the bridge of his nose in a gesture of weariness that tugged at her heart. Remembering Suzy, she quickly pushed the feeling away. She was here for her.

Just as Flynn started to leave, he must have sensed her presence. She felt his eyes upon her and turned back to face him. The vulnerability of his posture was gone in an instant, replaced by cool composure.

"Come, sit. Please. I thought I was the only early riser."

She sat at the other end of the bench, ignoring his amused smile. "Sometimes I like to get up early, some days I sleep in."

His gaze lingered on her hands lying in her lap and she could feel the calluses on the end of each finger.

"You're not married."

It was a flat statement which she didn't answer, only held up her hand to display fingers devoid of rings.

"What did you say you did for a living?"

"I don't recall saying. I'm sort of into music—"

"Oh, one of those groupies who follow rock bands around?" He looked unconvinced.

His skepticism riled her as much as his quick leaps to conclusions. "You got it. Only most of us zero in on one particular band. It's a fallacy that we follow any old band that comes along." *Now where did she pick up that gem?*

He seemed to swallow the fib. "To each his own."

"You mean it's not a very productive life?"

"I'm not one to judge. 'If at the end of your life you can say you've 'ad a good go at it, you're bloody lucky,' my old man used to say."

"He sounds very interesting."

Marshall snorted. "He was a tyrant, plain and simple. I couldn't wait to get away. Poor Damon, he stayed on, boot licking to the end."

"Damon? Mrs. Hopkins mentioned something about a brother living nearby."

He kicked his boot against the edge of a slightly tilted rock on the walkway. "Damon's four years younger than me. I hate it that he and I are at odds now. He's always been decent and helped the old man a lot while I was roaming around."

"Why are you at odds?"

Marshall studied her, speculation in his eyes. "I'm not used to talking about the rellies to strangers. But then again, you aren't going to be a stranger, are you? You sure are a good listener."

She smiled despite her effort not to. The spare compliment oddly warmed her.

"Damon was so certain he would inherit Rainbow's End. I was sure he would, too. But dad lived by the old school rule of the older son inheriting. In the end he gave it to me."

"That must have gone hard with your brother, to stand by and see you get what he thought he had coming."

"I'm sure it did. But I'd like to think the old man had other reasons to want me here. He knew this place was going downhill without new resources and the energy to make it work. Damon never had much push to make changes and didn't have a brass razoo to his name. He got dad's money, I got the land."

"That seems hard, but fair."

"If I hadn't had enough savings to add breeding stock and a new variety of apple trees, I couldn't have made it work. Dad never saved that much, the way things stood."

"Where is Damon now?" Flynn asked as innocently as she could manage.

"He bought the farm next door. It's a good place. He still isn't over it, though. Hates me guts."

To have something you thought was yours taken away—it was understandable his brother would hate him. But had Damon coveted Suzy, not so much for Suzy herself but as a form of revenge against Marshall? Is this what ended the marriage?

"Speaking of dislike, you don't care much for me, do you?" Marshall asked with a wry smile.

His abrupt change of subject jarred her for a moment, surprising an uncensored response.

"No. Not much." What caused the momentary flutter of her pulse when he stared at her so intently? Why was it hard to catch her breath when she looked at his shapely, sun-bronzed hands and imagined—*Stop it!* She almost said the words out loud to still her wayward thoughts.

Marshall regarded her, a hint of intimacy in his probing gaze. "I won't ask why you formed such a negative opinion on such a short acquaintance. That's your business. But I guess it might have something to do with me almost running you over on the road."

"That would be logical."

"You're a baffling person, Flynn Stevens. I can't believe you're who you pretend to be."

She shifted uncomfortably on the wooden bench. Something about being so near to this man, talking to him on such a close, intimate basis, stirred her senses in a way she hadn't known was possible. It was uncomfortable that he could get so close to the truth.

"What makes me so mysterious? Is it because I refuse to fall under your charm? Mrs. Hopkins says you have all the daughters of the local farmers swooning over you."

He laughed, a good, spirited sound that came from his chest. "Hoppy's a dear old girl. But there aren't any cockie's daughters around. That's why I had to...." He broke off, not completing what he was about to say. "She's trying to scare you away from any nefarious intentions you might have." He smiled and it jiggled something inside her center.

"I can assure you I have not a nefarious intention to my name." She tried to keep it light as he was obviously doing.

Marshall raised a quizzical eyebrow, his lips tilting at the corners just a little. "Too bad."

"That's odd you should say that."

"Why?"

The bantering was becoming uncomfortable. She found herself floundering and didn't like it one bit. The mood became somber and he broke the silence by asking, "What opinion did you form of my son?" His voice was hesitant for the first time. He turned away, but not before she saw a flash of pain in his eyes.

She cleared her throat. Oh how she wanted to tell the truth now, to no longer dance around the edges of reality. "I can't make snap judgments on a first meeting, but he appears to be a pretty normal little boy. Shy and lacking in self-confidence, maybe." *That could be your fault.*

He stood up, hands in pockets, and began to pace the sidewalk in front of the bench. "God knows I've tried to be a good father. I don't want to be a cold disciplinarian like my old man, but I can't seem to help myself. Every time I look at Timothy, I see his mother's weaknesses."

It was the first time he'd referred to Suzy, and Flynn held her breath, afraid to disrupt his reflection.

When he didn't elaborate, she forged ahead in an attempt to get him to open up to her.

"Maybe what you're seeing isn't so much a weakness as simply the undeveloped personality of a little boy. I don't believe we are preordained to follow the values or conduct of our parents. It's a choice we make. I certainly don't want to be like my mother."

He stopped pacing and looked at her. "Why is that?"

"She's in a business that takes her away from home ninety percent of the time. Always has." How much of her youth did Suzy tell him about? She dared not say too much. Something might register with him. "When I decide to become a mother, I'll be there for my child."

He sat close to her. "'When you decide to become a mother'? That's an odd choice of wording. When will you decide?"

She laughed at the serious expression on his face. "When I find the right man, of course."

"If you are close to thirty, it doesn't appear you've given it all that much thought. Aren't you a bit long in the tooth to wait?"

He was teasing her again in that dry, Australian way.

"I want to be sure, to be in for the duration. My mother and father were divorced when I was a baby." Was there much time left? Why hadn't she met the right man? Was the life of a musician the wrong place to find him? Perhaps. Seldom had she been intrigued by one of her kind.

Her attraction to this man was very disconcerting. *It's only because I've never met anyone quite like him.* "Getting back to Timmy, maybe he just needs time to adjust. He probably still misses—"

"No! He doesn't miss anyone. His mother has been gone for four years and not once in all that time has she bothered to come back to check on him."

Four years? That wasn't what Suzy wrote in her letter, or told her on the phone. The time she'd been away from Rainbow's End differed depending on who you spoke to. Suzy had claimed Marshall wouldn't let her near the boy. Someone was lying. She would ask Mrs. Hopkins later.

"I hope you can do something with my son. When I saw you on the road, all fire and ready to tear into me, I figured you for a scrapper. That's what he needs, some backbone. He's ready to turn tail and run when anyone frowns at him."

"Then don't frown at him."

He scowled at her and she laughed, pointing at his face. "See, that's what I mean. You resemble some ancient Viking war god when you scowl at people. It's scary."

An amused look replaced the frown on his face. "It doesn't appear to scare you."

"No. I grew up with Viking war gods and goddesses." She couldn't explain further about the tantrums and explosive dispositions of various music teachers and conductors she'd played under since childhood. There wasn't much that could intimidate her anymore.

"Just do the best you can. I'm wrapped up in work. Things aren't going too right. Call on Hoppy if you need anything. I'm in and out all the time." He gave her an abrupt salute and began walking toward the stables.

In other words, he didn't want to be bothered.

"I'll do what I can," she called after him.

He paused in mid stride and half-turned to look at her.

"To be truthful, taking care of children isn't exactly my line of expertise."

"I realized that from the first. But I pride myself on being a good judge of people and horses. If I didn't think you'd be a positive influence on my son, I'd never have asked you to stay on in spite of…"

"In spite of what?"

He looked disconcerted and walked back to face her.

She received the full impact of Marshall Beckett, with the slanted sun rays coming through the trees above. His dark eyes and the sun-browned skin fit well with his wide shoulders and narrow hips. The shadow of an overhanging tree branch hid part of his face when he moved nearer, giving him a closed, secretive look.

"You seem to be playing some sort of game with us. You don't fit my notion of an adventuress, or even a person who would answer that ad in the paper. Are you laying a porkie on us?"

Porkie? Oh yes, a lie. Flynn stood to face him. They stared at each other for a long time, neither speaking. Her pulse began to race at his nearness. "Let's get this said once and for all." She stepped back to give herself some breathing room. "I assume my private life is just that. Private. It's true I haven't volunteered much about myself, but you appeared to accept me—in spite of the conclusions you've drawn. I promise I'm not wanted by Interpol, I've no criminal past you have to fear. Beyond that—"

"Of course. You're quite right." His words were abrupt. He moved closer, tilting his head to look into her face.

She had nowhere to go. The back of her legs pushed against the bench. She put up her hands in defense when he reached for her.

"I wouldn't hurt you," he said, his voice filled with concern. "Why would you think such a thing? I only wanted to brush away the web caught on your collar."

He showed her the spider web with a small green leaf caught in it, dangling from his fingertips.

It was then Flynn realized she'd completely accepted Suzy's story of Marshall's violent temper.

"Thank you. It was just a reflex." She still felt the warmth of his hard fingers against the side of her neck, even though he had withdrawn his hand seconds before.

Marshall moved back to give her space.

Flynn spoke to push away the intensity between them. He had to feel it, too. "Will you allow me to be a bridge between you and your son? Please don't think about sending him away—for now."

He shot her a look of surprise. "We can start that way. I know the boy wants to stay here. He's got everything he needs. A comfortable, secure life with plenty of sunshine and fresh air and animals to play with."

"Is that what you feel is important to a child?"

"Mrs. Hopkins is essentially at his beck and call. He

has toys, a dog, even a pony of his own, though he's never ridden her. I've tried everything in my power to bring the boy out of his shell." His eyes showed only honest puzzlement.

Flynn took a deep breath. It was either now or never. It had to be said. "What about Timmy's mother? Perhaps he misses her more than you realize."

His jaw hardened, the muscles clenched beneath the taut skin as she watched him struggle for control.

In her professional life, she was able to control tantrums or walk away from them, but this was a powerful, disciplined man who was head and shoulders above anyone she'd ever had to contend with. She had to admit he would be a formidable opponent. No wonder Suzy lost everything.

"I told you, we don't speak of Timothy's mother around here—ever. I realize you're new, but it's a forbidden subject and closed to discussion." He held up his hand as she opened her mouth to protest. "Do not pry into matters that don't concern you." He spoke with cool authority, his voice saying he expected no opposition.

She swallowed past a lump in her throat. It was like she'd been slapped in the face. How she would have enjoyed telling him what he could do with his stiff-necked pride. No wonder Suzy had been so unhappy with him. He was arrogant and narrow. Flynn looked away, striving to regain her composure. When she turned back, she was ready to take him on again. "Very well. You've laid the ground rules. How about a deal, Mr. Beckett?" Flynn held out her hand toward Marshall.

"A deal?"

"I won't mention Timothy's mother in your presence again if you will be so kind as to stop questioning my motives for answering your ad."

He looked temporarily at a loss for words and then managed a wry grin.

"Suits me." He reached to encompass her hand in his.

She felt a current of electricity spark between them and knew he felt it, too, by the sudden look of surprise that back-lit his eyes.

As if burned, they dropped their hands and each stepped back.

"Would you like to see the stables?" There was a huskiness in his voice that he tried to clear away with a cough.

"Yes. I'd like that."

He turned to lead the way down the narrow descending walkway.

There were times when Marshall appeared hard and unyielding, and then she'd glimpse a vulnerability that completely disconcerted her. What was she getting into?

More important, how would she get out?

Chapter 6

Everything is so green." The little winding lane down to the stables was paved with charming rocks painstakingly set against one another. Tiny yellow flowers meandered between the stones.

"It is beautiful, isn't it?" Marshall said. "When I was a teenager I thought Tasmania small and provincial. I couldn't wait to get to the mainland. The more I traveled, the more I knew this was home."

"That must be a wonderful feeling." Flynn had intended the words as a scornful putdown until she recognized the hint of envy. *It must be special to know where you belong.* Both Mrs. Hopkins and Marshall had expressed their satisfaction about where they lived. Until lately, she hadn't realized she didn't know where she wanted to lay down roots and hadn't considered it important.

They passed a fragrant rose garden, bright with flowers in spite of its seeming neglect. "We—I hired a gardener to fashion an informal English garden with a gazebo. No one is here to take care of it now." He didn't say it had been Suzy's idea, but Flynn was certain it was. The stone pathway gradually conformed with the downward slope of the lawn, leading toward a large building she assumed was the stables. Marshall paused, allowing her to catch up with his long stride. "I've started to grow a new variety of apple trees of my own here. They've found a market on the mainland now." He pointed toward the orchard in the distance. "I'm starting a special breed of horse, too. Apples aren't nearly as interesting as horses."

She stood beside him, looking at the stables and the surrounding countryside.

When a farmhand approached them, Flynn watched the interchange between the two men. Marshall had a natural magnetism and everyone in his radius seemed to take on more animation just from being near him. To her discomfort, she discovered she was no exception.

From the top of his head to the wide shoulders encased by a plain work shirt, to the broad expanse of chest with the hint of reddish curled hair peeking above the first button of his shirt—the package that was Marshall had been enough to make Suzy fall for him and draw her out of her comfort zone. But why had it ended so abruptly and bitterly? Perhaps her diary would reveal something. Flynn had no compunction about reading it to discover the truth either. The two girls had always shared one another's journals and diaries. It had to hold the key to what happened, explain what caused Marshall to gain full custody of Timothy and make Suzy behave so strangely. *Suzy is all right. She's just being melodramatic by staying hidden until I get a chance to find the diary.*

Marshall was waiting inside the door of the stables. "Woolgathering again?"

Flynn rushed inside the stables and bumped into his chest. "Oops! Sorry." She was so close to him she felt his warmth burn into her cheek and stepped back hastily.

"So right. Takes a minute for your eyes to adjust, it's bright out there."

He introduced her to the horses. "Hold out your hand

and give them an apple." He reached into a barrel and pulled out one. She was startled when a horse stuck its head out of the stall.

"Don't be scared. They're almost part of the family. The only ones who might try to nip you are the studs. They're kept in another stable."

How could she tell him she couldn't take a chance with her hands? How would she explain musicians guarded their precious fingers and hands fanatically, and she was no exception?

"I'll—I'll pass, thanks. I told you I was a city girl."

Marshall shrugged. In the next stall Flynn recognized the horse that had nearly ridden her down on the road. The animal stood proudly, his head higher in his stall than the other horses, his coat shiny black.

"Sultan is the only stallion I keep in this stable." He patted the arched neck and gave the animal the apple.

"That's about the biggest horse I've ever seen." She eyed the animal with a certain amount of trepidation. "Especially from the middle of a road."

"Yes, well, I admit Sultan and I did get off to a bad start with you, didn't we?" He offered no apology as he lovingly stroked the muzzle of the horse.

They walked through the stable, out the back door and into the beginning of the orchard. Horses and black cattle dotted the landscape. Somewhere in the background she heard what sounded like a creek or river.

"We did get off to a bad start," he repeated, watching her. "But I think you're going to like it here. You could start by learning how to ride. That might encourage Timothy."

She heard the bitter disappointment in his words. Any son of his should be excellent in the saddle.

Flynn looked down at the ground, suddenly angry at herself for the jab of guilt. She wouldn't be here long enough to teach the boy all Marshall desired from a son.

Knowing the child was not being mistreated, just misunderstood, she had only to find the diary and wait to receive her papers and money. Then she'd be off.

So why did the guilty feeling persist?

"I've got to go into Hobart for a few days. Mrs. Hopkins will be in charge, of course. Please consider this your home for as long as you wish to stay."

Flynn looked up at him, disturbed that he might have tuned in on her guilty thoughts.

"You've got hair the color of Sultan." His eyes were focused on the thick braid that lay in front of her shoulder. His fingers wrapped around the plait, the knuckles of his hand pressing lightly against the top of her breast. She inhaled deeply, frozen immobile at the realization that she couldn't have moved away if she'd wanted to. His eyes reflected a hunger and something deep within her rose up to meet it. He bent close, as if to kiss her and then straightened, looking away into the distance.

When Marshal turned back, she saw he'd regained full control. "You said your father was a Mick." His voice was calm, his gaze steady.

She managed a nod, raising her hand to hide the racing pulse she felt throbbing in the base of her neck.

"Yes. My mother always referred to him as 'that black Irishman.' When I visited Dublin once, I discovered there were people who were fair, redheads like you, and then mine. Are you Irish?"

"Me?" He laughed. "Glad you didn't ask me old man that question. Pommy way back and now Aussie, and that's it. We call the English Pommy."

She refrained from telling him she knew that.

"You've no family now, except your brother? Pity you and Timmy can't be a little closer." Her innermost thoughts found voice but she didn't care. It was time he faced up to the fact he and his son were almost strangers. If she could manage to stay long enough, she wanted to help them. But in trying to do that, she didn't have time to dance around the subject or mince words.

Marshall hit his fist against his open palm, startling her. "Bugger it all! I'd give anything to get close to that boy, but he won't let me. He blames me for taking him away from his mother. She was the one who left him behind but of course I didn't tell him that. I've just about given up. He needs more than I can give him. Boarding school on the mainland may be the only way to go."

"According to Mrs. Hopkins, that would be a disaster."

Silence hung over them, heavy and oppressive. Flynn looked beyond the meadow, to the dark, blue mountains in the distance surrounded by puffball white clouds. Only the placid munching of nearby horses and the swishing of their tails broke the quiet surrounding them.

"If you'll excuse me, I know you have to get ready for your trip, and I want to see Timmy. You know, begin to earn my keep," she said lightly. "Thanks for the tour."

He tilted his head in a brief nod, and as she walked back to the house, she felt his eyes boring into her.

Why couldn't this seemingly intelligent man see what was apparent to everyone else? His son loved and needed him, and he needed his son just as badly. Both of them were stubborn beyond belief. Could she change any of that in the short time she would be here?

Chapter 7

The two days without Marshall's presence changed the atmosphere in Rainbow's End. A light seemed to go out and even Timmy moped around the house.

Every time Flynn came in from outdoors she was struck by a sense of coming home. The old house looked dignified and elegant in a timeless, comfortable sort of way. Through the arched doorway leading into the dining room, the long mahogany table covered with a crocheted tablecloth, the color of rich cream looked welcoming. She instinctively headed toward the kitchen.

"Good morning, Timmy. How's breakfast?" She didn't know what else to say. The boy sat in the kitchen alone, eating cold cereal and milk. The poor kid didn't have anyone to eat with. "I've just been out to see the horses. I'd like it if you'd show me your pony."

He looked at her, his serious dark eyes startling in his pale face. Suzy's hair, Marshall's eyes. "I guess so. I don't like her much. She bites."

"I'm scared of that, too. Maybe between the two of us we can talk her out of the idea. Let's take her an apple." Flynn waited until Timmy drank his milk and stood up. Her fingers itched to wipe the milky mustache from under his nose, but he probably wouldn't have accepted the contact.

Since Marshall would be gone for a while, maybe she and the boy could learn to talk to each other.

They walked out to the garden and Timmy stopped. "That was my mum's favorite rosebush." He pointed toward a large bush with yellow roses as big as dessert plates, their centers tinged with pale pink.

Was he trying to test her, to see if she was afraid to talk about Suzy?

"It's lovely. The best of the lot. Your mother had excellent taste." Flynn sat on a bench and looked at him standing in front of her. "You miss her, don't you, Timmy?"

He nodded. "Dad d-doesn't let anyone talk about h-her."

Flynn smiled. "I'd hate to go against your father's wishes. I bet he has a good reason. But I don't see what it would hurt to speak her name sometimes. It can be our secret."

She felt guilty going behind Marshall's back, but damn it, he shouldn't be so inflexible. What could it hurt? Every child needs a mother, even if it's only the memory of one. What mother wouldn't love this shy, beautiful child?

Timmy's face lit up and he gave her a wide smile so much like Suzy's that she wanted to ruffle the thick, cream-colored sweep of hair across his forehead.

Only his eyes stayed darkly serious. His father's eyes.

"Dad says I have to study. He wants me to pre-prepare for school in Melbourne."

"Do you want to go?"

He shook his head fiercely. "I like it here."

"Would you like to show me around?"

"C—could we see the new mare? Dad says she's huge!"

His father had given the boy a pony he didn't like and yet he wanted to see the new horse. Were they both just being contrary and stubborn?

"Sure. Where is she?"

Timmy pointed across the pasture. "Over there."

Flynn knelt on the soft grass, putting herself at eye level with him. "I'll tell you what. Let's study this morning and then we'll take a picnic lunch and spend the afternoon out in the fields."

She watched his eyes grow big with wonder, and it was all she could do to keep the tears from starting in the face of such happiness infusing his thin little face.

Approval and quality time, that's what his son needed. Marshall withheld it while professing to love the boy. It was apparent he did love his son, but why couldn't he unbend? Was it because Timmy reminded him so much of Suzy? What could she have possibly done to leave such bitterness behind?

೧೧೧೧

The cook had packed them a picnic lunch that would have taken a group of farmhands three days to eat. As they carried the basket between them, the sun made dappled patterns on the pathway, sifting down through thickly-branched apple trees. Flynn found herself wondering what it was Suzy had hated so much about this place. And yet, trying to fit her vibrant, fun-loving cousin into such a placid, serene setting was mind-boggling. Loud music, bright lights and swarms of people were more her forte.

"You knew my mum, didn't you?" Timmy asked as they sprawled beneath a huge tree to rest.

Unable to form a quick answer without lying, Flynn regarded him a long moment and then nodded. She couldn't lie to him.

"Yes, I did. A long time ago. Why do you ask?"

The boy always stuttered in Marshall's presence, and in hers, at first, but now he spoke carefully and precisely. "Mum showed me some pictures of when she was a girl. I recognized you."

The only pictures she could remember of them together was when they graduated high school. "Do you still have the pictures?" Marshall might have seen them. That would mean he was hiding the fact he knew about her and Suzy knowing each other. The thought had chills run up her arms.

Timmy shook his head. "Nope. She took her things when she left."

"What did she tell you? That we were roommates in school?" She didn't want to mention they were cousins unless she had to. Suzy might have left that out deliberately.

He made a wry face. "A girl's school. She told me. I can't remember it all."

Flynn laughed at his typical little boy response.

He turned his face away. "I miss her. A lot."

She wished he would look at her so she could connect more with him, but his gaze focused on the grass around them.

"Of course you do. There's nothing wrong with missing your mother. But she wouldn't want you to be sad, would she?" Flynn touched her hand lightly to the back of his neck where the collar left off. Marshall had that same vulnerable spot as the boy, one she had wanted to touch.

"I guess not."

"She's somewhere else right now, but you have your father. He loves you, too."

"He does n-not!" Timmy leaped to his feet, small hands on hips, and stuck out his chin the way Suzy used to in a fit of temper. "He hates me and I hate him back!"

What had made him imagine such a thing? Marshall was plainly at a loss about how to handle the boy, but the love he felt for his son was unmistakable.

Flynn swallowed and silently prayed for the right words. "Sit." She patted the grass beside her. "I know for sure your father doesn't hate you. I can't explain how I know that, but I do. He loves you very much."

"Then why won't he let me see my mum? Why does he want to send me away?"

"He's not doing these things to be mean. For one thing, I doubt he even knows where your mother is." *Damn you Suzy, how could you stay away from your child?* She had claimed Marshall would not allow her to see him, but Marshall said she'd never even tried. Flynn was inclined to believe Marshall, despite the fact he wouldn't allow Suzy's name to be mentioned. It was probably a defense mechanism to get her out of everyone's mind.

Flynn wished she'd never become involved. If it hadn't been for her restless indecision—whether to renew her contract for another five years or pursue some other interest—she would never have allowed this to happen.

"You didn't tell your father about the picture when you saw me?"

"No. He would have sent you packing like the others. I like you. I didn't like the others." She held her breath when he frowned. For a crazy moment it was as if Marshall Beckett looked at her from Timmy's eyes.

"Others? You mean the people your dad interviewed for nannies?"

He nodded.

"Thank you for saying you like me." *Traitor!* Her conscience stood on her shoulder and yelled. She cupped her hand over her ear to shut it out. She wouldn't be here long enough to help him.

"If I told him about the picture, he'd make you leave." He spoke with all the seriousness of a six-year-old. "I don't want you to go."

His words warmed her. "But little man, I have to go sooner or later. Even you must know that. I have a life somewhere else and I'm really just visiting Tasmania." She patted his hand to ease her words.

Privately she thought Timmy was right. The inflexible iron in Marshall's voice when he spoke about his missing wife screamed volumes and he would have kicked her out if he'd seen the picture.

"It'll all work out. You'll see."

Chapter 8

Marshall was waiting for them when they came back from their picnic.

She looked toward the tall, straight form as he watched them approach, and her heart beat faster. How would it feel to belong here? To have this man wait for her across a meadow with something besides cool politeness in his eyes?

She shook her head at the foolish notion and looked down at the boy. Timmy had a closed look to his face, greeting his father with respectful courtesy.

"Mmm. I see you two had a picnic." Had that sounded a little regretful?

"Timmy wanted to show me the mare. We never found her."

"She's probably run off to the back paddock. She'll be back. I'm surprised, Son. You didn't like the pony I gave you."

Flynn laughed. "I think he was curious about her size."

"She's different," Timmy said abruptly without further explanation.

Marshall shrugged and looked directly at Flynn. "Since I came home early, I thought we might go for a ride. I'd like to show you the place. That is if the nipper will excuse you."

"You mean ride a horse?" She looked at him doubtfully. "I don't know, I've never—" She looked down at her hands, rubbing her fingers over her knuckles as she inspected the neatly trimmed nails. It was always her hands. Even with gloves she feared causing problems with the delicate feel of her fingers on the strings of the violin.

"Hey, look at me." His voice held a gentle, cajoling quality. Surprised, she glanced up to see his head tilted in an endearing manner, a troubled expression on his face. "Surely a horseback ride won't infringe on that wall of privacy you've built around yourself."

"That's absurd! You've the wall built around you— not me." Belatedly she thought of the image she was trying to maintain. Timmy was listening with rapt attention. "I guess it wouldn't hurt—if you have a tame horse," she capitulated, not hiding the annoyance in her voice. "Maybe I could ride Timmy's pony."

Even Timmy managed a giggle at that one and Marshall laughed out loud. The sound seemed to startle Timmy. Had he heard it so seldom coming from his father?

Trouble was, she wanted to go with him. The man exuded strength and common sense, characteristics that would not have pleased her cousin but drew Flynn like a magnet.

Marshall grinned. The lines of humor around his eyes deepened as he took hold of her elbow and moved her along toward the stables. She turned back once to see Timmy watching them and waved.

"Did your trip to Hobart work out well?"

He stopped abruptly, his grip on her arm tightening, and she cried out in pain.

"What do you mean?" He frowned at her.

She pulled away from him, rubbing her elbow. What was the matter with the man? "I merely asked a simple question."

"You're a friend of Damon's, aren't you?"

"What?"

His eyes were unreadable, his lips drawn tight in an uncompromising line.

"I don't know Damon. I've never met the man." Now that she knew Timmy was all right, she had to get away. This was getting too deep for her. She had never allowed herself to become involved in the messy situations of other people's problems, and becoming enmeshed in Suzy's was proof she'd been right to avoid such matters.

"I—I guess I've been under a lot of strain lately. Sorry." His apology seemed lame, at best, and she had the distinct feeling he didn't entirely believe her.

Did he think his brother had asked her to spy on him? Was he delusional? Paranoid, like Suzy claimed?

She looked down at her hands once again. "I'd like a pair of gloves to wear."

"Of course."

She followed him into the stables.

"Here's Dolly. She's like a rocking horse."

The stable hand came hurrying forward. "G'day, Boss. How can I help you?"

"This is Ralph. Ralph, Flynn Stevens, Timothy's new nanny. Ralph's been here almost as long as Hoppy."

Flynn looked at the tall, stringy man and liked him at once. His face reminded her of a horse's, long and bony with big dark eyes. His Adam's apple bounced in his throat when he swallowed and a tuft of dishwater-blond hair fell beside his cheek when he dipped his head to acknowledge her.

"Saddle up Dolly for Miss Stevens, Ralph. I'll tend to Sultan."

Marshall was already outside when Flynn followed Ralph and her mount out into the open yard. She stopped short to stare at the giant black horse and the man standing close to him. They resembled something out of a medieval history book, an ancient Viking and his warhorse, ready to do battle.

The sun turned Marshall's hair into the familiar burnished copper she remembered from their first encounter. The aggressive stance with his wide shoulders and powerful legs spread apart, as if he owned the world, caught her somewhere in her center, warming her from the inside out.

When she walked closer, Marshall smiled and motioned Ralph away. He showed her how to use the mounting block to get up on the horse. She sat in the saddle, her eyes closed tightly as she expected anything but the patient, docile non-movement she felt beneath her.

Why had she suspected he would bring out a horse she couldn't handle? It was a foolish notion. Marshall Beckett could be hard and cold from one moment to the next, but she doubted pettiness was a practice of his.

As they rode into the meadow, she saw thick, casually-trimmed hedges of flowering heath bordering the farm along the edge of the roadway, in perfect contrast to the indigenous growth on the other side of the road. It seemed that Marshall had done everything possible to bring a softer side to farm life for Suzy's benefit, sparing no expense.

The orchards were set out in perfect rows of brilliant green trees. It made her think of goose-stepping marchers, moving in precision along with them as the horses continued forward.

They rode in silence. Sultan snorted from time to

time, and she assumed it was because he chafed at the leisurely, measured pace.

"We don't have to go so slow if you don't want to. I think I'm getting the hang of this."

He turned to face her, an eyebrow arched in amusement. "I see. After ten minutes you know all about riding a horse."

Her first instinct was annoyance at his tone, but when she looked into his eyes, she could see it was his dry style of humor.

Her smile answered him in kind. He was being very polite and patient to plod along so docilely when he probably wanted to fly through the meadow with Sultan's long body stretched beneath him. In her mind she pictured him as a centaur and she swallowed. *Get a grip. This man could be your enemy—Suzy's enemy.* It didn't escape her notice that she had to continually remind herself of this.

Chapter 9

It was late afternoon by the time Marshall pointed to a grove of tall, leafy trees. "Let's stretch our legs, or you won't be able to walk tomorrow." He put his hands around her waist and lifted her down from her horse as if she'd been weightless. A thrill spread from beneath his strong hands and sped upward to make her heart beat faster.

If he noticed her sudden intake of breath, he didn't show it. "You've done well, your first time out."

The approval in his eyes made Flynn move away, smiling at his praise. "You were right when you said Dolly was like a rocking horse. Thank you."

He spread a rolled-up throw on the soft, fragrant grass and they sat beneath the shade trees. As the silence blanketed them, Flynn became uncomfortably aware of the contemplation in his eyes. When he stretched out long legs and chewed on a blade of grass, she experienced a reaction—something akin to what Suzy must have felt being near him at first.

Reluctant to break the silence but with her curiosity getting the better of her, she cautiously asked, "Why did your father call this Rainbow's End?"

He leaned back on his elbow, regarding her thoughtfully. "My dad and I were a lot alike. Probably why we were constantly at each other's throats. Like me, he'd roamed all over Oz, even worked aboard sailing ships, anything to keep from a steady, boring job. Much as you do, I suppose."

She didn't correct him. What did it matter? It was the persona she had stretched around herself to hide behind.

"When he found this place, he came back to it often. He knew this was where he wanted to put down roots. He'd met Mum on one of his travels and brought her home. They never left again. It was his Rainbow's End."

"Sounds idyllic. But you said you traveled, too."

"Only after he made sure I went to the uni. No one argued with Dad when his mind was set. He wanted me to get a degree, and when I settled on engineering, he couldn't have been happier."

"But that didn't stop you from roaming?"

He shook his head. "I helped build dams from the top of the mainland to the bottom, but always moved along."

She was puzzled. Had his father been resentful of his son, losing his wife and having to care for Damon and Marshall when they were boys? Is that the reason why Marshall had felt the need to escape from Tasmania?

"Is Damon all the family you have left?"

He made a wry face. "Except for Timothy."

"How did you come by Rainbow's End if you didn't want to stay in one place?" The more she knew about the man, the more she could judge whether Timmy was really okay.

"I was mining near Alice Springs when I got the last letter from Dad. I rushed home, but it was too late. The old codger up and died and left the whole bloody rundown mess to me. Damon got all the cash. It was damn lucky I had a bundle, or I would have had to sell the farm to my brother." He laughed, the sound harsh with no trace of humor. "But I love this old place."

She was fascinated by the softening in his face. The hard planes of his cheeks and jawline eased, his long, sensuous mouth turned up at the corners in a near smile and his eyes held an unguarded, faraway expression.

He was certainly turning out to be more complicated than she'd first assumed. Her preconceived ideas were beginning to turn topsy-turvy, and she didn't like it one bit. For as long as she could remember, her world had been steady, albeit a bit boring. Life had been like a comfortable, elegant room, with everything in place.

It had been very satisfying—until now. Her restlessness had been coming on for a while, long before she had to think about her contract renewal. She just didn't realize how edgy she was until she received that phone call from Suzy. And thinking of Suzy, a lot of the things her cousin had told her were at odds with what seemed to be going on here.

Marshall's handsome ruggedness combined with a quality of arrogant superiority agreed with Suzy's assessment. But not his obvious care for Timmy and his frustration at their lack of rapport.

She had also called Marshall a womanizer. Even though Flynn recognized the flattering interest when he looked at her, she couldn't imagine him flirting and carrying on with a bevy of women. It didn't fit—didn't seem to be his style.

He sat up straight to look over at her. "You look puzzled. Was it something I said?"

She shook her head abstractedly. How had he and Suzy ever made it past the first year together? He was much too steady and serious for the Suzy she remembered.

His voice penetrated the fog of her thoughts, and she turned her attention back to him.

"Getting back to what we were talking about, Damon is still cranky even though you might say he got the best deal from the old man. He's just beginning to drop over now and again."

"Does he get on with Timmy?" She wondered if Marshall was the jealous type regarding his son.

"Ah, yes, Timothy thinks Damon is fair dinkum, and I'm happy for that. It gives me hope the rift between us will heal with time. His farm's every bit as good as this one, maybe better. He never had to spend a brass razoo after he bought it. Everything was in excellent shape, while Rainbow's End was dragging the bottom. I expect the old man didn't see any reason to update anything, or was too tired to."

"Looks to me like you've finally got everything you want from life."

"No!"

The explosive sound of his denial made her sit up abruptly and stare at him.

"It's not nearly what I want from life. I want a family, rugrats to fill the place with noise and laughter." He looked away from her, silence once again engulfing them as she looked at him, stunned by his vehemence.

She cleared her throat nervously. "You've got a start—with Timmy."

He made an impatient sound. "Even Timothy needs more. I know he misses—he misses his mother—but it can't be helped. She wasn't good for him—for us."

Her heart beat faster with the fear of him closing down again, just when she might learn something. "Maybe if he saw her occasionally."

He glared at her. "Impossible! She's gone for good."

Involuntarily, her hand flew to her mouth in alarm.

He softened his voice, turning the volume down a notch. "She was—*is* too erratic. When she left here, she was so disturbed that I conceded partial custody of the boy to her. She grabbed him one day and took him to Melbourne. Timothy told Hoppy he was left alone a lot in their apartment—which wasn't in the best part of the city. He lived on take-away and what neighbors brought by while she gallivanted around town, keeping late hours. Or so the neighbors said."

Granted, Suzy was vain and self-indulgent, but would she do that to her son? The son she had begged her to check on?

"It's a shame when a marriage dies." She fished for more information. He had already said a lot, both in words and voice, and she couldn't wait to be alone to think it all over.

"It was bound to be short-lived. Like fireworks that light up the sky, in daylight they become just loud noises. She's not the only one to blame. I had to whip this place into shape before I went bankrupt, and I spent a lot of time away. I went to the mainland to pick up new horses. And there were financial problems in Hobart to attend to. There was always a lot of hard yakka involved."

"I guess having a child didn't help."

He gave her a long, considering look. "I don't know why I'm telling you this. I've forbidden any mention of her since she left us. Figured it was better all the way around to forget her. Having a tot made it worse. She hated every minute of her pregnancy. Used to stand in front of the mirror, moaning and carrying on about her lost figure and what it would do to her skin."

Flynn noticed he still wouldn't say her name. She understood this about Suzy. It would have been horrifying to watch her once-perfect figure balloon out of shape with the constant worry of possible stretch marks after.

He stood and paced back and forth, his long strides eating the ground quickly. "It got to the point where I hated her. I hated her guts. It felt like she despised everything about me, including the baby—*my* baby she carried inside her." He stopped his pacing and began to stroke Sultan's flank. "For a while there, I even thought the little nipper wasn't mine."

"What? Of course Timmy is your child. His eyes are identical to yours."

Marshall stopped what he was doing and looked at her. "I know that now, but there were a lot of rumors about her activities while I was gone. Damon and others—" He broke off abruptly.

What about Damon? Did he suspect a fling between his brother and Suzy?

He sat back down and leaned against the huge tree trunk, their legs nearly touching. His expression was closed, cynical.

"The last straw was when she kidnapped the boy while I was in Hobart. I hired a detective and eventually tracked her down in Melbourne. She had left him with an elderly couple who could barely totter around. Just to keep him from me. That's when I made the decision to go to court."

Flynn couldn't absorb it all. What he was saying was completely opposite from what Suzy told her. Someone was lying—in a big way.

"Enough. That's my old life. Dead and buried." He hit a fist into his palm with a loud smack. His words were ominous in their finality.

She felt at a loss. He turned toward her and touched her shoulder, brushing back the hair from her damp neck. It was a gentle almost-caress, sending small shivers rippling through her body. The sensation was so unexpected that surprise must have shown in her expression. Marshall quickly removed his hand.

"I'm sorry. I didn't mean to startle you."

"You didn't. It was just unexpected."

He was so close she felt his warm breath against her cheek and wondered if he'd try to kiss her. He smelled good, like cinnamon tea, horse and shaving lotion. What would she do? Half of her wanted him to take her in his arms, but the other half still worried about Suzy.

Looking into his face, remembering the love for his son she saw reflected in his eyes when he thought no one was looking—that sort of behavior didn't mesh with Suzy's description.

Mesmerized, like a fly caught in a web, she held her breath, unable to move. He knelt in front of her, their faces on the same level. He held her shoulders lightly when he bent to kiss her. She felt the kiss clear down to her toes and a deep warmth surged up from somewhere in her center, moving in waves to every inch of her body. His kiss was light at first.

He nibbled softly at her bottom lip, his tongue moved slightly, encouraging her to open her mouth. She'd had kisses before but this was beyond anything she would have imagined. Their hearts thumped in unison as he held her even closer to his body.

When his kiss became more demanding, she felt her lips open beneath his and a low moan from him. She struggled to escape the tight bonds of his strong arms.

Immediately he released her and sat back next to her, regarding her with a twist to his mouth. "I don't know what came over me." His voice was low and husky. "I've never behaved like a randy teenager before, but something about you—from the first time I saw you there on the road—"

It wasn't exactly an apology but then she knew she

had been curious to feel his kiss. She scooted away from him, preventing any further contact.

Marshall sighed, a tired sound that went to her heart. "You're an odd one, you know that? I get the impression you want to like me, but then at other times it feels like you constantly have to remind yourself to hate me. Who are you? Why did you come to us?"

Flynn shifted uneasily on the soft, cushioned grass covered by the blanket. He had an uncanny way of getting right to the heart of things. She wished she could blurt out the truth, but somewhere between the picture Suzy painted and what she was seeing for herself there was reality. And until she could find that truth, she had no choice but to continue with her masquerade.

"I don't want you to get the wrong impression of me. Just because you're my employer, and just because I'm traveling around on my own. I don't—" She stalled for time, willing her senses to calm, unable to look at him.

He threw back his head and laughed. When he caught his breath, he looked at her, a long, speculative look.

"Is that what you think? What penny dreadfuls have you been reading?"

"Well, you did kiss me. And we barely know each other." She was confused by his expression. It was like he couldn't make up his mind whether to be amused or annoyed. The last thing she wanted was to sound like a prude, but she was almost thirty and had never had a serious relationship. She didn't know how to handle her feelings.

"Is it too ungentlemanly of me to observe you kissed me back?"

His voice was teasing, giving her much-needed space. Relieved, she answered in kind.

"Yes. That would be ungentlemanly. You took me by surprise."

"I did apologize."

Had he? "I may be traveling alone, but I'm not free with my favors. I'm not waiting to be picked like one of those apples in your orchard." Her voice was quiet with dignity.

He clasped his hands behind his head and leaned against the tree trunk. Part of his face stayed in the shade. "I never thought that for a moment. It just seemed like something—a mutual attraction between us, and a kiss was the way to express it."

"It's okay, not a big deal. Forget it." She was irritated by his casualness. For her there was nothing at all casual about the kiss. It had nearly melted the polish on her toenails, and she still tingled in places she hadn't realized were part of her body.

"Fine. Let's leave it at that, then. Please accept my apology. Do you want to go on with the tour or go back to the house?"

Feeling foolishly prim and prissy, she discarded her stance of indignation and smiled. "I'd like to see more of the place. It's lovely, from what I've seen so far." In spite of her misgivings and doubts, she didn't want to part from his company just yet. Maybe he would talk some more about Suzy.

He looked around the meadow, his eyes reflective. "Yes. I am proud of it. I had hoped someday to leave it to sons and daughters who would care for it as much as I do."

"You already have a son. That's a beginning."

"That's why I worry so much about the boy. I want him to be strong and self-sufficient, not babied and mollycoddled by women. He needs a bucket load of grit if he's to succeed."

"If he's anything like his father, he'll have plenty of that. Anyway, you haven't the right to plan his life in advance." Hadn't Dolores planned her life for her? Her mother had instilled an early sense of competition between them that led inexorably to her choice of career. She had never questioned it until lately.

"I know what's best for him."

"We don't own our children. Timmy may or may not wish to take over the farm. You didn't much like it when your father planned your life, did you?"

"Touché." He touched his finger to his forehead in a mocking salute. "I keep forgetting you're not as young as you look. You've a good head on your shoulders."

"Is that why you hired me on the spot?"

Marshall grinned and arched an eyebrow. "Partly." His gaze brazenly traveled down the length of her body, approval lighting his eyes.

She felt the heat of a flush come to her face.

He stood and proffered a hand. When his big hand engulfed hers, an electric shock traveled all the way up her arm from her palm. She held her breath, hoping he didn't notice the throbbing pulse at her throat.

"We'd best start up again if you want to see it all." He laced his fingers together and bent over near Dolly. Was she supposed to stand on his hands?

"There's no mounting block out here, so if you can't leap up on your own, I'd suggest you put your foot in here and let me boost you up." Amusement lit his eyes. "An' by all means, don't forget your gloves," he added in gentle mockery.

"Thank you for reminding me."

She let him lift her up so she could swing her leg over the saddle. After he mounted Sultan, she reined her horse back a step to watch him. He was so much a part of this place. Rainbow's End *was* Marshall Beckett. Had

Suzy somehow become a threat? Were she and Damon conniving to destroy him by taking away Rainbow's End? Could they do that?

She remembered Suzy's anger over the phone. It seemed almost misplaced when she listened to Marshal. Someone was stretching the truth.

Marshall looked back, his expression filled with concern. "Are you all right? If this is too much for you…"

A familiar surge of guilt about the way she was deceiving everyone washed over her again. She should never have bought into this crazy idea, but Suzy always sounded so plausible when she proposed some outlandish plan. And yet, watching the man in front of her, his face in the shifting shadows cast by the gently moving tree branches overhead, she thought how empty her life had been, how sterile of any emotional ties or support.

No matter what Suzy had stirred up, Flynn knew she had to see it through as far as she could.

It was time for some drastic changes in her life.

Chapter 10

For days after their horseback ride, Marshall appeared politely attentive but distracted. Mrs. Hopkins said they were having trouble with the old equipment up at the hydroelectric dam above Rainbow's End.

Flynn sat with Hoppy and Timmy on the veranda, sipping apple juice. From where they sat, the lawn sloped down toward the stables, and they watched Marshall supervising the horse training. It was a soft afternoon, the smell of roses thick in the air and a few clouds moving slowly across the blue sky.

"He enjoys caring for those animals, doesn't he?"

Mrs. Hopkins' thin mouth arranged in a self-satisfied expression of contentment. "Yes, he does. He is good with them, too. They trust him."

"Aren't they an expensive gamble?" Marshall had told her about his father being nearly broke before he took over.

"Oh, yes, they cost an arm and a leg, but he knows what he's doing. Already there are orders for breeding stock from spreads in the outback and contracts from Sydney for trained show horses."

Timmy spoke up, his voice thin and sharp in his excitement. "Dad's done wonders for this place. Both Hoppy and Cook say so."

They looked at the boy and he flushed from their attention, subsiding back into his quiet shell.

"That's great, Timmy. I wonder, has anyone told him how great it is that he's managed to save Rainbow's End?"

Mrs. Hopkins looked shocked. "Mr. Beckett would get his dander up if you did. He doesn't glorify praise, he likely resents it, tell the truth."

Flynn thought the housekeeper couldn't have been more wrong. Marshall seemed very much alone. She was sure he wouldn't accept sympathy in a million years, but there was that look in his eyes at times, of being apart from everyone else. *It's his own fault. If he weren't so arrogant and independent, he'd have people closer to him. Maybe it was the only way he knew how to cope.*

෧෨෧

Tuesday came around again. Suzy had said she'd look for her at the churchyard on a Tuesday afternoon, but didn't specify which date. Would she be there today? Would people recognize her? Regardless, it appeared her cousin didn't want to be found for one reason or another.

"I'd like to go into the village to poke around when I have some time off," Flynn said to Mrs. Hopkins. The days had sped by and she needed to get her passport and traveler's checks straightened out. It was the first time in her entire life she'd ever been without a cent to her name, and it surprised her she was not more ill at ease at the thought. Swept up in the hum of activity on the farm, she had postponed going into town and entering the real world again. It was a ridiculous notion, and she shoved it immediately from her mind.

"Of course you should go to town. I never thought of it. You must have purchases to make. There isn't much to the village, but we do have a bank, a few shops and a post office. Ralph Junior goes to the post office once a day, if you need to post anything at some time."

"Thanks. I'd just like to look around." She'd been isolated on the farm and was surprised she hadn't felt restless. Although she missed her violin, it amazed her to realize she thought of it as more like a security blanket than as an instrument.

"I am sure you need an advance on your pay. I reminded Mr. Beckett and he gave me this envelope for you."

Flynn felt relieved she hadn't had to ask. She needed to call her agent, to check if there were any messages, and get him to call Dolores for her so she could avoid a long conversation. She would tell them she was taking a holiday. She might even buy a new dress.

"Can I come with you?" Timmy asked.

Mrs. Hopkins looked surprised. "No, munchkin. Miss Stevens must have many things to deal with first, without worrying about you."

"Maybe next time, sweetie." They didn't know her all that well, and she was glad they were cautious and protective. Although kidnapping seemed far removed from this peaceful setting, the elder woman had already mentioned she was afraid Suzy might eventually try it again. Was Marshall worried about that, too?

The idea sent chills down her arms. If she had to guess, Suzy was to blame for at least half of what had happened between her and Marshall. Her cousin hated the farm and her pregnancy, that much was clear. What else was there to bind her to her husband?

"Let's go inside and rest a bit, Timmy. You can work on the studies Miss Flynn set out for you and later I'll read to you." Mrs. Hopkins looked down her nose at her and Flynn felt chastened for not thinking of it sooner.

"Now might be a good time for me to go into town, then."

"Will you be back in time for dinner? Mr. Beckett seems to look forward to the new arrangement of eating with you and the boy. Before, he always had work to do, and the little vegemite ate in the kitchen with me."

"Couldn't you eat with us?"

"Maybe once in a while. But Cook and me, we've been best friends for years. We enjoy our tucker together."

Of course she'd return in time to eat with Marshall and Timmy. It had become the highlight of her day. If she was not mistaken, it was Timmy's highlight, too. Even though the boy didn't say much, he showed a quiet delight in sharing time with his father, with her acting as a buffer between them. It forced both of them to be politely sociable, on their best behavior in front of her.

It was a beginning.

⌀⌀⌀

Ralph Junior drove her to town in one of the utes, as they called the truck. She was getting used to the odd phrases they used and only once in a while did she have to remember something and look it up in her book later for the meaning

It was her first experience riding in a flatbed truck, but she decided jouncing over the rutted road was kind of fun. She tried to strike up a conversation with the young man, but he was as shy and taciturn as his father. The two were tall and thin as poles, with long horsy faces and wide smiles that endeared them to her right away. Junior couldn't have been more than eighteen.

"Could you let me out at the bank? I'll find my way around from there. When will you be back for me?"

He grinned. "The missus says I'm to wait. I'll be at the arcade. You can't miss it."

If it was like every other noisy arcade, she was sure she wouldn't.

She entered the bank, and after her explanation to the manager that she was staying at Rainbow's End, he offered to let her use his phone to call her agent. It didn't take long to get through to him.

"Hi, Marty. It's me, Flynn."

The line wasn't clear, but his typical scolding tone was unmistakable.

She pictured the short, rotund little man, chewing on his wintergreen candy. His clothes, his office—probably his home—smelled of the strong flavor. Maybe he shouldn't have tried to give up smoking.

He wanted to know where she'd been and what she was going to do about renewing her contract. When he found out she was in Tasmania, the line went dead for a long moment.

"Marty? You there? I needed time off to weigh my options. I've been working the orchestra circuit for half my life, and there may be other things out there in the world to examine."

"What?" His voice sputtered like a fizzling fire-cracker in a cup of water.

She smiled into the receiver, knowing full well he couldn't wait to repeat all this to her mother.

As if he read her thoughts, he said, "What about Dolores? She'll fall apart, she'll foam at the mouth, she'll—"

"Don't be so dramatic. My mother will be fine. Once she gets used to the idea of me doing something else besides playing violin."

"But you've never done anything else. What will you do?"

"Why do I have to do anything? At least for a while. I have some money put by. Who said anything about quitting? I just want to think over my choices. I might want to get married—have a houseful of kids."

"Married?" His vocal range went so high he would have qualified as a fine soprano. "Dolores never mentioned—are you seeing someone?" His voice was full of suspicion.

Flynn didn't know whether to laugh or cry at the thought that he'd never regarded her as a red-blooded woman. Not only was he defending his livelihood, he was always overprotective of his clients, especially the younger ones. Much like a grumpy, elderly uncle.

"No, of course I'm not seeing anyone. At least not right now." She tried to keep the picture of life at Rainbow's End from intruding.

"All right. I'll fax everything to you. Send me a phone number for emergencies."

She swallowed hard. That would be all she needed, to have her mother calling and interfering. Without a doubt she'd spill the beans about her relationship with Suzy and her career.

"No phone. I'm on a farm way out in the boondocks. I lost my cell phone and anyway they don't work here all the time I'm told. I'll keep in touch. Gotta go now." She glanced toward the bank manager who was cooling his heels just outside the door.

Flynn hung up gently on Marty's sputtering voice.

As she walked around town, the quiet, old-fashioned dignity of the shops and the clean streets charmed her. In one dress shop she tried on a few outfits and fell in love with an apple-green skirt and white blouse trimmed with the same green. She counted out her money and still had a bit left over. An outdoor restaurant beckoned and she sat for a while under the umbrella and drank cider.

Unable to put it off any longer, she headed up the hill toward a towering church. Old graveyards had always been interesting to her, even as a child. Suzy used to call her morbid.

She passed by the native stone church building and entered the courtyard encompassed by intricate wrought iron fencing.

Spotting a wood-and-iron bench, she sat down and looked around at the elegant topiary figures carved from trees and bushes, at the roses so splendid with their extravagant blooms.

"What took you so long? I've been waiting in this damn place forever. Gives me the willies." Suzy's voice came from behind Flynn, close enough to brush against the hair on her neck.

Chapter 11

Flynn nearly fell off the bench. "You scared me to death! Do you always have to be so melodramatic?"

Suzy laughed.

Caught between righteous anger and relief to see her after so long, Flynn hesitated a moment while Suzy wrapped her arms around her.

They held hands as they sat on the bench.

"I've not been able to get away for a while," Flynn commented into the silence. She didn't remember Suzy being so quiet.

"Did you find the diary?" Suzy looked around furtively before removing the floppy black hat and veil wrapped around her face and neck.

"Never mind the thanks for coming here. Do you realize what a mess you've sucked me into? And don't you think that getup's a little over the top?"

Flynn felt the gentle caress of Suzy's fingertips against her cheek.

"Just like my little cousin. The world can crash down around her head and she's thinking of a dress code. That diary is important. I need it!"

Flynn wanted to grab Suzy's shoulders and shake her. Suzy could cause so many problems and never offer a hint of gratitude or apology.

"Everyone thinks you've disappeared. For good."

Her cousin laughed again, the sound mirthless and dry. "Perfect. But you know what? Someday I might disappear for good, if you don't locate that diary for me."

"I'm surprised you didn't ask about Timmy first. That's mainly why I'm here, isn't it? To tell you if your ex beats him senseless every night before bedtime?"

Suzy sketched an impatient gesture with her long, slender fingers, as if brushing away the idea. "I wasn't worried about anything like that. I know Marshall loves him."

Flynn sputtered, closed her eyes for a second and thought of her violin. When she was a child, frustrated by her isolation and her mother's involvement in a career, she had pretended to have violin strings inside her, stretched from the top of her head to the tips her toes. When she was upset, she mentally touched her inner strings until she felt a sense of calm and serenity.

"Okay. Timmy's doing fine, not that you asked." Her voice was composed—just.

"Good." Suzy seemed preoccupied with other thoughts.

"I like Rainbow's End, Mrs. Hopkins and Marshall. Timmy's an absolute dear. This village is quaint and sweet. I can't understand why you didn't like any of it."

"Good God! I never would have expected that from you. Not after you've traveled half of Europe and lived in Paris for a year." Suzy leaped to her feet and paced back and forth on the stone walkway in front of the bench.

The familiar wave of envy returned to Flynn as she watched the lithe, tall body, the immaculate clothes without a wrinkle, the chic leather boots that just touched the hemline of her elegant, swirling skirt perfectly—out of a page of *Vogue*.

"This is a provincial town filled with provincial, small-minded people. Rainbow's End was my prison and Marshall Beckett my jailer. Surely only a day or so would show you that."

She stared at her cousin. *I wonder. How would she look ten or fifteen years from now, with lines of discontent etched permanently in that fine, ivory skin?*

The thought surprised her. Was the newly-awakened perception of her cousin allowing her to see Suzy as she truly was? Selfish, wayward, shallow—those negative qualities Flynn had defended against throughout the years.

She tried to concentrate on the positive things about the woman in front of her, but it wasn't working. "I don't see that at all." She held on to her patience, but it wasn't as easy as it used to be. "Now sit here and tell me everything you've left out. Where've you been, and why have you dragged me into this mess?"

Suzy flopped down gracefully and took Flynn's hand in hers, bringing it to her cheek in an old gesture of friendship that tugged at Flynn's heart, in spite of not wanting to be moved.

"I know, I know." Suzy spoke in a rush of breathless voice that was so familiar. "It's even more of a mess than you imagine. Have you met Damon yet?"

"Marshall's brother? No."

"I'm not surprised. They're on the outs now. It's not exactly about Rainbow's End, though that is a part of it."

"What is it, then?"

"It's about Damon and me."

"What about you and Damon?"

"We're in love." Suzy looked away. "He's going to marry me. But first he's set on getting Rainbow's End back. It really does belong to him, you know."

"It most certainly does not!" Flynn's temper flared. "Marshall's father gave it to him and provided Damon with the money to buy his own place. That was more than fair."

"Fair? Did you say fair? That's Marshall's warped point of view you've been listening to." Suzy's voice rose with outrage, building up to the frenzy she had shown over the telephone. "Damon deserves Rainbow's End for staying by that dreadful old man's side all those years, taking care of the place."

"Come on, Suzy. Be reasonable. The property was Mr. Beckett's to do with as he wished. Damon shouldn't have stuck around just for what he could get out of their father."

Her cousin made an unladylike snort through her perfect nose. "A lot you know. You've had everything given to you on a silver platter."

"Stop it! That's hateful, and you don't mean it. I've been working on my own since I was seventeen. Before that I studied every day of my life. I gave up my childhood for my violin. I've never even taken time for a serious relationship. You of all people know that."

"I'm sorry, Flynn." Suzy leaned in close to her and put her arm around her shoulder. "I'm going through such turmoil, you wouldn't believe it, but I didn't mean to take it out on you. You're my best friend. We're closer than mere sisters. If Dolores hadn't taken me in when my parents died, well, I don't know where I'd be now. I'm depending on you to help me."

"But how can I help? Can't you just settle for seeing your son on a schedule, like most divorced couples, and let it go? You're wrong about Marshall. He would let you have visiting rights with Timmy."

Suzy shook her head. "You would think so, but he

won't. It's because I tried to take the boy away. The courts are on his side. So far."

"Okay, that's a hurdle we have yet to come to."

"Not only that, he'd be livid to have his suspicions confirmed. He caught Damon and me kissing once. Ever since then he's suspected something was going on."

"Sounds to me Marshall had reason enough to. Can you blame him?" How painful it must have been for him, to think of his brother and his wife together. Flynn couldn't fathom how Suzy wound up hating him so.

"I need the diary. It really is important to me."

"What's so crucial about it?"

Not a word of concern about Flynn's life and what she might be missing by leaving the orchestra so precipitously. Suzy had no way of knowing she was on leave.

Suzy's head turned away with practiced flair, and the fine, silky, blonde hair fell across her cheek, hiding her expression. "I wrote personal things about Damon and what I was going through. He'd never forgive me if he knew. He'd be furious. The point is someone could find the diary and it would be all over for me and him too as far as getting Rainbow's End back."

"You always were one for exaggerating."

"No! I'm serious. I've got to get it back. It could blow everything up in my face."

"There are lots of places to hide something little like that. I'm surprised you don't remember where you stashed it."

"It was a long time ago. The doctor gave me prescriptions to help my depression, and sometimes I just forgot stuff. I've tried to think of everywhere I might have hidden it. The attic—gee, I hated the dust in that place. Not the library—that's completely Marshall's. Have you tried my room?"

"No. It's locked and Mrs. Hopkins has the key on that big ring she keeps on her belt."

A strange light glinted in Suzy's eyes. For the first time in her life, Flynn was nervous and the tiniest bit afraid around her cousin. Resolutely, she pushed the uneasy feeling away as she listened to Suzy.

"She takes that stupid ring off when she goes into town. Always leaves it on the highboy in the dining room. I might have stashed the diary under the mattress, or you can look under the bureau drawers. I've taped letters under there before. Damn it! Why can't I remember where I put it?"

"I still say you're exaggerating. The diary can't be a matter of life and death like you tried to convince me over the phone."

"You don't know how wrong you are." Suzy took her hand and squeezed. "Forget the diary for a minute. I need money. I need money to live until Damon gets this all straightened out."

"You're not staying at Damon's farm?"

"Of course not. Damon doesn't want us to be together right now. I'm sure it's only until all this blows over. I'm staying on the mainland, in Melbourne. I could stay in Hobart except Marshall goes there all the time on business. Damon thinks it's too risky, my staying at his farm. We can't cause a scandal. It's important to have this stupid little village on his side."

"Why?"

"You're not going to tell Marshall any of this, are you?" Her eyes narrowed as she regarded Flynn in a long, searching glare.

When no response was forthcoming, she made a wry face and continued. "Damon's going to contest the old man's will. Says he has a good case because the local jurors will agree that since he stayed here all his life and Marshall left, he should have the farm."

"And Damon won't take care of you while you're waiting this thing out? I think you've put your trust in the wrong man, Suzy."

The large blue eyes glistened with unshed tears and the voice sounded on the edge of hysteria. "Don't talk to me about judging men, Little Miss Virginity."

The words stung as much as if Suzy had slapped her, but Flynn refused to give her the satisfaction of knowing she'd hit the mark.

"What do you want from me? I lost everything over-board on the ferry coming here. I'm just waiting for my papers, and as soon as Marty faxes them to me I'm gone. Whether I find your precious diary or not."

Suzy sighed. "You can't go yet. I need you as a go-between. I should have gotten much more out of my set-tlement with Marshall than what I did."

"I won't have anything to do with that kind of thing. That's strictly between you and Marshall. This is beyond the outside of enough."

"I can take the boy back if I want." Suzy's voice was quiet and ominous.

Flynn briefly closed her eyes, reaching for calm as her heart raced at the threat. The thought of Timmy being jerked between the two of them, his living with Suzy in some apartment house in Melbourne, being cared for by strangers, was appalling. Her cousin had lost all sense of reality.

"No, you can't take him back. The courts gave him to Marshall."

"On grounds of adultery. He and that wicked witch of a housekeeper claim they saw me in a compromising situation with the overseer who once worked for Mar-shall."

"Suzy! Did they see that?"

"I'm not admitting anything. But, god, was he handsome. Better looking than Damon even, and younger."

"I can't believe I'm hearing this." Flynn put her hands over her ears.

Suzy reached out and took one of her hands down. "Then hear this, *Cousin*. I can pull the same thing on Marshall as he did me. You're living together, under the same roof. Very careless of my ex, wouldn't you say?"

"But that's stupid. I'm the boy's governess, for God's sake."

Suzy tilted her head back and laughed so hard, tears streamed down her cheeks. Composed once more, she carefully wiped the tears away from her mascara-lined eyes. "You're smashing, Flynn. You really are. Don't you imagine I could prove you are no more a governess than I am?"

"You would dirty my reputation for your own ends?"

"I don't want to." Her voice held genuine reluctance—underlined by cold steel. "But I will if I have to."

"I haven't told Marshall about my career or anything about my life. I let him think I was a sort of vagabond, traveling around Australia before I ran out of funds. You're the one who suggested this farce, remember?"

Suzy's eyes rounded and then she laughed again, a harsh noise that grated. "Oh, that's too good. You? A vagabond? And you're pulling it off? That's priceless. Does Dolores know?"

Disgust and disappointment churned Flynn's stomach and twisted her heart at that moment. Suzy's superficiality had never been more transparent than it was right then. Her deception would cost Marshall dearly. Flynn had hoped to leave quietly, with no harm done, before her subterfuge came to light.

"That was your wonderful idea," she reminded her again. It was obvious Suzy didn't recall anything about advising her how to dress or how to approach Rainbow's End. Maybe it was the pills she admitted to taking, but the lapse in memory was frightening. "What do you want from me?"

Suzy leaned back and sighed.

Flynn's fingers twitched as the urge to wrap them around that long graceful neck and squeeze grew. She clenched fists in her lap, appalled at the sudden need for violence.

Silence stretched between them. In the distance a baby cried fretfully and the sounds of children playing in a nearby park wafted on the breeze.

With a sigh of capitulation, Flynn broke the silence. "I'll look for your diary, but that's all I can help you with. As soon as my passport and money come, I'm off. I don't care what you do then, but don't involve me."

"That's fine with me. I don't blame you. You always liked your life nice and clean. It must be like living in a little spare room."

"You say mean things. I may forgive, but I don't forget."

Suzy shrugged. "Doesn't make much difference. Nothing will change. We'll always be cousins."

"But not friends." Flynn's voice was filled with resentment and regret. Suzy looked at her, puzzlement in her eyes.

Her cousin stood, dusting her hands and her clothes in preparation to leave. "I'll call Marshall and ask for money. There's nothing else to be done."

Flynn got up and faced her. "You're not going to tell him about our relationship, are you? The fact we're cousins? Can't you wait until I'm gone?"

"I won't say anything about us. It wouldn't be in my

best interests, now, would it? Not until I get my hands on the diary."

She had unwittingly given Suzy a trump card. Her cousin now knew she had defended Marshall, was drawn to Timmy and not prepared to leave Rainbow's End yet. And worse, Marshall would surely evict her if he knew the truth.

Suzy kicked her shiny booted toe at the courtyard stone under their bench. "If you leave now, you'll be throwing Timmy away. If the courts don't give him to me, Marshall will put him in a boarding school 'to shape him up,' as he was so fond of saying."

"I'm not throwing Timmy away. You did that when you left without regard to anything but your hormones."

She watched as Suzy nonchalantly bent and flicked at a little up-turn in her hem. When she straightened, her eyes were cold, her mouth set. A chill settled in Flynn's veins. It was like looking into the eyes of a stranger. A very hostile stranger.

"No matter. Motherhood never agreed with me. Do what you have to do. I'll do the same."

"Why did you drag me down here? Why did you turn my life topsy-turvy? What purpose did that solve?"

"The diary. I need someone to find the diary for me. Lacking that, I figure some idea might pop into my head."

"Such as that silly one about Marshall and me cohabitating? Puh-leeze, I hope you can do better than that."

"I'll be here most every Tuesday afternoon until you find it."

Flynn tried to grasp the circuitous method to her thinking process. Suzy had not given up any of the ideas that would get Damon back in Rainbow's End and her on the winning end for helping him do it.

She couldn't have hated and feared her cousin more if Suzy had suddenly grown a tail and horns.

She was capable of everything she threatened. And more.

Chapter 12

The once-bright day had now turned sour. After taking leave of Suzy, Flynn tried to calm down by window-shopping again but finally gave up and went to find Ralph Junior at the arcade.

He glanced at her package. "Hmm. You bought Timmy a prezzie?"

"A what?"

He chuckled self-consciously. "A present. Did you get Timmy a present?"

"Lordy, I never thought of that. No, I bought a dress. I only brought a few clothes with me." She held up the bag to show the name of the shop.

"No worries, the boy has all he needs. My mum used to shop there." He pointed to the bag she was holding.

"Used to?" She'd always seen Ralph and his son together, but assumed they had more family in the village.

"She's crippled bad with rheumatism. Doesn't much get out of her chair now. She's a battler who takes care of us all in spite of her problems."

It was the longest conversation she'd had with any of the farmhands on the property, and it made her feel good that Junior was willing to talk in spite of his shyness.

They rode the remainder of the way back to Rainbow's End in silence.

No one was about when she entered the house, which probably meant Marshall wasn't home and Timmy played in his room. Flynn had to talk to someone, so she looked for Mrs. Hopkins. They had taken to sharing a cup of tea in the late afternoon. She approached the breakfast alcove, noticing the tea fixings on the table, but the little room was empty.

The old fairytale of *Goldilocks and the Three Bears* came to mind when she pulled up a chair. Sitting at the table in the room always gave her the sensation of being in a small boat, floating in a sea of brightly-colored flowers, thick, green ferns and ivy of every description outside and in. The area jutted out in a hexagon shape from the house, away from the porch, circled on three sides by waist-high connecting windows. The sun never entered the room directly. A huge oak stood watch outside to shield it.

How would it be to share a cozy, candlelight dinner here with Marshall? As if the thought conjured up the person, Marshall's voice filtered through her thoughts. When she stood to face him, his presence seemed to overpower the dainty little room.

"Are you feeling all right, Miss Stevens? Your face is pale."

"Thank you. I'm fine." She motioned toward the plate of Cook's delicate, flaky pastry and the pot of tea, desperately hoping he didn't notice how his closeness had suddenly affected her.

"Looks like Mrs. Hopkins forgot to drink her tea this afternoon."

Marshall pulled up a chair across from her. "It's not for Hoppy, it's for you. I thought you'd be home about this time. There's not much to do in the village."

"That's very thoughtful." Flynn reached to pour the steaming brew. Guilt washed over her and she fervently prayed her meeting with Suzy wasn't stamped all over her face for him to read.

Marshall regarded her over the rim of his cup, his eyes serious. "I just had a swim in the river. Why don't you join me sometime?"

Her attention immediately went to his hair, darkly damp, curling against the nape of his neck. Her fingers itched to touch him there, in that little hollow behind the neck. It looked so vulnerable, so little-boy-soft.

"Brr! No thanks." Her hands rubbed her arms in exaggerated motion. "I put my hand in that river once and had chill bumps all day."

He laughed. "You're a real puzzle."

"Do you fancy yourself a puzzle solver?"

"Maybe. I'd like to give it a burl."

"A what?"

His lips spread in a wide grin. "Give it a go. If you stay around long enough you'll learn that us ockers have a word for everything. We should have our own dictionary. For all I know, maybe we do."

"It's charming. Ralph Junior said something about his mother I thought might be a compliment. He said she was, oh, yes, he called her 'a battler.'"

"Mmm. She's that, all right. Had seven kids before she got struck down with rheumatism. A real Aussie battler, that one. The real McCoy."

They were silent a moment, watching a cloud of butterflies swarm down on the rose bushes in front of the windows.

"It's beautiful here. You're lucky to have found your niche." Funny words coming from one who disdained niches, but it was true. He was luckier than anyone she knew. Once, when she chided her mother for their never having roots, her mother had said, 'My dear, vegetables have roots. Do you wish to be a vegetable?' It made sense at the time, but now she was not so certain.

She wanted to tell him about Suzy, about their relationship, the wild threats her cousin made. But one look into those eyes, one lingering glance at that strong jaw, and knowing that humorous expression would turn to granite was enough to stop her.

He would toss her out in a moment if he knew all that she had to tell him. She wasn't ready to leave Rainbow's End yet. Her position was still precarious, without money or papers, but that wasn't uppermost in her mind. Most of her concern was for Timmy. Marshall would send him away to school, or even more destructive, Suzy and he would go to court to fight over the boy.

How could she stop what was happening here? She had to warn him somehow. The thought of Marshall's life being torn apart, Rainbow's End taken away from him, filled her with despair. It didn't belong to his brother who had never helped to make the farm prosper before Marshall took over.

Suzy was right on one thing, though. Flynn had created a serene, comfortable box for her life, much like a neat little room. Why did she think for a second she might break out of it? Why would she even want to, when it had offered nothing but comfort and security her whole life?

Marshall reached a long arm across the table and slid his hand lightly down her cheek. "Why so sad? Do you dislike having tea with me so much? Or does being alone with me upset you?"

She trembled at the feel of his callused palm against her flesh. *Being alone with him might have been intolerable in the beginning, but not anymore.*

The realization came as a surprise as his light touch sent ripples of pleasure through her.

"I'm worried about Timmy. He's such a sweet child. And you two love each other so, but you just can't—"

Marshall took a sip of his tea and sighed. "This would work better with a shot of rum in it. But, no, we can't get together on it. Maybe it's because I've spent so much time away. My father let Rainbow's End fall down around his ears, and I've had to work around the clock to whip it back into shape. I'm surprised Damon stood by and let that happen."

"Your father might not have listened to anyone. Apparently his thoughts were with you."

His mouth straightened into a grimace. "I know. I didn't deserve his concern, either. He must have known he was sick, setting his money aside to give to Damon instead of putting it back in the place. Dad and me, we got under each other's skin. I never thought he cared a rat's arse about me. It's one of the reasons I left and didn't return. He was cold and distant—that was his way."

"Do you suppose you're the same way with your son without realizing it?"

He shifted on the chair, obviously uncomfortable with the question, or was it impatience at her attempted analysis? When he looked into her eyes, his expression was one of so much sorrow she longed to reach out and caress his face, touch her fingers to the damp curl that threatened to fall over his forehead.

Instead, she clasped her hands tightly in her lap.

"I know you're right. He's a good sort, a right fine boy, and I'm proud of him."

"Have you ever told him that? Children need to hear the actual words. They aren't very good at guessing, and when they do, they usually make the wrong assumptions." Where did those words of wisdom spring from? From her own ongoing difficulty with her mother?

His hands tightened around the teacup until she feared the fragile china would break.

"Is it because he looks so much like Su—his mother?"

The look he directed at her was sharply speculative. Had she gone too far? What did it matter, anyway? Soon all their problems would be settled one way or another.

He turned to gaze out the window, his deep timbered voice muffled as if something was lodged in his throat.

"You may have something there. Every time I look at the boy I see her."

"Does it hurt so much, losing her?" She hadn't wanted to ask the question, but the words came out slowly, as if by their own volition. It dawned on her she envied what Suzy might have had with Marshall before she threw it all away.

He focused his gaze on her once again. "That's not it at all. I don't want him to be like her. She was selfish, willful and completely thoughtless of others."

He had that right. Cocooned in her own little world of music, had she been so obsessed with ensuring her comfort and stability that she'd ignored Suzy's faults all her life, or had she seen a new Suzy emerge in the churchyard?

"Maybe you're trying too hard. Maybe if you let him, he'd be more like you."

"Could be. I'm not a patient man, though. Nothing was ever gained through timidity and meekness. That's what I see in Timothy, and I don't like it."

The boy certainly didn't get his timidity or meekness from either Suzy or Marshall. "Are you confusing patience with weakness? It's not the same thing, you know.

When a person is strong in his own right, he can afford all the patience in the world."

A dark coppery brow etched upward with unexpressed skepticism.

"I tried patience with Suzy. It didn't work. She hated it here. Hated me, Hoppy, the whole works."

"But why? Why did she hate everything?"

Marshall turned away and then back again, covering the flash of pain she saw with a wry expression. "We—*I* had nothing here to offer her. She thought of Rainbow's End as her prison."

The same word Suzy had used.

"We met in Melbourne. At the races. I'd taken a few days off, looking for breeding stock for Rainbow's End. She was there with some bloke, and God help me, I thought the sun shone outta her arse once I saw her standing there."

A stab of jealousy pierced Flynn, thinking of how that must have been.

"Do you still love her? Is that why you're so angry?" As much as it hurt to think about it, maybe she could persuade Suzy to give her life here another try.

His burst of laughter was short and harsh. "'Struth, no! Her beauty was a curse. Underneath all that perfection was emptiness. No, not emptiness—poison. The woman was, *is,* filled with demons out of her control. One day she'd be on a high and then the next she'd be down in the dumps. I was afraid to leave the boy with her. When she shot through with the young'un, dragged him away to Melbourne, I had to go after them. That was the end."

Flynn swallowed through a tight throat. Was this strong, stalwart man ruined for life? Could he ever learn to trust again? For him not to mention Suzy's infidelities, those Mrs. Hopkins hinted at and Suzy herself bragged about, spoke volumes about the man himself. How the years with her must have eaten at his pride and self-respect.

It was difficult to finally admit the Suzy she had known in childhood was gone. Her cousin sounded mentally ill, but it was something Suzy would never admit to or seek help for.

If Marshall found out about her own deception in coming here, her kinship with Suzy, would that be the final blow? Would he turn sour and withdraw forever?

She had to get away, before it all hit the fan.

Flynn impulsively reached across the little table to hold her hand over his. She couldn't help herself. She needed to touch him, feel his warmth, the hardness of his bones beneath the tanned, firm skin.

"I'm sorry this happened to you. But without her, you wouldn't have Timmy. Aren't you at least glad for that?"

He looked startled at her sudden gesture and turned his hand around to cup hers gently. "That I am. Without kids, without a family, my love for Rainbow's End is empty— devoid of meaning. That's why it's so important Timothy be strong and honest and reliable."

Reluctantly, she pulled her hand away. "Marshall, I've got to leave soon. There's no way else to say it. Something's come up and—"

His expression was unreadable. "Does it have anything to do with your going into town today?" She opened her mouth to answer him but he spoke first, answering his own question. "Of course it does. I hope nothing's wrong."

Mutely, she shook her head. He had enough worries on his shoulders without imagining problems she might have. "No. My mother's worried. And I do have certain obligations." How close dare she come to the truth?

Would Suzy blurt it all out the next time she talked to Marshall? At least Flynn wouldn't be here to see the look of betrayal in his eyes.

"I thought you couldn't have been the homeless type you claimed to be. So why the pretense?"

The ring of a telephone interrupted the conversation. Mrs. Hopkins appeared almost immediately at the open doorway. "It's for you, Mr. Beckett." Her voice sounded angry, her thin lips in a straight line.

Flynn had a burning, sinking sensation in the center of her stomach. She knew without a doubt it was Suzy.

Chapter 13

Her first instinct was to run upstairs to her room and throw her belongings together. Get out of the house. She didn't trust her cousin not to blurt out the truth. But there was still her passport and money to contend with.

"I thought you'd gone forever," Marshall said into the phone.

Rooted to the spot, she couldn't help but listen.

"You'll never get away with it! The whole idea is outrageous. This is lower than you've ever crawled before. I'm warning you, Suzy, I won't let you do it. An' if you try, I'll make you wish you were never born."

His voice was raised in passionate outrage but as Flynn listened, he gradually subsided into intense, teeth-clenching composure. What did Suzy say that would make him so furious as to lose control? Was it about their kinship? Her threat to take him to court because he was 'living in sin' under the nose of his child?

Flynn's inaction was repaid by having her avenue of escape taken away. Marshall slammed down the receiver and in quick, angry strides, headed her way. It was too late to retreat.

She tilted her chin, ready to face whatever came. Her

body ached, felt pummeled and beaten, her nerves stretched taut.

She had to leave. Whichever way it turned out, that was inevitable. She had grown fond of Timmy, of Rainbow's End, and, yes, Marshall was the biggest part of the regret and loss she felt at that moment.

He grabbed hold of her arm and pulled her back into the little alcove, dragged out her chair and pressed lightly on her shoulders to make her sit. Pacing back and forth, his movements in the tiny space caused the corner of the tablecloth to fly up with every passing step in a most disconcerting way and added to her sense of dread.

Tentatively she stood and put a hand on his arm to stop him. His eyes were anguished pools of darkness when he looked down at her, tracing his fingers lightly along the side of her cheek and under her jaw.

"What is it, Marshall? Tell me what's the matter."

"That was Suzy. I don't believe she can carry it out alone. I'm not sure she is alone. The threats she made…She sounded too bloody confident. She wants to meet me. Not here, though."

If Flynn could have grabbed Suzy right then, she seriously doubted she could keep from doing her cousin bodily harm.

"Marshall, sit. Tell me what she said."

He ignored her command, agitatedly running his hand through his hair in that endearing gesture she couldn't get enough of. Everything right now seemed to be viewed from a misty sadness of resigned departure.

"I don't know how, but she's been spying on me, somehow. Says we are—you and I—are cohabitating. Shacked up."

"What?"

"I know. It's ridiculous. It's that stupid ad I put in *The Herald Sun* last year. Hoppy warned me against it, but I wanted someone permanent in Timothy's life. I wanted kids without investing in a lot of courtship and muddled emotion. There wasn't anyone around here, so—"

"Exactly what did the ad say?" The welcome distraction from the subject of Suzy gave her time to think. She had to tell the truth before she left—she owed him that much. It was obvious Suzy hadn't told him.

"You came in answer to it. Why do you play the innocent now?"

"I don't know what you mean. I told you, I didn't see the ad. A friend told me about it." Now was her chance to explain how Suzy had set them both up, but she couldn't do it.

He looked away for a while, reminding her of a little boy caught out in mischief. When he turned back and took her hands in his, he leaned over and kissed her palms. The warmth nearly took her breath away. She wanted so badly to draw his big hands close to her cheek, to kiss each knuckle, glide her lips gently along the length of each long, strong finger. *What am I thinking?* Never before had she allowed such sensuous thoughts to intrude upon her life.

Until she met Marshall Beckett.

"I thought you knew. I didn't just advertise for a nanny for Timothy. I advertised for a wife." His voice was hesitant at first, firming with resolution at the end, his mouth a straight, stubborn line, his jaw jutting forward.

"A wife?" Her voice rose several octaves, and she swallowed, struggling for control. "You advertised in the paper for a wife?"

He looked chagrined. "'Struth, it was all I could think of to keep us together. Hoppy was in the hospital with double pneumonia and I was a newly-divorced father with sole custody. I had to turn Rainbow's End into a paying concern or we'd sink like a brick. An' then there was Damon lurking on the sidelines like a bloody vulture, ready to pick my bones. I didn't know what else to do. I needed a wife."

"It obviously didn't work out for you. No wonder Mrs. Hopkins was so indignant when I showed up on your doorstep."

"I wasn't put out a bit." He grinned unrepentantly. "I assumed you knew about the ad. I mean, why else would you be here? There's nothing wrong with traveling around the world on your own. I just thought you had grown tired of taking care of yourself."

"Maybe that's partly true, but it wasn't exactly like that, you see—"

"I don't care if you've been around the block. You're not a mallee root, anyone can see that. Your bearing, your attitude, it's all ridgy-didge."

"But—"

"I couldn't believe my luck when you answered that ad. It's why I didn't push it. I wanted to give you time to like us—to get to know us better."

His words echoed in her head like sibilant whispers of condemnation. Part of her felt ashamed for lying to him, part of her wanted to be indignant at his presumption she would answer such an ad in the first place. Part of her floated in euphoria at his praise.

How could there ever be anything between them? Her mother and father had a loveless marriage. Dolores became a shell of her former self, all because she wouldn't allow herself to love or to demand love in return. Flynn had vowed never to fall into that same trap.

"There's something I've got to say to you." She wrung her hands, nervous about what she was about to say. "You should know that—"

He touched his lips to hers, preventing her from speaking further. At first it was hesitant, and then it turned into a kiss that lifted her off her feet, held tight in his arms. The mixed emotions he'd voiced flowed over into that kiss. He feathered the seam of her lips with his tongue, seeking entrance. Before he could go further, she pushed away, fearful she couldn't absorb all the raw emotion of his kiss.

His grip loosened in the face of her struggle, and he slowly let her down until her feet touched the floor. She stood transfixed, breathless, unable to think.

He looked at her, the expression in his eyes dark and unreadable. "You can't leave us now. Suzy could win anyway."

"Don't you see that's the only way? It would stop her accusations if I left."

"No. It wouldn't stop her. Something in her voice told me she was mouthing words from someone else. I wouldn't put it past Damon to be behind this."

"But how can they harm you? It has been settled, hasn't it? You've full custody of Timmy. Your father willed you Rainbow's End. How could anyone take it away from you?"

"It's possible. These settlements tucked away in the bush can be reclusive. Their moral standards are quite narrow compared to the outside. I don't know how well the community liked Damon, but he was here when I wasn't. An' everyone knows a child needs a mother."

"I wish I knew how to help you." If she could locate that accursed diary that Suzy wanted so badly, she could hold it over her cousin's head and make her leave Rainbow's End alone in exchange for the book. When had her loyalties changed so drastically?

"I'm sick to death of it! Everything's turning sour. The bank in Hobart is holding back on my loan. The hydroelectric system in the dam above us is giving trouble. I'm supposed to help remodel parts of it and oversee replacements before the rainy season. Timothy lives in his own little world that doesn't include me. An' now this." He threw up his hands. "What a bloody mess."

She laid her head against Marshall's chest and wrapped her arms around him in an intimate gesture of comfort that shocked her even while she did it. His heart beat beneath her cheek, his chin lightly resting on the top of her head.

After a while, he took hold of her shoulders and gently pushed her away, his eyes searching hers questioningly. "I've been chewing over an idea, since you're obviously not answering my ad for a wife. A business proposition. Come to dinner with me tonight. I need to talk to you after I've thought some more on it."

Flynn hedged. "Is that like a date you're asking me on?" She struggled to keep it light. Getting in deeper every hour she stayed, she had to put a stop to it, and now. But what to do? How? Her indecisiveness must have shown on her face, because he lifted her chin to peer into her eyes.

"Come on. You have to let me take you out at least once before you leave us. Where's the harm?"

His words cut to the bone. "Okay, I guess."

"That's my girl."

Chapter 14

Flynn sank down on her bed wanting nothing better than a good cry, but the much-sought-after sobs were buried too far inside her to come to the surface. Her eyes remained dry and empty, her sadness too intense for tears.

Suzy was no longer the lovable, madcap cousin she remembered but an angry, petulant harridan bent on ruining Marshall, even if her own son was hurt in the process.

What could she do? What kind of business proposition could Marshall come up with? There was always money from her trust fund or investments to bribe Suzy with. It was obvious he had a stiff-necked pride and would never accept anything like a loan from her. Besides, the little witch wouldn't stop until she'd told Marshall the whole story of who Flynn was and why she was here.

The only feasible way out for everyone was that she leave right away. Without the diary and without her help inside, Suzy would have a more difficult time making good on her threat. Would that be equal to an ostrich sticking its head in the sand?

Flynn's life had always been neat and compartmentalized. She knew what each day would bring. She carefully scheduled every detail to get her through the months, the years. That was, until she let Suzy talk her into this adventure. Her life up until then had been planned ahead like a well-ordered chess game.

It was time for Timmy's lesson. She knocked and then entered his room. When they had first started he'd been hesitant, not volunteering any answers to the questions from the book they read together. As the days passed he became more self-confident and started taking turns with her, reading out loud. Marshall had given him a laptop for his lessons.

While she sat in an armchair with Timmy sprawled on the carpet at her feet, he listened to her with rapt attention. She read from a book in his little collection on the bookshelf by his bed.

He thumped on the carpet with eagerness "No! No, that's not the way of it at all." Excitement gleamed in his brown eyes, so like Marshall's.

She enjoyed teasing him. Sometimes she left out passages deliberately to see if he'd been listening.

"Oh? You mean I'm not reading it correctly?" The story was one of his favorites. She loved the way he pounced on the mistake if she left out a line or changed the wording. It was a good way to keep his attention.

When she looked up, she saw Marshall leaning against the door. How long had he been there? Before he realized she was watching him, she espied a haunted, wistful look in his eyes, which he quickly hid by clearing his throat.

Timmy leaped to his feet, standing at attention.

"Shouldn't the boy be out playing in the sunshine if he's finished with his lessons?" Marshall's vulnerable look was now replaced by a cool, steady appraisal. "I don't want him coddled."

Her temper rose and she quickly choked back a reply. The last thing her young charge needed was to hear adults arguing.

"Coddling has nothing to do with it. The story is a part of his lessons."

Flynn heard Timmy swallow audibly.

"Do as your father says, Timmy. Run out and play now."

When the door closed gently behind him, she spun on Marshall, her voice quaking with indignation. "Why can't you see Timmy hangs on your every word, just waiting for a speck of encouragement? What we were doing was part of his lessons. It's a good way to develop his enjoyment of reading as well as make sure he's paying attention. Did you notice he wasn't stammering when he spoke? No, of course you didn't notice."

Marshall frowned at her, but made no reply as he walked across the room in several long strides and looked out the window.

What a proud, lonely man. The thought came unbidden to her, and she tried to push it away. She didn't want to pity him. He was too arrogant for his own good, for his son's good. She watched him looking out the window, knowing he watched Timmy run across the yard with the dog. She too had stood looking out the window at the boy and dog a number of times.

"I don't know what gets into me. There's just something about the boy that bugs me."

"It's because he looks like Suzy. He can't help that. He has your eyes, a way of looking at things that is unmistakably you. He has your laugh, when he lets it out."

Marshall turned back from the window to give her his full attention.

"Yes, I see that. But there is a weakness in him, and I don't want that. He has to be strong and self-reliant."

"He's still a child! Give him a chance to grow at his

own speed. He's bright and smart, he'll get there in time."

"An' you're such an expert with children?"

She refused to be intimidated by his scowl. "No, not really, but I've been there. I have a very judgmental mother, and it hasn't helped me over the years. He's frightened of you."

"Scared of me? I've provided him with a secure home, given him everything most kids would give an arm and leg to have. I've tried to do my best by the boy."

Her voice softened. "I know you have. But Timmy doesn't know that. There has to be some meeting ground between you two. You're very much alike in many ways—perhaps that will always be the problem. But you are the parent. You have to help both of you overcome that obstacle."

Marshall took her hand and brought it to his lips. "Thank you."

The simple gesture started a pulse fluttering in her throat. There was no apology, no promise to do better in the future, but she knew he understood. For now, that had to be enough.

"If we're going to go out tonight, I have some things to do." She shooed him out of the room so she could straighten up and put the books back, something Timmy usually did.

The house was quiet when she returned to her room, and she decided to lie down to read for a while. She woke in a panic, horrified to see darkness outside her windows. It was after six. Leaping to her feet, she shucked out of her clothing and dashed into the shower. After what had to be the quickest shower in history, she slipped on her buttercup-yellow, scooped-neck dress, ignoring the slight wrinkling on the bodice. She could have worn her new garment but she'd bought that outfit to wear around to meet Suzy. She didn't know why it should matter, but she wanted Suzy to see she wasn't sticking to the blue jeans and boots routine that her cousin had suggested would work best.

She ran a comb through her hair, looking at her mirrored image, dissatisfied as always, even though the color of the dress was flattering to her dark hair and gray eyes.

It was said a woman began to favor her mother after a certain time in life, and Flynn continually inspected herself for such a likeness. Thankfully, she hadn't seen it yet. Dolores was too severe-looking to be beautiful. Tall and reed-thin, her mother had dark hair precisely streaked with white at the crown, as if she had used an artist's brush. She had a regal bearing that went well with her professionalism and might have been called striking.

Flynn had inherited her father's wide, gray eyes, though. She'd heard that often enough from her mother, over the years.

"Why should it make any difference what you are wearing?" her reflected image asked her. Before she could leave, she must find that infernal diary. When she did, Suzy would leave them alone. Surely she would. Flynn's legs trembled so much that she quickly sat down on the edge of the bed.

She would miss Timmy. A lot. The little boy and his shy vulnerability had wrapped around her heart. What would happen to him? Even though she knew Marshall loved his son deeply, he was so sure the boy needed more structure in his life to mold his character. The poor child would probably be sent to a boarding school. Timmy didn't need more discipline. He needed unconditional love.

Still, she had her own life to lead. She looked down at her hands, suddenly missing her violin. It had been so much a part of her life. She had grown to depend upon the instrument to communicate her moods, soothe her spirit, and give her comfort.

When she went downstairs to meet Marshall in the living room, she was unprepared for his stunned look of admiration. He strode toward her and engulfed both her hands in his.

"You look like the fairest jonquil from the garden." His voice was gruff as he offered the compliment.

She smiled up at him, trying to keep the sadness from creeping into her expression. Marshall was extraordinarily attractive, exuding a sensual masculinity he seemed completely unaware of. His hair was slicked back from the usual rough tumble of curls over his forehead. He seemed as much at ease dressed in dark pants and a white linen shirt as he was in his work clothes. The boots he wore were shiny with polish.

He drove down the country road, quiet at first, but the silence didn't feel uncomfortable between them. She leaned against the seat in the Land Rover and inhaled the fresh air, the heady rich smell of damp vegetation.

"You're beginning to like the country, I can tell."

"Oh? How?"

"Just observations I've made."

"Hmm." He'd been observing her. A shiver of anticipation ran up her spine.

"You don't appear to be the sort who would be content here, though, without cultured things to do."

"Like what?"

"Like going to the opera or ballet, or those fancy boutiques to shop in."

That might have been her life before she came here, but now? She looked out of the window before answering.

Her throat constricted and she realized that under different circumstances, she could be very happy at Rainbow's End. But there was her music. She wouldn't give that up for anyone. Would she?

"Please don't judge me with…with others. I like it at Rainbow's End. It's so peaceful and serene. And I've grown very fond of Timmy."

"You're doing wonders with the boy. I had my doubts at first, but you've even won Hoppy over. I set her straight about the misunderstanding with the ad in the paper."

"That's good." Warmed by Marshall's praise, she was all the more saddened about leaving. Most of all, she hated the inevitable bitterness and anger she would leave behind when Marshall found out about her true identity. It would be another reason for him not to trust anyone ever again.

"Where are we going?"

"The next village over. I hope you like Eduardo's. His place is the best we have. As a restaurateur, he's a genius. I'm always surprised to see he's still here with us and not in Sydney, where he learned the business."

When they reached the outskirts of the township, she noticed it was somewhat larger than the village closest to Rainbow's End. It seemed to rise out of nowhere, nestled between two hills. They passed a park edged with giant elm trees interspersed with lights shining down on adults sitting sedately on benches, talking while children played.

When they walked into the restaurant, every head in the dimly-lit room turned in their direction. She supposed they did make an unusual-looking couple. Her petite size made him seem even taller.

The maitre d' fawned over Marshall. *How often did he bring someone here?* The thought was unwelcome and she pushed it away. The table where they were seated seemed to exist in a world of its own. An indoor waterfall cascaded over moss-covered rocks surrounded by lush, tropical ferns and orchids. A fine mist sifted lightly over the plants, enhancing their fragrance. A cream-colored spotlight played softly over the scene as if the moon had suddenly appeared from behind a cloud just for their benefit. "Oh! It's lovely."

Marshall grinned smugly, not speaking.

"Do you come here often?" She hated the need to know if he'd brought Suzy here.

He shook his head. "No. Don't have time. My tastes are simple. This is as close to gourmet as I want to be. But I met Eduardo in Sydney and told him about the specialness of Tasmania and here he is."

She laughed. "Your cook at the farm is excellent. I'm surprised you can keep anyone that fine, I mean—"

"I know what you mean. I met Thelma when I was in Alice Springs. Miners would come from miles around to eat her tucker. When her old man passed away, she hated it there and wanted to get away. One of the first things I did after moving back here was to send her a plane ticket. She and Hoppy get on like a house on fire."

"One big, happy family, hmm?" The twinge of envy made her ashamed. It had been obvious from the first that all of his employees doted on him, but did he have to be so darned smug about it?

"Oh no." He laughed, touching her lightly under the chin with his finger. "You're not baiting me tonight. No arguments."

She'd hoped to keep their relationship on its usual testy, unsure footing. It would be easier to say goodbye that way.

Just then the waiters brought the first course and she didn't have to answer.

"I hope you like it. Green turtle soup laced with white wine." He smiled at her appreciative sniff of the steamy fragrance.

When the waiters brought on the broiled crayfish, delicately golden and swimming in butter, it tasted like the best lobster she'd ever eaten. She savored every bite of the rich, tender meat. There were individual loaves of dark, crusty bread, warm from the oven, and a casserole of scalloped potatoes and sour cream sprinkled with chives and parsley.

Just when she thought she might have to unzip her dress, the waiter brought out the dessert with a dramatic flourish.

Marshall laughed at her expression. "It's a specialty of the chef. You should feel honored. He's never served it to me."

The waiter lit the small bowls of sherbet and cherries with extravagant drama and quickly disappeared into the background. Above the blue flame they stared into each other's eyes.

They sat a while, listening to the gypsy violinist playing in the distance. Her hands longed to jerk the instrument away from him and play it the way it should be played, although she must admit, to the untrained ear, he probably did a fair job of it.

Abruptly the futility of her life overwhelmed her and a cloud of depression became smothering. *What do I want? To go on playing for a room full of strangers for the rest of my life? What is the point?* The traitorous thoughts had never consciously entered her head before, and she wondered where they had come from.

Marshall interrupted her gloomy reflections. "Let's go sit in the park for a bit. We need to talk."

Chapter 15

Outside, the night had turned cool. Marshall took Flynn's sweater from her arms and draped it across her shoulders. They walked in silence, listening to the night sounds of the little village. Dogs barked, children shouted and played. Couples sat on benches along the street.

In the park the trees loomed overhead, hiding the canopy of stars, turning the area into a shielded coziness. He led her inside the plaza a few feet and they sat on a bench.

"I enjoyed dinner very much. Eduardo's was a revelation. I could imagine him in Paris if he wanted work there."

"He does stick out like a sore thumb. Sometimes it's hard to believe he could be satisfied here in this valley."

Satisfied. Was that a good word? She wasn't sure anymore.

When he didn't seem inclined to speak further, she broke the silence. "About the ad..."

"Mmm, yes. Back to that. I need a wife. I want to leave a legacy for sons and daughters. Someone to care about Rainbow's End when I'm gone. None of the women who answered the ad seemed to fit. Either they didn't like us, or we didn't like them."

"Did it ever occur to you that love should figure into your plans somewhere?"

The old-fashioned street lamp a few benches away spilled its creamy, soft light over the narrow brick sidewalk.

A pained expression washed over his features. "I tried that with Timothy's mother. I will never let myself get so out of control."

"But everyone's not the same. You must know that."

"I thought I knew a lot. She burrowed so far under my skin I almost never got her out. I won't go through that again for anyone."

"You did get her out, though, didn't you?" It didn't sound like he was over Suzy.

"I sure did. I think a relationship based on mutual respect and interests should be enough to hold a marriage together. It was good enough for the old man and Mum. That's why I advertised. There's no need for emotional poppycock to get in the way of selecting a missus."

"And love doesn't enter into it?"

His line of thinking brought back so many memories of her mother and father's marriage, the bitter arguments and eventual separation. She wanted to tell him why she felt as she did about marriage, but if he didn't know the futility of a loveless marriage, what could mere words do?

They sat so close together she felt his warm breath against her cheek. She longed for his arms to embrace her, for his lips to caress hers, in spite of his words denying a need for love.

When he leaned away to look at her, his dark eyes reflected her thoughts, but he said, "Love muddies the water. Now, passion is okay." A smile played at the corner of his mouth.

"Burying your feelings so you won't be hurt again is kind of childish, wouldn't you say?" She wanted to kick him out of the self-pitying role he'd adopted for himself.

He stood and paced back and forth in front of the bench. The glow cast down from the street light created a larger-than-life being, half in the dark, half in the light. His voice, deep and angry, didn't help dispel her sudden anxiety.

"What the hell do you know about my feelings? Love is for teenagers. Love puts blinders on a person, handicaps them. Who needs it?"

His words were sharp and cutting. But were they set in stone?

He unnerved her. No man had ever had that effect on her before. She tried for lightness. "Okay, that out of the way, what did you want to say to me, then?"

He smiled at her. "Nothing I rant and rave about scares you, does it?" He cleared his throat. She watched his anger dissolve, leaving a visage that looked remarkably like Timmy with a case of the shies. "I have a business proposition to offer you."

"I'm listening." She patted the bench next to her. "It's much easier to listen to you when you aren't swaggering back and forth in front of me and muttering curses."

"Was I doing that?" A grin quirked the side of his mouth, his eyes alight with amusement. "You're the first person who has ever had the—"

"Ever had the guts to tell you?" She smiled back at him as he sat down.

"Suzy told me on the phone yesterday that she wanted more money. God knows, most of my savings are tied up in the horses and new trees. She went on to say that if

I had anyone staying here, taking care of our son, besides Hoppy, she was going to court to press adultery charges. Apparently her attorneys advised her she would probably get custody of Timothy and half of Rainbow's End."

"Suzy said that?" *Would she go that far?* Suzy knew perfectly well who was staying there. For heaven's sake, she had arranged it. A flash of anger speared through Flynn, leaving her almost breathless at the suddenness. *Had that been her plan from the beginning, to use me as leverage to get more from Marshall?* It was hard to believe Suzy's principles had deteriorated so much over the passing years.

"Can she do that?" It was rotten playing the innocent, but she had passed the point of no return when she failed to confide in Marshall about her relationship with Suzy.

He shrugged. "I don't know. It would be bad enough if all she did was try. I'd have to spend money I don't have, defending myself in court. She's using the same tactic I used to get rid of her. I didn't actually accuse her of infidelity in court, although I should have—for the record. She went off with the overseer for a couple of weeks. Almost everyone knew of it. I had given her every spare razoo I had at the time, just to be rid of her." He smacked his fist into his palm, and Flynn jumped at his sudden vehemence

"I know damn well someone's behind all this. She doesn't have the attention span of a gnat to focus on Rainbow's End like this. She flits from one thing to another like a bloody dragonfly."

"So who do you imagine is prodding her?"

"Damon has already threatened to contest the will, and I betcha there are people who think my brother is due more than just money."

For the first time since she arrived, Flynn wanted to

meet Damon. He must be something special, to drag Suzy away from Marshall. But then again, Marshall's brother didn't sound all that steady and reliable. Qualities Suzy would probably have sneered at.

"About my business proposition. Would you consider becoming engaged? I don't think we'd have to go as far as to actually get married. It's just until Suzy gets off my back."

Numbness stole over her. Was she hearing right?

"The only other way is for you to leave, but I don't know what that would do to Timothy just now." He took her hands in his. Little shocks of electricity ran up and down her arms as she absorbed the hardness of his hands, their strength.

"Don't put a guilt trip on me, Marshall. Timmy can manage, as he's always had to, without a mother. He has Mrs. Hopkins."

His jaw tensed. "You've done a lot with him in such a short time."

"I understand what you're saying, but a mock engagement? Would that eventually lead to a mock marriage if it didn't stop Suzy? Do people have marriages of convenience anymore? I don't like being used." Regret overpowered her as she struggled to keep her voice steady. She barely knew Marshall. Yet deep inside she wanted his proposal to be real.

"I don't see how that is using you. When you came here, you said you had nothing special going on."

She jerked her hands out of his grip. Was he always going to hold that against her?

"I honestly thought you came in answer to my ad for a missus, so that part isn't as shocking to me as it may be to you. I'm working part-time on the hydroelectric system at the dam, and when I finish the contract, I'll pay you better than if you'd worked as a nanny."

Is that all he thinks about? Paying me off when my duty is done? In fairness, the person she pretended to be would jump at the chance to live in comfortable surroundings—if only for a little while. She couldn't have it both ways. She either stayed in the character of the persona she adopted or, as he so bluntly said, just leave.

How was it between Marshall and Suzy at the beginning? He obviously had the capacity to love deeply at one time. Did Suzy ruin that for him forever? No one in Flynn's life had appealed to her like Marshall, despite what she'd first thought of as his arrogance and superior attitude.

It was at that point she made up her mind to accept his offer.

The decision struck her like a blow. She wasn't ready to return to her career, couldn't bear to think of her sterile existence. Entertaining strangers she would never know, moving from one luxury hotel to another, not caring about what the rooms looked like anymore or the exquisite food to be found in her travels. It was all a sham, especially if you didn't have anyone who prized you above all else to share it with.

Without her being aware of it, she had grown to care for Marshall Beckett more than anyone else she had ever known. The thought that he didn't reciprocate her feelings—and might never—left her frightened but steady in her resolve.

Maybe he could learn to trust again. There was no way she could leave Timmy now. Not until Marshall understood that he and the boy belonged together, that the boy could flourish under his attention if, as a father, he learned to love freely.

Yet Marshall had said he didn't believe in love. Didn't want to muddy the waters with out-of-control emotions. Wasn't that what love was all about? It was why she'd never had a serious relationship. She couldn't reconcile herself to a loveless marriage like her mother and father.

Marshall was explaining how he would take care of her needs, continue with her salary and at the end, when she wanted to leave after the danger from Suzy had passed, settle a lump sum on her. He would just explain to everyone concerned that they had realized they were not compatible and canceled the wedding. She supposed from his point of view these were logical, sensible pleas to get her to agree.

But each of his calm, cold words struck her like stones. He was an empty shell of a man. Suzy had ruined him for anyone else.

Before she could change her mind, before he said anything more hurtful, she blurted out, "I'll do it."

For a second Marshall continued his obviously pre-pared speech and then stopped and looked at her, his eyes slowly blinking as she watched her words finally register with him.

"You will?" His voice echoed his disbelief.

"I've grown fond of Timmy. I don't want you to send him away. As far as Suzy goes, I don't know what she can do to you, but I'm willing to help you put a stop to it. You said she wasn't a good mother. I don't want to see her get him any more than you do. Or Rainbow's End, either."

He just stared at her, his initial silence unnerving. "Are you sure? When you first answered the ad, I couldn't believe my luck. Then when you said you didn't know about the marriage part, I believed you. When you said you had to leave because of Suzy's threats, I didn't know what to do, but I couldn't just let you leave."

"It's a business proposition, yes?" She tilted her chin up, not wanting him to guess her feelings. Not after the cold, calculating way he described his vision for a successful relationship. "You must promise not to send Timmy away. Otherwise it's no go."

He smiled, relief showing in his expression. "Done. Besides, you're afraid to be alone with me. You need my son as a buffer."

They both needed buffers.

"I want to be clear about something." Heat suffused her face and she felt foolish. "We, I mean, you kissed me. We're on a date now. How do we reconcile that with our business proposition?"

Grinning, he touched her hair and pulled out the ribbon at the nape of her neck.

When it was freed, he leaned forward and put a strand to his lips. She caught her breath, her heart thumped so loudly she was certain he could hear it in the quiet park.

"You are a lovely, desirable sheila. Surely you feel something for me. What's the harm in that?"

She slid away toward the end of the bench. *Good lord, he meant it when he said he wants a live-in nanny and a lover with no emotional strings attached.* What he didn't want was a companion or someone to love and love him back—to share his life on equal terms.

"No! That's out. When I marry, I'll marry for love. I want someone who will love me back." She struggled to keep her pain and anger in control. "You said it was a business arrangement. You can't have it both ways. I'm not going to be anyone's broodmare. If you want children, it will have to be with the next person you marry."

"You Yanks have a way of getting right to the center of things, don't you? You're right, though. We shouldn't complicate things with anything physical between us, even if you agreed."

"Damn straight. It could get very tangled and

sticky." She wasn't sure she was ready for commitment, herself.

What she was about to do was a risk. Was she really willing to go that far? To set aside her career for months on end? To take a chance on losing her heart to Marshall and his son and then leave them behind, some terrible day in the future? What did he have to lose, compared to her?

He didn't want anything more complicated than a business arrangement with a little fling on the side if possible. However, he did want someone to bear his children.

She was gambling all or nothing. She would stay on and hope he didn't find out about her past until she decided on the right time to tell him. Maybe she could get through that wall he put up against love. She could not and would not settle for anything less than Marshall Beckett's heart and soul.

Without even knowing it, he already had hers.

Chapter 16

After a night of tossing and turning, her dreams crashing together without making a shred of sense, Flynn determined that morning she would search in earnest for Suzy's diary. But looking for the elusive book was tougher than she imagined. She dressed hurriedly and while the family slept, she checked most of the books in the library. The attic stairs appeared to be tucked up into the ceiling of the hallway, with a rope pull dangling down against the wall. When one pulled the rope, the stairs should gently descend to be climbed. That put them out of the way when not in use. It would probably be a noisy business, and a job best done when she wouldn't be interrupted. Suzy's room was the best place to look, but Mrs. Hopkins kept it locked, at Marshall's orders.

Flynn waited impatiently until the housekeeper went out to do errands. Unable to believe she'd been reduced to petty theft, she took the ring of keys Mrs. Hopkins left on the highboy in the dining room. She managed to justify her guilt by the need to find Suzy's accursed diary. Thinking herself alone, Flynn stood in the hallway in front of Suzy's room. Timmy was in his room reading, and Marshall must have gone out with one of the trucks.

There was no telling when he would return. It made her decidedly uneasy, but Suzy's room was the most likely place for the diary to be. She took a deep breath and then tried each key, until finally the last unlocked the door and it squeaked open.

It was eerie. Once she let herself in, she detected the faint smell of Suzy's perfume, lingering. Some of her clothing still hung in the closet. A thin patina of dust covered everything.

Pausing at the big curved window, she noticed the window seat was covered in the same material as the bedspread. *Did Suzy sit here and look out onto the world, like a caged bird, wishing to be elsewhere?* The room was beautiful, with large closets and vibrant colors. Her cousin must have designed it herself. One of the large, gold-flaked mirrors over the dresser had been broken. Had Suzy flung something at it in a fit of pique? *Seven year's bad luck, Cousin.*

It was odd that Suzy had her own room. Why was it kept locked and unchanged? Was it a shrine? Had he thought at one time she'd come back? Or was it just an uncomfortable reminder they all wanted to avoid facing? Whatever the reason, the first chance she got she would see the room was thrown open to air out.

Flynn peered under the bed and then lifted the mattress to see if anything was hidden there. She had to hurry. Marshall could return at any time, or Mrs. Hopkins might come home early.

She stood on a footstool and was reaching up in the closet when she heard a noise downstairs. Her legs trembled so much she nearly fell as she stepped down. She ran out into the hall, grabbing the bunch of keys as she went, and turned the key in the lock. *Dear Lord, it's not the right one!*

The keys jangled, seeming as loud as bells in the

quiet house. Was Marshall downstairs? How would she explain going into Suzy's room?

The sounds of Marshall coming up the steps echoed ominously just as she found the right key and locked the door. As quietly as she could she ran to her room, easing the door shut behind her. He hesitated outside in the hallway for a fraction of a heartbeat but then moved on past Timmy's room to his own.

In the following days, she was seldom alone with Marshall with always the buffer of Mrs. Hopkins or Timmy, suiting her just fine. Ever since the night of their date, he hadn't said anything more about their engagement. Had he changed his mind?

She helped Timmy with his schoolwork. Because of Suzy's abduction of the boy, Marshall had decided it would be safer for the child to be home-schooled. There was less risk of Timmy being taken from Rainbow's End. Often they took walks around the yard and down by the horses. He still had that closed, cautious look sometimes that didn't allow her to come close. *Like father, like son.* Would it ever change?

When Tuesday came around, she hitched a ride into the village with Ralph and waited impatiently at the churchyard. She needed to talk to Suzy more than ever, especially after that threatening phone call. An hour dragged by, until Flynn gave up and went to meet Ralph to go home.

It was late afternoon by the time she returned, and found Mrs. Hopkins sewing in the library. Needing company after being alone in the churchyard for so long with nothing but her dour thoughts for company, Flynn sat down across from the older woman and silently watched her for a moment.

"I didn't know about his ad wanting a wife."

Mrs. Hopkins smiled at her. "It didn't seem as if you

did. After you'd been here for a while, I began to see that. Mr. Beckett told me later that you didn't know."

Flynn would have liked to explain how Suzy had roped her into the mess, but she knew the housekeeper would be duty-bound to tell Marshall. "I only heard about Rainbow's End needing a nanny."

Mrs. Hopkins nodded as she kept sewing.

"You thought I was an…an adventuress, searching for a husband and security?"

Mrs. Hopkins stopped sewing and looked at Flynn. "I'm not one to pass judgment," she said stiffly. "I just work here, the same as you."

"You and I both know you're part of the family. Marshall thinks the sun rises and sets on you, so don't tell me that."

A smile creased the face of the housekeeper and her eyes softened. "I suppose you could be right."

After a few minutes of silence, Mrs. Hopkins said, "You've made quite a difference in the short time you've been here. Timmy's taken a real shine to you and seems to have come out of his shell. As a matter of fact, Mr. Beckett said just as much the other night."

He did, did he? "Thank you for telling me. Timmy has come to mean a lot to me. I never thought much about kids, never been around them much." *What kind of nanny hadn't been around kids? Had she said too much?*

Mrs. Hopkins bit off the end of the thread, unperturbed by her confession. "You haven't fooled any of us about your background, dear. It's as plain as the nose on your face you come from a good family but you know nothing about children. Isn't there someone who will be worried about you? You're free to use the telephone. Mr. Beckett wouldn't mind in the least."

Flynn squirmed uncomfortably in the big chair. "My mother and I, we, we don't get on too well. I've let her know I'm okay, but I'm not a teenager, you know. I'm perfectly capable of—"

"Yes, yes, I know." Mrs. Hopkins folded her hands over her sewing. "I'm glad my old man and I never had children. They can be such problems."

"And such a joy to have a complete family about."

Mrs. Hopkins smiled. "Yes, there's that. I had my share of pleasure helping raise the Beckett boys. They were a handful at times, those two."

"Didn't you ever want a family of your own?"

"We decided, early on, not to. Mr. Hopkins was older than me, quite a bit older. On one of his days off he went fishing and never came back. I believe he had a heart attack out there on the lake. I hate the water, and I hated thinking of him passing on like that, all alone. Falling into the cold, dark water." She shivered, rubbing her arms as if she had goosebumps. "They found the overturned boat but never found him. I was grateful when old Mr. Beckett asked me to come here to live."

"What about Damon? I haven't met him yet."

She regarded Flynn with a steady gaze. "That's surprising. He has an eye for beauty, that one. Even though he and Mr. Beckett don't get on that well, I find it very odd he hasn't found an excuse to come for a visit, or met you somewhere out in the paddocks."

"Nope. Haven't seen him." Flynn leaned forward. "Do you think he should have inherited Rainbow's End?"

Mrs. Hopkins took a deep breath and shook her head emphatically. "Certainly not. Old Mr. Beckett had the right to choose who he left the place to. Marshall needed roots, not that he would have admitted it in a thousand years. Mr. Damon lacks the drive needed to bring Rainbow's End to a paying concern."

"Do you suppose offering this place was his father's way of getting Marshall to come home to stay?"

"Yes, I believe it was. But he did try to be fair. He gave Mr. Damon all the cash he could scrape together, a very generous amount. Nearly sent Rainbow's End bankrupt with all the scrimping and cutting back he did before he died. He settled an amount on me, too, but I didn't need it. I lent it to Marshall to help him. He's long ago repaid me."

Flynn couldn't help notice how Hoppy addressed Marshall by his name and used Mr. with Damon. Did that hold a hidden meaning?

"Did Mr. Beckett love Damon and Marshall the same?"

Mrs. Hopkins made a face. "I don't know if love entered into it. Old Mr. Beckett wasn't much for showing his feelings. He was crotchety and unbending in his youth, and old age just magnified those qualities. But I'm sure Mr. Damon felt the same amount of caring the old bloke gave to Marshall. He treated them both the same."

"Until he gave the farm to Marshall."

"'Tis the eldest who inherits."

Flynn took a deep breath. *Here goes nothing.* "What about Marshall's wife, Suzy?" She waited for an answer, afraid she wouldn't get one.

Mrs. Hopkins was quiet for a long time. Her bony fingers played with the material on her lap, as if she was toying with the idea of how to answer.

"He doesn't allow her name to be spoken here."

"I know that, but we're alone. There may be reasons I should know about her."

"I can't think of any." Just when Flynn thought that was an end to that, Mrs. Hopkins relented. "We all loved her at first. She was like a beautiful doll come to life. Marshall worshiped her."

Her words cut deep, but Flynn forced herself to hear them.

"But all that beauty was only skin deep. She hated it here. Towards the end, she began to consider us her jailers." Mrs. Hopkins sighed. "Mr. Beckett tried to give her everything, including far more freedom than was circumspect." Her thin lips narrowed until they almost disappeared.

"He bought her a little sports car in an attempt to make her happy. Sometimes she took off for Hobart, or God knows where, and was gone for days on end with no explanation on her return. All of us here could tell he didn't like it. They fought a lot. She didn't care if we heard the arguments. She reminded me of a spoiled brat, pushing to see how far she could go."

It was such a pity that Suzy had clashed with everyone here. Mrs. Hopkins had been ready to accept her and obviously had wanted to care for her. It was truly remarkable she stayed all through her pregnancy.

"Did she settle down a bit when she became pregnant?"

"The one thing Mr. Beckett insisted upon was her staying put. When she told him she was expecting, he took her car keys. He made sure she didn't tear off again, and maybe wreck the car and herself in the process. It was for her own safety. He stopped working on the farm, too. Took her to shows and buying trips to Melbourne. God knows that man tried to please her."

Flynn's heart contracted in pain at the thought of what he had gone through. *How will he ever open himself up to love again?* In spite of all that happened, did he still love her cousin? It was entirely possible. Suzy had that effect on everyone she met.

"I can see she was a difficult person to live with, but don't you think it a bit drastic he should kick her out after Timmy was born? That's like...like he just wanted a broodmare and then was done with her."

Mrs. Hopkins snorted derisively. "Where in the world did you hear that? Suzy accused him of that very thing many times during her pregnancy, but as soon as Timothy was born, she left. Of her own free will. It wasn't until later she came back and demanded alimony and kidnapped the boy."

What a relief it would be to tell this woman the truth about her and Suzy and why she came to Rainbow's End. But if she did that, Mrs. Hopkins would take the information to Marshall. It would certainly be the end of his business proposal, or any other type of proposal.

Flynn had never been comfortable with subterfuge. She and Dolores always bumped heads over the issue. Her mother maintained there were politics in any phase of life, especially careers, whereby the absolute truth wasn't always appropriate. She missed Dolores sometimes, her acerbic wit and her well-meaning meddling, but they got on a lot better via telephone or letters. What would her mother think of Marshall Beckett and his engagement of convenience? It was hard enough wondering what Dolores would think about her having a job as a nanny.

By the time this crazy thing was over, by the time Suzy had her diary and was satisfied, she and Marshall would go their separate ways. What was the point of involving her mother? Flynn was better off saying nothing.

When the diary was once again in Suzy's hands, maybe her cousin would go off into the sunset and leave the Becketts alone. If she did have a fling with Damon, it was just that, a fling. She would eventually tire of him, just as she had everyone else.

But was Flynn prepared to bet her future on that very thing?

Chapter 17

Marshall missed dinner for two evenings in a row. No one saw him on the premises and no one seemed concerned. Flynn continued to supervise Timmy's lessons. He was a fast learner, when he decided to apply himself. They spent sunny afternoons near the stables, or walking in the meadow. The big sheep dog accompanied them everywhere, once he became used to Flynn. At first she was uneasy, he was so overwhelming with all that hair and size.

"He won't hurt you, Miss Flynn," Timmy assured her for the umpteenth time. "He's trained to work with the sheep and he's very well behaved."

Her mother was a cat person and couldn't tolerate any other animal. Her childhood memories always had a Burmese or Siamese cat in the apartment, and they never seemed to start out as kittens. Aloof, unlovable, just like their mistress, was how Flynn remembered the cats.

"I'd love a pup of my own." Timmy stopped to look at the dog walking sedately just in front. "Shep made puppies with a dog on my uncle's farm one time, but Dad wouldn't let me have any."

As if the mention of his uncle conjured him up, a tall, dark-haired man on a bay horse leaped the fence on the far side of the meadow. He dismounted gracefully and sauntered over to them. When he came closer, Flynn realized it had to be the notorious Damon in the flesh.

And what interesting flesh it was, too. He was as tall as Marshall, but slim and wiry, reminding her of the Siamese cats she'd just been thinking about.

She and Timmy watched his approach. Although Timmy had a cautious look on his face, she could tell he liked his uncle.

"G'day, Tim, old man, how's my favorite nephew?" He bent with solemn grace to shake the hand Timmy proffered. After the greeting, Timmy ran off with Shep, leaving Flynn alone with the man. She started to call out to the boy, but Damon stopped her.

"He'll be all right. Let him go."

She turned to face him and frowned. Was every Beckett so bossy?

He grinned and put his hand out. "Name's Damon Beckett."

"I know. I'm Flynn Stevens."

He held her hand too long, his gaze insolent and familiar. "You don't seem to be the sort of woman who usually answers my brother's ads."

"How do you mean?"

He shrugged, his shoulders barely moving beneath the trim corduroy jacket. He looked like he was playing the part in a novel titled *Lord of the Manor Born*. Flynn smiled at the notion.

"Such a lovely smile."

When she didn't reply, he took a pack of cigarettes out of his jacket pocket and offered her one.

"No, thanks."

He helped himself to one and lit up, letting out the plume of smoke with unfeigned satisfaction before he turned to her again.

"You're different, what can I say? Different is different."

"Have you met all the ladies who answered his ads?"

He laughed. "You betcha. I make it my business to know what my dear brother's up to. Stupid idea that, bringing strangers in."

"Marshall said no one marriageable lived within miles of here."

"How very true. But, 'struth. He goes to Hobart, he travels to Melbourne. If he wasn't such an arrogant jerk, he'd have women dropping off the bloody vines for him."

Even though she didn't want to hear a brother speak of another brother in those terms, there was a grain of truth to what he said. Marshall was very off-putting, for the most part. Living in his house, it hadn't taken her long to see behind that gruff exterior to the pain he was hiding. But if it hadn't been for her prior knowledge of Suzy and the havoc her cousin had created in their lives, she wouldn't have had second thoughts about leaving after the first week.

Belatedly, she noticed Damon had subtly led their walk away from Timmy and the dog. She turned back to keep an eye on the boy. It was hard to stop herself from sneaking looks at Damon from under her lashes. Did he have anything to do with Suzy not showing up for their last scheduled meeting? Moreover, had Suzy told Damon about her? It wouldn't seem so. She didn't think he would bother hiding such knowledge.

From the way Suzy spoke about Damon, the man had a surprising hold on her. To Flynn's knowledge, it had always been the other way around in Suzy's relationships. She was fairly certain that neither Marshall nor Damon knew about the existence of the diary. What was in it, that Suzy was so fearful it would get into the wrong hands? It wasn't like her cousin to lose something valuable and secret. It showed more than anything else the state of her mind while she was here. Unstable to say the least.

"So, how long are you in for?"

Cheeky sod. "I'm Timmy's nanny, " she said emphatically. "I plan to stay until I've done my job properly." *The nerve of the man!* What she wouldn't have given to tell him she and Marshall were soon to be engaged. That little tidbit might permanently wipe the smile off his face, if all Suzy had said was true. But it wasn't her place to tell him, and since she hadn't seen Marshall in two days, it was quite possible he'd changed his mind.

Damon cleared his throat delicately. "Ahem, I see. In that case, would you like to go out with me some evening?"

When sheep grow leather coats. She smiled sweetly. "No, I don't think that would be appropriate." What kind of slime was he? Persuading Suzy to think she would be Mrs. Damon Beckett and then coming on to a stranger?

"Well, then, I suppose you'll be off soon, like the rest of them."

Flynn shook her head. "I don't think so. I like it here." Something about this man made her want to defend Marshall. "In fact, I enjoy your brother's company, and I hope he enjoys mine."

Gravel crunched under the wheels of an approaching vehicle. Timmy's face broke into a broad smile. Marshall had come home.

In long, impatient strides, Marshall stood in front of them. He glared at Damon. "To what do we owe the pleasure of your company?"

Geez, he could have said hello to me first before lighting into Damon.

The two men stood practically toe to toe, legs spread, chins in the air.

"Hello, Marshall."

Timmy ran up and then skidded to a halt, his shyness taking over his first burst of enthusiasm.

"Hey there, Sport." Marshall reached down and ruffled his hair, never taking his eyes from Damon.

It struck her then how bad it must have looked for Marshall, coming home to find his new fiancée chatting with his brother, who might have slept with his wife. Was he jealous of Damon? Did he think she was another Suzy? The idea at once pleased and saddened her.

Damon turned to look at her, his gaze traveling insolently up and down her body. "I see you're breaking in a new nanny." He stressed the last word mockingly. "Very charming, too. The loveliest of the lot, I'd say."

Before she finished deciding where a well-placed kick would do the most hurt without causing serious injury, Marshall put his arm around her shoulders and drew her close.

"You have that all wrong. Flynn and I, we've decided to tie the knot. We're engaged to be married. Just some immigration papers to work through." He leaned down, tilted her chin with his hand and kissed her soundly.

She kissed him back. At first it was a show of defiance toward Damon, but Marshall was very skilled at what he was doing, and it didn't take long before she threw herself into the idea. When she came up for air, she placed her hand on her chest in an attempt to stop her runaway heart beats.

Damon's mouth had dropped open. His pale blue eyes widened and he sputtered. A quick look at Marshall's face showed he was enjoying his brother's dumbfounded expression as much as she was. She decided to twist the knife a little by putting her arm around Marshall's waist and squeezing.

Quickly regaining his composure, Damon put out his hand to her. "Allow me to be the first to congratulate the lucky couple." Only his narrowed eyes showed some other emotion than happiness.

"Thank you." Flynn looked for Timmy, who, thankfully, had wandered off to play with the dog. It might take some real explaining to get him to accept her in the role of mother. Especially since it would be only temporary, at best.

"When is the wedding? I hope I'm invited." Damon finally turned to face his brother, a challenge underlying his voice.

Marshall shook his head. "As I said, there's a waiting period. Anyway, we'll have a quiet ceremony in Hobart. We don't plan to invite anyone."

It would never come to a wedding. The engagement should be enough to get Suzy and Damon off Marshall's back. It was sad to think her first-ever engagement was a farce, to be swept under the rug as soon as she left Rainbow's End.

"Come on, Timmy. Time for lunch." Marshall beckoned to his son and whistled for the dog.

Damon gave her a mocking bow. "I'd better get a move on. I've an appointment in town. Good meeting you, Miss Stevens. Congratulations, Marshall. See you later, Timmy, lad." With a jaunty wave Damon walked toward his horse, mounted and again jumped the adjoining fence between their properties.

Flynn watched him leave. He was obviously arrogant, but the feeling in her gut told her it seemed unlikely he would be a physical threat to Suzy.

"Cheeky bastard," Marshall muttered to his receding back, echoing her earlier thought.

Flynn's eyes twinkled teasingly. "Aw, I kind of liked him."

He swerved to look into her face, his brows pulled together like thunderclouds. When he saw the teasing glint in her eyes and lurking smile at the corner of her mouth, his expression lightened and he grinned.

"You wouldn't be the first to fall for his charm."

"He's not my type." Making Marshall jealous was not the key to his heart.

"Good."

It was a surreal moment, as if she stood aside from her body and watched the little family of three walk together toward the house, the dog loping ahead. It was a good sight to see. The fact that it was only playacting didn't seem so important right then.

Mrs. Hopkins came out on the porch as they drew closer. "Time for lunch," she called out. "Timmy, come in and wash up."

Obediently he ran up the steps.

"We'll be there in a minute. Don't wait for us."

Marshall guided Flynn toward a bench in the garden brimming over with heather and low creeping plants. A few rose bushes struggled to bloom but looked sadly neglected.

Her thoughts turned to the lovely gardens in England, which in turn made her homesick for her music. She didn't miss playing to an audience so much, but she did miss her fingers touching the strings, the sounds that came from the delicate piece of wood at her demand.

"I take it no one here is a gardener."

"Too bad, isn't it? We all have other pursuits, but I'm afraid gardening isn't one of them."

"Mind if I give it a try?" *Why did I say that?* She'd never touched earth in her life, if she could keep from it.

"Great idea. Give you something to keep you busy. You must be bored out here in the sticks, with only a handful of people to talk to."

I should be bored out of my mind, but I'm not.

"What you said out there, the business arrangement we have, I guess it's still on?"

"Of course it is. That's why I was in Hobart. My solicitor is drawing up the agreement right now. I don't think we'll need to go that far, but we must make our engagement official in case we are challenged by anyone. It will also give us an out."

She understood and agreed with the legalities he set in place to protect them both in their business arrangement, but the remoteness of his words still hurt. "I should hope so. I'm not marrying anyone for business reasons. Not ever." Her vehemence surprised him, judging from his puzzled look.

"Would marrying me be that terrible?" His tone was light, but his eyes were serious.

"I wouldn't describe the idea as terrible, but you did lay out the guidelines that you would prefer. Sex without intimacy and a mother for your children, no emotional ties involved. Am I right?"

His grin was wicked. "I think that pretty well sums it up." His voice became more serious. "You're wonderful with Timothy. You're strong yet you look so fragile. A real good wicket. You'll find your Mr. Right someday. Me, I've no intention of getting involved with anyone who might bail at any minute."

"Nothing in life is guaranteed."

"But that's the problem. Nothing in my life is absolute, and I don't like it. My son pines for something he can't have. Rainbow's End is solvent for now, but with Suzy's threat...who knows? Damon wants to take Rainbow's End for his own, and you might pull out any minute without warning."

"Why don't you just take one thing at a time? Timmy will get over losing his mother. Let him grieve and get it out of his system. It's clear she's a disturbing influence and shouldn't see him."

Marshall stopped and looked into her eyes, as if searching for something elusive. "That sounds reasonable. If the boy doesn't decide I'm the culprit and take it out on me. What about the ex? How do we make her disappear?"

Flynn thought for a moment, desperately searching for the right words. "Suzy threatened you—us—with blackmail. We both know it probably wouldn't work, but it could cause a lot of trouble and embarrassment. So we agreed to a mock engagement to defuse the situation. If it comes to that, I suppose we could marry and have it annulled later, if the engagement doesn't stop her."

"You'd do that for me—for us?" His look was skeptical and it angered her.

"You don't know anything about me. I've never been married and certainly hoped for a real wedding the first time round, but yes, if it comes to that I would marry you. I don't want Damon to get Rainbow's End and I don't want Timmy to go away." She broke off, realizing too late she'd said too much.

His brows came together in a frown. "What do you mean? I know Damon wants the farm, but there's no way in hell he can get his hands on it."

"No, of course not. What I meant was I didn't want Suzy to be able to split this place apart by taking half of it. It is a possibility."

"After all this is over, you will leave. Timothy is growing fond of you."

"I know, and that saddens me. But if I've been able to help him, and help you both to grow closer, it won't have been for nothing."

He didn't look convinced.

"Someday I hope you'll meet the woman you have

carved out of your imagination, who will make everything just peachy for you." It was a struggle to keep her
voice steady. She hated the idea of him settling down
with another woman.

He sat next to her and took her hands in his. She
loved the way he absentmindedly rubbed her knuckles
between his callused thumb and fingers.

"You have obviously lived the life you wanted to,
going walkabout, looking for adventure. This can't be
much different for you, except you'll stay put for a
while."

*Is that all? How can you be so sure of me? Of who I
am?* She swallowed past the dryness in her throat. It was
her own network of lies that she brought here. No need to
blame him for buying into it. "That may be true. But if
you want a pretend engagement before a pretend marriage, you can't have it both ways. It's strictly business
with no hanky-panky."

"I assure you, I have no designs on your virtue."

His tone was so dry, it was hard to tell if he was
laughing at her or offended.

Had she overplayed her hand? She hoped not, but as
far as she'd been able to figure out, the way to Marshall's
heart was through a regained trust in the vows of marriage. If he took her for an easy roll in the hay, he would
never learn to trust her. Again, it was all or nothing. She
suddenly realized she couldn't abide any other way.

"To set your mind at ease, I'll make sure something
of that nature is put in our contract, if it goes that far." He
stood, his voice formal, shutting her out.

"Do you think it will harm Timothy, when we eventually split up?"

"I hope not. There's no denying he's already formed
a bond with you, but anything you can give him in the
way of steadiness and—and caring—shouldn't go amiss.

He'll adjust when the time comes."

A mixture of emotions overwhelmed her with shocking intensity. She wanted to win Marshall's heart before he found out about her and Suzy. Could he learn to love her? Would he forgive her for lying? She feared it was hopeless, but worth the gamble. When had she realized she loved him?

"We had your brother going, though, didn't we?" She changed tack, not wanting to think about the ending before there was even a beginning.

Marshall grinned. "We did, didn't we? I don't know why he should care, but it really threw him off."

She knew why. It probably threw his and Suzy's little game right out the window. It interfered with their grand scheme to get Rainbow's End back and ruin Marshall in the process. Doubt niggled, though. Suzy had so misrepresented her life at Rainbow's End, from the very beginning. Was she telling the complete truth now?

The next move was up to Suzy. Flynn needed only sit back and wait for the fireworks when her cousin heard about the engagement and impending marriage.

Chapter 18

Tuesday arrived again, and this time Flynn was certain Suzy would show up. News of her impending marriage to Marshall would surely bring her cousin out, ready to fight.

As she sat in the churchyard, she rethought her options. It was uncomfortable taking such a horrendous chance on her future. Any number of things could go wrong. If she didn't renew her contract with the orchestra, it would take forever to get work with them again, in spite of her tenure. They had an enormous waiting list.

Suzy didn't show—again. That made it two weeks since she—or Marshall—had heard from her. Had something happened? Memories of Marshall's rage while talking to Suzy on the phone flashed through her mind. Could Marshall become incensed enough to actually harm her cousin?

☙❧

When she returned to the farm, Mrs. Hopkins and Timmy were already seated at one side of the table. Marshall drew out the chair for Flynn to sit next to him, which was uncharacteristic. He usually sat alone at the head of the long mahogany table. Half way through the first course, he stood and cleared his throat.

"If I could have your attention, please."

Flynn's heart pounded and she felt cold chills settle in the middle of her stomach. *He was going to make the announcement. It was now or never. Should I stop him? Can I control him once I give up my freedom and my name? I'm in a foreign country with different customs and laws. I will be at his mercy.* Perversely, the idea was not displeasing. Looking into his unsmiling face, seeing the tension around his eyes and mouth, she couldn't move, couldn't speak.

"I know this will come as a shock, but Flynn has agreed to be my wife. We'll be married as soon as the immigration papers are sorted." He sat down and returned his attention to his meal.

Only the melodious sound of the grandfather clock ticking away broke the silence in the room.

Timmy appeared bewildered. He looked across the table at Mrs. Hopkins, then at Flynn. "Will you be my new mum, then?"

Poor little mite. He hadn't had a mother since before he could remember. She felt like coffee dregs, knowing that if this didn't work out she could leave, but he'd be stuck with his life—again—without a mother.

"I'll try, Timmy. I'd like to help your father take care of you." This seemed to satisfy him. She chanced a look toward Mrs. Hopkins, whose expression was unreadable.

Three pairs of eyes settled expectantly on the house-keeper. "Congratulations to you both." It was clear the woman had reservations.

The meal dragged on, the tension in the air so thick it was hard for Flynn to swallow. She imagined the others were also having problems adjusting to the new plan. This arrangement didn't seem to please anyone.

Marshall was doing it as a way out of his dilemma. No one wanted him to lose Rainbow's End. She was going along to thwart Suzy, to keep Timmy home and privately for herself, to delay making a decision about her life.

Mrs. Hopkins probably felt her authority would be undermined now. She'd been managing the household for more years than Flynn had lived. And little Timmy, what did he want? He had the same inscrutable look on his face as his father. If he was happy with the announcement, he certainly wasn't showing it.

Mrs. Hopkins finally spoke again. "Will we have the ceremony here, at Rainbow's End?"

Flynn had the distinct feeling the housekeeper wished she'd taken her meal with Thelma in the kitchen, like she usually did. She wriggled uncomfortably in the straight-backed chair, feeling the weight of Marshall's gaze upon her.

"No, that's a lot of trouble for everyone. We could always go to Hobart, get it done quietly."

A lot of trouble. Get it done. Flynn's stomach lurched and she pushed the plate of food away from in front of her. It was a business arrangement—she'd had a hand in making sure of that—but still, he could pretend a little. At least around others.

Marshall's eyes were slightly crinkled around the corners, the aloof, cool look gone. He was teasing her.

She smiled weakly, and without understanding why, she knew without a doubt he had thought about the possibility of Damon and Suzy showing up at any wedding ceremony held at Rainbow's End, and the disruption they would cause.

"I've an excellent idea." Marshall announced. "As part of an engagement present, I'm taking Flynn to Hobart for a weekend."

"You're what?" She felt her mouth open and close. Nothing else came out.

"It's customary for the betrothed couple to go on a pre-wedding trip. Get to know each other, that sort of thing."

Flynn looked at Mrs. Hopkins, who smiled and offered no help at all. Timmy still sat with an amazed expression on his face.

Well, then, two could play at his little game. "Sounds like a great idea," she said sweetly. "Although I appreciate surprises, maybe we should have discussed this together."

Marshall waited, his eyebrow curved into a high arch and his mouth twitching as if he wanted to laugh.

"I'd like Mrs. Hopkins and Timmy to come with us, as well. It will be a grand outing for the whole family."

She'd caught him off guard. He frowned and she smiled back at him. *Go ahead and try it, but you won't intimidate me.*

"We—ell, I reckon that could work."

"Yes!" Timmy kicked his legs against the chair, his eyes alight with excitement. "Does that mean we can come too? Can we?"

Marshall looked at his son. "I don't know…"

"Do be a dear and let them come. We all need a vacation." She touched her hand to his arm. Didn't he realize there had to be some playacting if this engagement was to achieve anything at all?

Marshall raised his glass and waited for everyone to pick up a glass in turn. "A toast then, to my lovely fiancée and our future together." His tone was gently mocking, but the expression in his eyes was like a tender caress. "I don't see why they can't come with us. Good job you thought of it, my dear." He brought her hand up to his lips just before she saw his sardonic grin.

❧❦❧

Two days later they left for Hobart. As they traveled along, with each passing mile the tight coil of tension that had taken up residence in her stomach eased. Flynn listened to Timmy and Mrs. Hopkins laugh and joke in the back seat. She glanced over at Marshall. The tight worry lines of the past week had disappeared. Instead, there were the familiar crinkles of amusement when he looked in the rearview mirror at his son.

"You've made quite a difference in our lives."

"I hope this doesn't upset Timmy," she whispered. Eventually when she looked back, he was fast asleep, clutching to his chest the stuffed wallaby he never let out of his sight. It was the last gift Suzy had given him.

Marshall turned to look at her. "It's a bit late to carry on about that. Timothy likes you. He'll adjust to whatever the future has in store for him."

Content to let the silence blanket them as they sped down the highway, she leaned her head back against the seat and closed her eyes.

Her dream wedding was meant to be a splendid affair, since she'd waited so long for it to happen. She had thought she'd be marrying for all the right reasons. Dolores would be livid if she found out she was left out of the planning of it. Maybe she would never have to know. An engagement should be enough to get rid of both Damon and Suzy.

There was always the possibility Suzy would retaliate by telling Marshall everything. Flynn knew that. The make-believe marriage was destined to end in disaster. If Timmy came out ahead, it would be worth it. And there was that narrow chance at claiming Marshall's heart. But she didn't have much faith in that happening.

Chapter 19

When they arrived in Hobart, they drove through the city, Marshall acting as a tour guide as they made their way to their accommodation for the weekend.

He pointed toward a group of newer buildings. "There's my office."

Flynn peered out the window. "I hadn't realized you had an office here. I wondered why you spent so much time in Hobart."

"There are many facets to running a farm and raising show horses which require hands-on maintenance with imports and exports. Someday I want to be able to hire an agent and not have to make so many trips here."

He took them to the hotel he always stayed while in town. The desk clerk and baggage boys all knew him and scurried to do his bidding.

The lobby was quaintly old-fashioned, decorated in dark mahogany, with colorful couches and pillows. Not many people lounged around. One elderly woman with bluish hair sat at a reading desk. Several children played quietly in a corner near a nanny with a book in her face.

"I've reserved rooms for us on the second floor, where I usually stay. Let's have a bite to eat in the dining room first and then go upstairs." He motioned for the baggage boys to carry up their luggage. The dining room was quietly elegant. They weren't very hungry, though, and all ate sandwiches and salads.

After that, the elevator took them up to their hall-ways and Marshall showed Hoppy and Timmy their room.

He pulled Flynn along down the hall, his fingers pressing into her elbow. "Your room is here." He started to unlock the door.

Flynn touched his sleeve. "Could I have a peek at your room?" She had the distinct feeling he had already made reservations before she insisted they invite Mrs. Hopkins and Timmy to come along.

He looked embarrassed. "Why? A room is a room. They're all the same."

At her arch look, he set down the luggage in the hallway and reluctantly opened the door. Flynn entered the room and, with hands on hips, tried to keep her laughter from welling up. The unmitigated gall of him! He'd planned it all in advance.

"My, my, this looks surprisingly like a honeymoon suite. What exactly did you have in mind for our pre-engagement trip?"

Marshall sat on the edge of the huge bed. The spread was decorated in hearts and flowers, which matched the curtains hanging at the windows. Cut flowers were everywhere.

He had the grace to look sheepish, a wry grin on his face. "I thought I'd surprise you. When you invited Hoppy and Timothy I called to make alternative arrangements, but they only had the one extra room available on this floor, so I guess I'm stuck with this."

Her heart hammered in her chest. She was flattered and at the same time annoyed he assumed she would fall into his plans so easily. "Look, Marshall. We discussed this before. I'm going to be married someday, and it will be forever. What you propose is a fling until we are ready to part. No way."

A voice whispered he might learn to love her if they shared intimacy, but another little voice cautioned it wasn't the way to capture this man's heart. It was all or nothing.

"This engagement agreement is not going to be effective if we don't make it look real," he countered.

"Maybe. But the playacting you do here will have to be continued back at Rainbow's End. Are you up to all that subterfuge? I'm not sure I am."

"Sounds interesting." Marshall strode to the window and looked out over the street. After a while he turned back to her, his gaze steady, speculative. "I was a bit rash with this idea. It won't wash. She—Damon—whoever is in this scheme—I doubt they'll buy into it. Even if we married and they can prove our intention to deceive the court, they can request our marriage be annulled and we'll be back to square one, with Suzy in the driver's seat. God, I wish she was…"

Gone forever? Dead? What did he wish? In spite of the harsh words left unsaid, Flynn understood Marshall's torment. He'd given Suzy everything he had, and still she demanded more. If she really wanted time with her son, in spite of Marshall's misgivings, he would have found a way to let them share time together. But Suzy didn't want that, and everyone knew it. Flynn was afraid even Timmy knew it, although he seemed inclined to blame his father.

She looked at the king-sized bed and then back at Marshall. She'd held on to her virginity this long, not necessarily because of morals but more a lack of interest in anyone special and a lack of time to spend looking for that someone. Even if she might be the oldest virgin in captivity, she wasn't about to surrender to a man who wanted to make love to her with no strings attached.

"You're probably right. How can we pretend to be a loving, engaged couple?" How ironic. She came to Rainbow's End with so many untruths and half-truths and yet here she was, balking at this innocuous deception.

"On second thought, why shouldn't we be able to pull it off? We're both adults. We struck a deal. I've never gone back on my word. I don't see any other way to get Suzy off my back." Marshall stood tall, larger than life, the street lights from outside the large window silhouetting his body. Legs apart, shoulders back, his chin tilted upward in that stubborn look she'd come to recognize, her heart gave a few extra thumps and she had a hard time turning away.

He was gorgeous, with an underlying rough-hewn arrogance she thought had gone out of date. Could she hold her own with him for however long it took to see this through? When they discarded the arrangement like so much baggage along the way, would she feel free? Or devastated?

Feeling alone and cut off from the others, Flynn swallowed past a lump in her throat. As if understanding her hesitancy, he smiled. A disarming smile that slashed white across his tanned features and wrinkled the corners of his eyes.

"What now?" She asked.

"What do you want to happen now?" While his smile remained at the corners of his lips, his eyes were pensive, serious.

Flynn sat on a chair, absently running her hands across the exquisite tapestry surface. "I have to be honest with you." She hesitated, on the verge of telling him about her reason for coming to Rainbow's End. But the look of approval in his eyes stopped her. He wanted to make love to her, that was clear enough, but would he be thinking of Suzy? He'd been deceived by her cousin enough not to trust anyone ever again, and here she was, about to tilt his world upside down again. What would happen to Timmy?

Now was not the time to tell him about her past with Suzy. Things had to be set right between father and son first, and then she had to find that damnable diary. After that, he would ask her to leave and then she could get back to her own life. Somehow the prospect didn't appeal to her as much as it should have.

"I'm waiting," he prompted. "What must you be honest about? You aren't getting cold feet, are you?"

"I always thought my marriage would be glorious. With the long, white dress, and friends and family attending. I realize this is just make-believe, but can you understand my reluctance?"

Marshall sat on the arm of her chair and took her hand in his, rubbing his callused fingers across her knuckles. "Someday you'll have that perfect wedding. You're a beautiful, caring woman, and I don't know why some bloke hasn't already snapped you up."

She fought back the tears that threatened her equilibrium. "Thanks."

He trailed his hand over her neck and under her hair, sending ripples of pleasure through her body. Leaning forward, he kissed her gently. She bent into his chest, inhaling the smell of after shave and man. He was the first to break away and stand.

"We'll only be here a few days. I've some business to attend to. It's true, you do have a perfectly good room next door."

"Good, that's settled then." Flynn walked across to the door. "What's on the agenda for tomorrow?"

"I've a meeting with my banker in the morning. Why

don't you three go shopping, explore the big-smoke for a bit. I'll see you about dinner time."

She swallowed her disappointment. "Fine with me." She'd hoped he'd spend some time with them, show them around. Why should she be disappointed, when she'd set the rules?

A knock on the door startled her. He opened it to admit room service, wheeling in a small table with a bottle in a silver container and two glasses.

"What in the world?"

He shrugged. "Wouldn't be an engagement celebration without champagne, would it? I forgot to cancel my previous order."

"We must keep up appearances." The irony was apparently lost on him as he poured the glasses. They sipped their wine in silence, both lost in thought.

After the champagne, she went to her room. It was big, lovely—and lonely.

All night she kept waking up to the sensation of Marshall's presence in the next room—so close. One time she lay there, listening, expecting to hear his even breathing.

If she'd stayed in his room and he slept on the couch as he promised, he might have had one arm flung off the couch, a thin sheet pulled over him.

She pictured herself taking an extra blanket from the foot of the bed and draping it lightly over him, the pale illumination coming in from the window, casting shadows and light across his face.

His lashes against his cheek, his expression peaceful. He would look a lot like Timmy at that moment. The tug of passion between them was growing and she wasn't inclined to stop it.

⌘

After Marshall left the next morning, Flynn, Hoppy and Timmy took a bus into town.

Mrs. Hopkins sighed. "'Twould be a lovely walk. "But this sea air always gives my arthritis a turn for the worse."

"The bus is fine with me." Flynn had hardly ever ridden a bus in her life except for the one to Rainbow's End. It turned out to be an interesting experience.

"That's Mt. Wellington over there, and Mt. Nelson is in that direction," Mrs. Hopkins pointed out.

The city had a nineteenth-century atmosphere Flynn found quaint and charming. Hobart seemed to be situated on a high bank, with mountains on one side and the waterfront spread out on the other side.

She inhaled the early morning air, fresh and crisp, with a decided smell of tide water. As the bus lumbered along, they saw small boats of every size and shape moored alongside huge sailing boats.

"Can we ride in a boat?" Timmy asked. He'd been silent for the most part, his wide eyes taking in all the new sights.

"Your father promised he would take us sightseeing," Flynn answered. "I don't see why a boat ride couldn't be managed." She smiled at his happy look.

Flynn and Mrs. Hopkins dragged a reluctant Timmy from shop to shop. Although he didn't complain, he was clearly bored.

"We'll take you to the chocolate factory," Mrs. Hopkins promised.

It sounded like an excellent idea to Flynn, ever a lover of chocolate. She considered cutting short their shopping expedition immediately, but Mrs. Hopkins wasn't all that enthusiastic.

They looked at clothing while Timmy sat on a bench, waiting.

She held one dress to her face and inhaled the sweet odor of the material, feeling the softness against her cheek. It was the finest weave of wool she had ever seen. The cloth was exquisite, able to be worn summer or winter. "I guess we'd better stop," she said after purchasing a soft, fern-green two-piece dress. Even if the marriage plans were a sham, she wanted to look nice on this trip, for Timmy and Hoppy.

"I'd like to get you a negligee, child. As my wedding gift."

"I really...you shouldn't...I have plenty of nightgowns and..." She always slept in pajamas.

"Rubbish. A marriage must start with new things. Here, this pale blue number would be lovely on you." The housekeeper held up a diaphanous gown that had an equally thin inner layer of material that wouldn't hide a mosquito within its folds.

"Oh, no, Mrs. Hopkins—I couldn't possibly." This was bad. How many people would they hurt when Marshall called off the wedding and she left Tasmania?

"You can call me Hoppy. You're practically one of the family now."

Without asking permission, Mrs. Hopkins beckoned to the saleslady to wrap up the gown and negligee and charge it to her credit card.

"Thank you. That's very sweet of you, it really is." How could she ever have thought the housekeeper dour and severe? Since she had removed herself from her cozy nest of security with the orchestra, Flynn was learning a lot about the real world.

When they had finished shopping, they carried their parcels to a nearby sidewalk restaurant overlooking the harbor. The seafood bisque was delicious, and the boats in the harbor revived Timmy's enthusiasm.

"How far is the chocolate factory?" Mrs. Hopkins asked the waiter.

"It's about a twelve-kilometer drive from here, but you'll never get in. You must book well in advance."

Timmy's mouth straightened in a set expression so like Marshall's it tugged on Flynn's heart. She touched her hand to his. "We'll find something better to do."

"I shouldn't have promised. I had no idea we had to call ahead." Mrs. Hopkins patted Timmy on the side of the cheek with her hand. He pulled away from them, his disappointment evident but silent.

If only the boy would throw a tantrum once in a while, at least it would be some sort of communication. Instead, he was a closed book, a mini version of his father.

Back at the hotel, Flynn rested a few minutes in her room before deciding to seek out Marshall and deliver some of the gifts they'd all bought for him. She knocked tentatively on his door, and when there was no answer she tried the handle. It wasn't locked, so she pushed it open.

He lay asleep on the sofa. Just as she'd imagined the night before, he looked vulnerable, his dark, silky lashes against the tan of his high cheekbones. She resisted the strong urge to settle on the carpet next to the couch and lay her head against his hand drooping off the side. The packages rustled noisily in the quiet as she put them gently on the bed.

He sat up. "Wonderful. You found something."

"Lovely stores, lovely clothes, we had a great time. Only sad part was that Hoppy promised Tim a visit to the chocolate factory, and we couldn't go."

"Why?"

"The waiter at the tea garden said you must book ahead."

Marshall made an impatient gesture. "We can fix that, right enough."

He picked up the phone, put a call through and spoke with someone. When he hung up, he turned to her. "I just talked to my banker. He knows the manager of the chocolate factory and said he could make it right for us, but they're closed for two weeks. Renovations."

"Darn! We kind of promised Timmy."

"We'll come back again. You sound as disappointed as he is."

"Hey, I wouldn't miss a visit to a chocolate factory if you tied me to the bed."

"Mmm...not a bad idea." His mock leer made her laugh. He could be so thoroughly charming when he didn't have that moody, closed look.

That night he took them out to a restaurant that specially catered to children. Timmy was surprised and delighted when he was weighed before he ate and then weighed again afterward to see what the charge would be for the meal. He chuckled about it all evening.

"Do you s'pose we might ride in a boat tomorrow?" Timmy asked his father.

Flynn met Marshall's startled glance over the boy's head. She figured he was remembering only a short time ago when Timmy would never have ventured to ask a question in front of everyone for fear of being rebuffed.

"That's a great idea. I'm sorry about the chocolate factory, son. We'll all come back here again, I promise."

Timmy's face lit up and he impulsively ran and hugged his father.

Before the boy could retreat, Marshall ruffled his hair and kissed him on the cheek. A long moment passed, and Flynn knew they all were experiencing a lump in the throat, the same as she.

Marshall and his son had changed directions and

seemed to be heading together, but not on a collision course.

"That's settled, then. Now that we've finished eating, I suggest we go down to the docks and walk off our dinners. Hoppy?"

"Oh, not for me. I'm practically bursting at the seams. My aches and pains have gone walkabout for the time being, and I could do with a long night's sleep. Come on, Timmy. Be a good lad and show me to my room. You could do with a story, couldn't you?"

Timmy looked reluctantly at Mrs. Hopkins then back to Marshall and Flynn. A little tug on his sleeve decided him.

"Okay. Can we go early in the morning?"

Marshall nodded and touched the boy's cheek with a gentle hand. Timmy's eyes grew large and he stood, as a restive colt might, liking the caress yet a trifle nervous.

It was a good sign.

A light fog had settled in as they walked along the waterfront, the streetlights laying down a patina of creamy mist over them. Marshall walked protectively close to her, making her feel warm and safe. If it wasn't for Suzy and her problems, things might have been different between them.

At times like this it was easy to forget Marshall had advertised for a wife so he wouldn't have to become emotionally involved. All he wanted was a nanny and someone to bear him more children. He had made it abundantly clear from the beginning that he wanted no part of love.

The night air crept through her sweater.

"It's a lovely night, but I'm getting a little chilly."

"Let's go back, then. It feels so comfortable with you, not having to yak, just being together."

He stopped walking and turned her toward him.

"Flynn—" He broke off at her questioning look and brought her close to kiss her. She put her arms around him, lost in the moment, the need within her was so great.

Marshall was the first to pull away. "It's damnably easy to forget our agreement."

"I know."

He escorted her to her door. "I'm meeting a few mates at the pub. We used to hook up every time I came to Hobart, but I've not had time to spend with them of late. Don't wait up for me."

She turned to go inside. "Don't give it a thought. I've been wanting to watch Australian telly anyway." He wouldn't allow it on the farm, saying it was a waste of time and deadened the brain. The hookup was only for Timmy's lessons.

As a parting gesture, he said, "Order anything you like from room service," and then closed the door behind him.

She wanted to throw a book at his retreating back. *How dare he just go off to be with his buddies?* The absurdity of her thought made her giggle, and she decided to read rather than watch the television.

Sometime during the early morning hours she awoke with the feeling she was not alone. She rose up on her elbow and pictured him lying on top of the covers on the other side of the bed, bootless but otherwise clothed. She saw herself getting up carefully and spreading a cover over him as he slumbered into the night.

What would have happened if he'd asked to spend the night with me? The thought was worrisome. She needed to have this all settled, to get back to her life as she knew it. But would it ever be the same?

Chapter 20

After a light breakfast, the four of them packed their luggage back into the car and journeyed down the Tasman and Forestier Peninsulas. They passed rolling pastures dotted with placidly grazing cows. The hills surrounding Hobart were heavily timbered, with dark and light greenery covering them.

Glancing sideways at Marshall, Flynn was gratified to see the lines of worry smoothed away, replaced by a look of contentment.

They traveled down a little strip of land to the south of Tasmania proper, arriving at a tiny resort village on the isthmus between the two peninsulas. The quaint log cabins Marshall had reserved were located a mere stone's throw from the towering cliffs that dropped off into sheer nothingness. Mrs. Hopkins bustled about, putting their things to order in the cabins.

"Come, walk with me." Marshall took Flynn's hand and led her along the jagged coastline, away from the center of the little village.

"Won't Mrs. Hopkins worry about us?"

He shook his head. "No. She saw us leave, and she's keeping an eye on Timothy. She won't like being so close to the cliffs."

"It's really peaceful here."

"I'm glad Hoppy came with us. Did you know she lost her old man in a boating accident? Ever since then she's been fearful of water."

"She told me a little about that, and how she and her husband decided not to have children."

"That surprises me. She never speaks of him anymore."

They came to a large flat rock nesting at the edge of a point overlooking the sparkling water far below. Marshall laid down his jacket and motioned for her to sit. He sat beside her and they looked out over the water.

"It's a beautiful place," she whispered, not wanting to dispel the sense of calm and quiet.

His shoulder touched hers, and he pulled her close, turning her head so that his lips lightly touched hers. When she didn't back away, his kiss became demanding, his tongue searching for hers, his fingers tracing under her chin and caressing her throat.

She closed her eyes and allowed herself to savor the moment.

"You are so desirable. You've no idea how much I want to be with you. In every sense of the word."

The huskiness in his voice echoed the heartbeat throbbing in her ears. She wanted him, too. Desperately. But not without love. He was offering sex without intimacy. No doubt the same thing he offered those other women who answered his ad in the paper. He had given Suzy his heart. Flynn would never settle for less.

Reluctantly, she pushed him away.

His expression was startled for a moment, but his eyes held a mischievous glint. "That's right. We've a business agreement." He tweaked a strand of hair that had fallen across her forehead and leaned away from her, staring out upon the water, and finally said, "I think you want me, too."

She cleared her throat. He would never know how much. "I admit there's an attraction between us. But I expect you to be honorable and stick to our agreement."

He answered her with that devilishly-raised eyebrow, a quirk to his lips. "Guess we'd better head back now."

Marshall had rented a small sailboat, with plans to spend the day sightseeing in and out of the various coves. They had to plead with Mrs. Hopkins to come.

"You know how I hate water," she argued.

"Please, Hoppy. Dad will take care of us," Timmy begged.

"It won't be the same without you," Flynn pleaded.

"I'll come in when you say the word," Marshall promised. "Look at how peaceful the water is, barely a ripple anywhere."

"Lordy, I don't know why you three pester an old bird like me to death."

Flynn looked over her head to Marshall, and he winked in return. It was obvious the housekeeper's crankiness hid her pleasure in their display of affection for her.

When they were all in the boat, Marshall edged the craft out of the mooring and into the open water with expert ease. The boat glided effortlessly along, the wind whipping in the sails as Flynn stood at the bow watching the countryside slip by, smelling the cool, clean air. Intense happiness flooded over her, which both startled and dismayed her.

A brisk breeze came up, giving her an opportunity to study Marshall as he became absorbed with what he was doing. The white T-shirt he wore molded to his shoulders and chest. Muscles rippled beneath the fabric as he worked the ropes, and when he turned suddenly to smile at her, his teeth were a slash of white against the tan of his skin. His coppery hair stirred in the wind.

He stood on the rolling deck, feet planted apart, looking every inch a Viking warrior, arrogant and supreme—ready to face anything. She would carry this picture of him the rest of her life. A strange melancholy descended upon her, erasing her former exhilaration. A sense of loss intruded on her contentment.

At first Mrs. Hopkins held tight to Timmy and stayed put on a bench fastened down in the center of the boat. Marshall knelt in front of them and put his hand on her shoulder. "Hoppy, ease off. I wouldn't ask you to come out here if I didn't think you could handle it. Can't you trust me?"

She managed a wan smile and seemed to relax a fraction.

Flynn admired his compassion for the elderly woman. He showed patience for his employees, his horses, and others. Why was it so hard to show some for his son? At least he was beginning to change on that.

"How'd you like to steer the boat for a while, Sport?"

The boy's eyes shone bright and a large smile lit his face. He disentangled himself from Mrs. Hopkins' grip and ran to his father's side. Marshall placed his captain's hat on Timmy's head, chuckling when it came down over his ears, but the child wouldn't let his father remove it.

Flynn found it difficult to swallow and her eyes burned with unshed tears as she watched Marshall turn his body to shield Timmy from the salt spray, once in a while reaching out to steady the wheel.

After sailing up and down the bay for the better part of the morning, Marshall put into a small, secluded cove. Mrs. Hopkins and Flynn unpacked the lunch provided by the restaurant.

When they'd finished eating, Timmy went below

deck to play with some toys he had brought along.

"Want to go for a walk on the beach?" Marshall asked.

"What a great idea." Mrs. Hopkins punctuated her enthusiastic words with an elaborate yawn. "Go on, bugger off, you two, so I can take a little snooze. Like as not Timmy is probably already snoring down below, after all this sea air and sunshine."

"I'd like that," Flynn said.

Marshall climbed down the ladder fixed to the side of the boat and waited for her to follow. Before she could guess his intention, he grabbed hold of her and waded effortlessly through the shallow water with her in his arms. At the edge of the beach he started to set her down and then paused. She turned her face up in question and he kissed her lingeringly.

"Marshall! Mrs. Hopkins will see us."

"Don't you think she'll probably expect it of a newly-engaged couple?" He laughed at her blush.

She looked back at the boat. It seemed a long way off. *Had he brought other women here?* There were those women who answered his ad. And Suzy. It hurt to think of her cousin here with him.

They walked up the beach until Marshall cut in toward a path leading inward on the little island.

"Hold up! You're walking too fast." The path was narrow and he walked ahead with a masculine protectiveness that was so much a part of him.

"Sorry. Must have been woolgathering." Marshall never lost an opportunity to tease her about the phrase she'd used the day she came to Rainbow's End. He slowed his long strides until she caught up to him. It wasn't much farther until they entered a clearing. The area was completely surrounded by large trees, some of their branches drooping with flowered vines that filled the air with their scent. On the ground, long, silky grass vied with tiny purple and pink flowers to make a carpet at their feet.

"It's lovely!"

"Yes, very."

She looked up at him and saw he was looking at her with a steady gaze. A warmth spread over her and she turned away, trying for normalcy. He took the rucksack from his back and lowered it to the ground, loosening a tightly-rolled blanket.

He spread it out at the edge of the flowers and she self-consciously sat down. Far away in the distance the sound of lapping waves trickled through the dense growth. Marshall touched her shoulder and pushed her gently back on the blanket. They lay side by side on their backs, looking up at the round patch of blue sky dotted with clouds above them.

"You are so beautiful, sweet Flynn." He touched the side of her cheek.

She lay still, hardly breathing.

"You aren't afraid of me, are you?"

Unable to speak, she shook her head. Truth be told, she was more afraid of herself, of these new emotions threatening to overwhelm her.

He rolled over onto his side, his head propped up by his hand, and combed her hair away from her face with his fingers. He bent his head down to kiss her and when she didn't resist, wrapped her in his arms, his kiss more demanding.

Instead of listening to what her body insisted she do, relax into the kiss and enjoy what he was offering, she pushed him away.

The problem of Suzy needed to be resolved, her own network of lies exposed, before anything could happen between them.

"I keep forgetting. We aren't really engaged." Although he smiled, his eyes stayed serious.

"I know, and we have an agreement."

He pushed himself to his feet and offered her a hand up. "Come. I want to show you something."

They walked through the woods a short way to see a deep-water pool nested like a jewel within its setting. Flowers and ferns were everywhere. The water looked cold and dark, yet clean and inviting.

Marshall appeared smug, pleased at her exclamation of delight.

Had he brought someone else here? It shouldn't matter. She had no right to question.

As if finely tuned to her thoughts, he spoke into the stillness. "You're the only one I've ever brought here. In my wild days, when I worked on the tuna boats, I discovered this little hideaway and spent hours here, reading and thinking."

"It's a magical place."

"Want to go for a swim? It looks colder than it really is."

"Okay." She began to unzip her outfit to get to her bathing suit she wore underneath and then stopped. "Do you have a suit?"

He laughed, the sound ringing through the woods, startling flocks of birds. "You are such a delight. I never bought into that 'world-weary adventuress' persona you've adopted. Yes, I'm wearing cozzies."

At her questioning look, he smiled. "You'll see, but I'll be decent."

She let the soft material of her outfit fall to the ground and felt her bare skin heat up where his gaze touched her.

"Beautiful!" His voice was husky, like honeyed gravel.

"You too." She appreciated his wide, muscled chest, dusted with a fine sprinkling of curly, coppery hair, and his long legs. His upper body was tanned, an indication he often worked on the farm without a shirt.

What he called cozies apparently was the brief swim suit like tight boxer shorts.

With what seemed like a great deal of effort, she faced the pool, reluctantly turning her back on the masculine embodiment of perfection and the swimming trunks that highlighted his virility.

"Watch out for the center, it's deeper there. Best to stay around the edges." He put a hand on her shoulder, concern in his expression. "You do swim, don't you?"

She laughed. "A little late for that question, wouldn't you say?"

The water was shockingly cold when she dove in, but her body soon adjusted. They swam around the edge of the pond and turned on their backs to float.

Flynn closed her eyes to let her thoughts wander. She missed her music. *Where is the orchestra playing this week?* Surprisingly, she didn't miss that part of it at all, she just missed playing her violin. It had been an element of her life for so long. *Can I just walk away from it and my career, when and if the time ever comes to choose?*

The water felt silky and smooth on her body. Above, the trees provided a canopy with colorful birds dotted here and there among the leaves, all making raucous noises.

"Thanks for going along with this engagement like you have. You'll be suitably paid for the time involved and the strife." Marshall's voice was cool and distant.

I want it that way, don't I? "You're welcome. I agreed mostly for Timmy. I don't want anything to upset his life right now. And it's not fair if you should lose Rainbow's End because of her." She struggled to keep her voice as stiff and remote as Marshall's.

"That's kind of you to care. You haven't known us long." His tone was dry, skeptical. *Does he think I'm only interested in the money? That this is just another job to me? Well, let him think that. It will be easier all the way around when he finds out the truth, or when I leave, whichever comes first.*

The conversation was becoming awkward. Flynn planed her palm forward to splash him.

Marshall sputtered, shaking the water from his hair. "You little rascal!" She began swimming toward the forbidden center to elude him, but before long she felt a strong grip on her ankle and was pulled downward. Marshall's iron grip held her fast as she turned around in the water and tried to twist away.

He lifted her out of the water, his arms around her waist and under her knees.

"Put me down, you nut!" She laughed.

They swam side by side for a while. Their bodies bumped together in the silken water, his skin warm and smooth against hers, and as she was about to spin away, he drew her close. His hands moved over her body, touching, caressing, in slow motion with the drag of the water against his hands.

She ran her palms over his chest, relishing the feel of muscle beneath her fingers, circling his ribs with her arms. His breath hitched audibly at her touch. Long, hard legs moved between hers, entwining together as they floated as one. Water teased their faces when they kissed long and deep, her pulse racing even more when his tongue began a relentless search, to which she boldly responded, molding her body against the length of him.

"Flynn, sweet Flynn." The spoken caress tickled her ear.

They moved toward shore and lingered at the edge of

the little pool, ankle-deep in lush grass, while they toweled their bodies. She rubbed the cold away until her skin tingled, then she brushed her towel over his shoulders and down his chest. Marshall closed his eyes and tilted his head upward toward the sun sifting down through the branches. She wanted to touch her mouth to the hard little pebbles of his nipples. She would never love him more than at this moment.

How would it be to let him make love to her? As if in answer to her question, he touched a finger beneath her chin, tilting her chin up to look deep into her eyes.

"Let me love you, Flynn." His voice was husky. She could have drowned in his eyes, tempted beyond belief.

"You mean make love to me?"

Marshall looked puzzled. "It's all the same, isn't it?"

She turned away. "When you discover the difference, then maybe we can talk about it."

The spell broke at the harsh cry of a gull out on the water. The look he gave her was indecipherable and then he motioned her on toward the blanket. They sat while he poured tea from a steaming thermos. They drank enough to warm them and then, as one, lay back. He took her gently in his arms and held her close, smoothing back the strands of damp hair from her face. For a while he was content to hold her, and she thought about how it would feel to be cared for and held this way the rest of her life.

His hands cupped her face while he rained kisses over her, his lips became more insistent, his mouth hard and demanding. Their bodies blended together with a sweet warmth enveloping her, moving through her body in waves.

His fingers roamed the slender column of her back and left a fiery trail as they moved. As if against his will, he broke away, his breath ragged, his eyes closed.

She leaned to kiss his eyelids softly, her moist lips

playing over his forehead and cheeks. He groaned and pulled her closer.

"Flynn, I…I care for you very much. This feels very real, as if we really are engaged."

"I know. I feel the same for you. But we've issues that can't be ignored. When I marry, I want a wedding dress—the whole works. I want someone who can't bear life without me and who will love me back."

"You deserve all of that and more. I felt an attraction for you from the moment I saw you. That hasn't changed. But as you said, there are many obstacles in the way. You know my views about love, and I promise I'll never lie to get to you. As far as I'm concerned, there's nothing more shameful than deception. I hate it that we have to deceive about our engagement, but it's the only way out I see."

She put her fingers on his lips to stop him from speaking further. What would he think about her network of lies? It was an absurd question. She already knew what his reaction would be. All his bitterness came because he either still cared for Suzy or didn't trust anyone because of her. She was always there between them.

Would there ever be a time when she wasn't?

Chapter 21

Flynn awoke the next morning to sunlight streaming between the drapes pulled back from her hotel window. Marshall was sitting on the couch, reading the morning paper, with a cup of coffee on the end table.

"How in the world did you get in? Haven't you ever heard of privacy?" Her protest was only a pretense. It was nice to wake up and see him first thing in the morning. "Mmm. That smells good." She sat up in bed pulling the sheet higher around her shoulders.

He winked. "Been waiting for you to wake up, sleepyhead. The maid let me in. We *are* engaged after all." He poured a cup of steaming coffee from the pot and brought it to her.

He was dressed for home. The neckline of his white T-shirt came just above the top button of his russet-brown shirt, his jeans just tight enough. He looked so fine, it brought a lump to her throat. Flynn turned her head away and sipped the coffee as she fought to collect her composure.

"I see you're dressed for Rainbow's End. Are we leaving soon?"

"This morning. Soon's I can get Hoppy and the boy

started. They can be slower than a snail sometimes."

Flynn understood his impatience. "What are you going to tell everyone—about us?"

He shrugged. "They have to know something. Bugger it all. I hate this subterfuge, but there's no other way around it. Unless I give in to her demands, Suzy means her threats and will follow through if provoked. I don't want to believe it, but Damon might somehow be behind it all, as well."

"You don't know that." Suzy as much as told her Damon was involved but then Suzy was a consummate liar at best. At worst her sense of reality was totally warped. If she hinted that Damon might be involved and it wasn't true, did she want to be the cause of even more bad blood between the brothers. It was getting so complicated. She'd have to hedge around the truth.

" I know you don't like lying to anyone. When it's over and I leave, you can explain that we just decided it wouldn't work. Couples break up all the time. Besides, everyone in town probably knows about it now, if Hoppy told Thelma."

Marshall paced the room "Damon seemed the only one put out about it. God knows what Suzy will think."

"Does it matter?"

Marshall didn't answer and her heart tripped in her chest. *He still has feelings for her.*

"Damon will probably be back to congratulate us again. He seems to have taken a shine to you." His tone sounded so noncommittal she didn't know whether he was joking or serious.

"He didn't appeal to me in the slightest." If she hadn't known about Suzy and Damon, she might have stepped right into it, trying to tease him, make him a little jealous. It would have been a disastrous move.

Marshall's mouth twitched in amusement, or at least

she hoped that was what it was. His eyes were secretive, closed to her.

"With this business arrangement, we'll have to do quite a bit of acting to make it work. There's a lot at stake here." She couldn't bear the thought of Timmy being sent away, which would surely happen if Suzy took Marshall to court and tried to get custody of the boy.

What would he do if he lost Rainbow's End? These shouldn't have been her problems, but because she was connected to Suzy, they had become hers. The one thing she wouldn't do was walk out on them. She would stay to see it through, no matter how it turned out.

Even as she mentally made excuses for her involvement, she had to face the truth. She loved Marshall. She hoped he would open his heart to her, someday before it was time for her to leave. But if he still wanted a broodmare for the family he craved, it wasn't going to be her. She wanted children with him, but only if he loved her as much as she had learned to love him.

කකක

With the passing days, life on the farm became normal and calm again. The farmhands accepted her as the woman of the house and gave her the respect due the position. One by one they came to her, to wish her welcome.

Her deep-seated shame at her deception made her increasingly uncomfortable each and every day. Marshall was attentive in a polite, remote manner. An outward show of affection was apparently not expected from either her or Marshall, which was a relief.

In a way.

One evening, at one of Marshall's now-rare appearances at dinner, Mrs. Hopkins and Timmy pretended to continue eating as she questioned him, but she knew they were listening.

"You're working awfully late, Marshall. You're not overdoing it, are you?" She forced her voice to sound solicitous, wifely. What she really wanted to know was whether he was avoiding her.

He acknowledged the questioning looks from around the table with a resigned sigh. "I apologize if I'm not giving my lovely fiancée the full attention she deserves." His look was unrepentant, his raised eyebrow a silent challenge for her to disagree. "Truth is, the mare I ordered from the mainland is ready to foal. We think it'll be twins. I need—Rainbow's End needs—this new bloodline. It will be the start of a new era for us."

"Can I see it borned?" Since they had returned from Hobart, Timmy no longer seemed afraid of his father, although he was still wary. They were both learning.

"Don't see why not. It could happen late at night, though. Sure you're up to that?"

Timmy sat straighter in his chair and folded his hands across his chest, thrusting out his chin in a duplication of Marshall's familiar gesture. Everyone laughed and Timmy looked around the table, puzzled but unperturbed.

"Just wake me. It's 'portant." He ducked his head and went back to playing with the food on his plate, plainly uncomfortable by the attention focused on him.

At the end of the meal Hoppy took Timmy away from the table. Before Marshall could stand up to leave, Flynn placed a halting hand on his arm.

"Is everything okay? I—we—hardly ever see you anymore." Had she done anything to make him withdraw?

"I didn't want to say anything in front of the boy, but the mare's having problems. The foals are big, and one is turned the wrong way. To make matters more complicated, I'm needed at the hydroelectric plant. Did I tell you I helped them set it up and get it started? Well, the system is getting old, and with predictions of an unusually heavy rainy season this year, it's well and truly time for it to be overhauled. I just haven't had the time to do anything about it, and now it has come to the point where I have no choice but to make time."

He really did look tired. Now that she thought about it, she hadn't heard him laugh for a while. She longed to smooth the lines at the corner of his eyes, kiss the top of his head, anything just to touch him. Resolutely ignoring the possible consequences of her actions, she quickly got up from the table, stood behind him and put her hands on his shoulders, rubbing and massaging the tense muscles there. After a moment she felt him relax.

"Ahh...that feels wonderful." Marshall reached his hands up to cover hers. "Thank you. For understanding. I know this can't be easy for you. I'll bet you can't wait to get back to your own life. Suzy should have heard about our engagement by now. All I have to do is wait for the uproar. That's what it'll take to sort this mess out. You shouldn't have to put up with this for too much longer."

Even though he was being honest, his words still hurt. She did have a life before Rainbow's End, but it was one she could barely remember anymore. *Where is Suzy?* She must have known Flynn would be furious about the telephone call, but as soon as news about the engagement leaked out, Suzy should have already made contact. And an explosive one at that. All her plans, and Damon's, could go up in flames. Flynn was sure Damon would toss her cousin aside when she was no more help in his bid to get Rainbow's End back. Was Suzy's absence an ominous sign?

Every Tuesday Flynn had made excuses to check the churchyard. It had started to become awkward, since she always had to catch a ride with Ralph or Junior. There were only so many excuses she could reasonably come up with, without seeming suspicious, and she was fast running out of them.

"Don't worry about me." She was standing so close, the temptation to run her fingers through his thick hair was almost irresistible. The weather lines at the back of his neck beckoned to her, wanting to be caressed. She balled her fists, refusing to succumb to desire. "My life's on hold. I needed a break away from things." He had never asked about her past. *Didn't he care?* The silent accusation wasn't fair. She was the one who had laid out the ground rules from the beginning, that he not question her about her past.

ೠೠ

It started to rain. Marshall had gone out and Mrs. Hopkins took Timmy with her to visit a friend in the village. Sitting in her room on the window seat, Flynn watched the lightning flashes through the trees. *Now's as good a time as any to look for the diary.*

She located a flashlight and then pulled down the swinging doorway to the attic with the attached stairs. It was the only place she hadn't searched for the diary. If ever she found it, she was more than determined to read the cursed book.

The air choked her when her footsteps disturbed the patina of powdery dust on the floor. Flashes of lightning through the dingy dormer windows caught the dust motes rising into the air. She flicked the flashlight upward and discovered a light fixture with a bare bulb hanging from the rafters. Luckily it worked, lighting up all but the farthest corners.

The first trunk was filled with old clothes. The clothing was feminine, probably his mother's. His father must have saved them after she died.

The next few boxes were filled with old dishes and whatnots. A scurrying noise in the corner caught her attention. Although she always said mice didn't frighten her, she'd never come across one in person. The closeness of the room was getting to her. Just a few more boxes to look through.

All of a sudden she felt a presence in the room. Swinging around in a panic, she caught her heel in a rough place between the floorboards. A strong hand held her arm, keeping her steady. She looked up to see Marshall's scowling face.

"What are you doing up here? It could be dangerous."

What did he mean? Was that some sort of veiled threat? Did he suspect Suzy had hidden something in the house?

"I love old attics." Her heart thudded in her ears. Another thunderclap sounded close to the house and she flinched. He pulled her close.

"We've never been hit by lightning yet."

Flynn felt the vibration of his voice through her cheek pressed against his chest.

"I'm not afraid. I like storms." She didn't want to push away from the warmth and comfort he brought, but she had to.

"I thought you were out with the horses. Is the mother all right?"

He grinned. "That's why I came back. To get you and Timmy. She's foaled and the three are doing fine."

She hugged him. "Wonderful! Timmy will be so happy. That's the start of your new stable, isn't it?"

"Our stable," he corrected with a wink. "All the dreams of Rainbow's End are tied up in that one little filly. If she produces what I think she will, we'll have a whole new breed of racers for the mainland."

She brushed her dusty hands on her jeans. "I'm ready."

"Good. Timothy should be back by now." Marshall had gone ahead, holding her hand when he switched off the light. He stopped just as they reached the downward doorway. "An' in the future, if you want to come up here to rummage around, feel free. Just make sure you tell someone where you are. You could trip on one of these beams, break a leg, and yell for help until you're blue in the face. No one would hear you unless they were in this wing of the house."

Very quietly she let out a huge sigh of relief. It seemed her flimsy excuse of curiosity was acceptable.

The last step of the rickety ladder called for a small leap and Marshall stood below to catch her. He held her for a long moment, his eyes filled with an emotion she couldn't decipher.

Timmy had returned and was playing in his room on his computer. He jumped up when he was told about the new foals. "Can one be mine? Can it?" He looked out at the rain and shrugged on his jacket without being prompted.

"You have a pony. I bought you one, remember?"

Timmy wrinkled his nose. "She's mean and hateful and always wants to bite me."

"Maybe that's because you don't pay her any attention."

I hope you think about what you just said. The same could be said about his relationship with his son. Flynn intervened before the argument turned serious. "Come on, let's go. We may be missing something."

From the beginning she'd noticed the only time Marshall paid serious attention to his son was when they argued. She didn't know much about kids, but maybe Timmy had picked up on that and decided bad attention was better than none. It was a terrible habit for both of them, and she longed to help them break it.

"Flynn's right, you know." Marshall knelt in front of Timmy and put his hands on his son's shoulders, looking at him eye-to-eye. "These foals are important. They're the new beginning for Rainbow's End. I don't see why you can't have one until it's grown. Then it will have to fulfill its specialty as a racer. You'd like that, wouldn't you?"

Timmy didn't squirm under his father's hands but stood still, thinking for a long moment. He nodded. "Good job, to grow into a racer."

Marshall stood and pointed to the raincoats on hooks near the doorway. "Hold up. Better grab your *drizabones.* It's fair bucketing down."

She didn't miss the note of worry in his voice. The dam and hydroelectric plant must be playing on his mind.

They hurried through the downpour to reach the stables, where Ralph had seen them coming and opened the gate for them.

"Evening, Boss. The mare's doing well."

Ralph was a dear. Tall and cadaverously thin, he reminded her of childhood tales of Ichabod Crane in *The Legend of Sleepy Hollow*. He was part of the family, the same as Thelma and Hoppy.

The mare stood by restively when they trooped in to see the foals. Tears came to Flynn's eyes when she took in their beauty and grace. Long-legged, tall and gangling, they were not the least alarmed by all the attention. "They're beautiful!"

Timmy looked up at his father for permission and when Marshall nodded, the boy walked over to touch them.

"They're right li'l beauties, at that. Going to be rangy and tall like their mother. The sire is from the finest racing stock on the mainland."

"The father isn't here at Rainbow's End?"

"No. That's the wonder of technology for you. The mare was artificially inseminated in Melbourne before coming here. If it works out well, we'll use the same sire each time, for consistency."

It didn't sound like much fun to Flynn. The sparkle in his eyes told her he understood without her speaking. It was uncanny, sometimes, how they tuned in to each other's thoughts. She hoped he missed her thoughts about Suzy.

Suzy. Tomorrow, rain or shine, she was going to the churchyard. Her cousin had to show up sooner or later.

Chapter 22

It was Tuesday yet again, and although Flynn didn't know if Suzy had shown up while they were in Hobart, if her cousin missed their meeting today, that would make it four altogether. She felt certain Suzy would show up this time, if for nothing else but to ask about the impending marriage and her diary.

Flynn cared deeply for Marshall and Timmy and felt so much at home at Rainbow's End. But now, even if she had a chance of making Marshall love her, their relationship was already doomed. Eventually she would have to tell him why she came here, her history with Suzy, her career. And when she did, he would never trust her again.

Her trips into town were becoming commonplace, and she caught a ride without comment. Though she had always offered excuses why she needed to go into town, she had started to get the distinct impression that nobody really cared if she didn't offer any. The awkwardness she felt each time was a waste of worry. Such was the respect for everyone's privacy.

The sky was overcast. Rain poised on the edge of the dark clouds, ready to let loose at any moment. The impending moisture already permeated the air.

"I'll meet you at the arcade in two hours, if that's

okay with you." She got out of the truck at the church-yard.

"Sure thing. I'll be finished by then." A gap showed between Junior's top front teeth when he smiled, just the same as his father's. Both men were so shy it was hard getting two words out of either of them at times.

Before she could slam the door, Junior reached across the seat to hold it open. "You'll be okay? Looks like a cloud buster coming."

Flynn pulled her jacket tighter around her. "Sure thing. I'll be fine." It was just a few blocks from the churchyard to the center of the little village, but it always seemed more. The church sat in the middle of a large acreage with tall trees and strange, topiary bushes all around it. Even in the daytime the churchyard had a dark, forbidding air. Suzy had chosen wisely for a meeting place. Flynn had never met another soul, as many times as she'd visited here.

At first she sat on their designated bench, listening to the busy birds getting ready to hide from the storm. The wind whipped leaves from the trees and snarled in her hair in spite of it being tied against her neck with a rib-bon.

After sitting impatiently a while, Flynn paced in front of the bench, up and down the stone walkway. The sky grew darker.

Suzy wasn't coming. She knew her cousin had to question the marriage. It would have thrown her crazy plans into a complete shambles. So what would keep her away? Her cousin must feel betrayed, even if it wasn't logical.

An oppressive dread settled over her. She could bare-ly breathe. Lightning flashed and the wind rushed around the corners of the tall, gray buildings.

She looked back into the churchyard one last time.

Her eye caught a flash of bright cloth caught in the bushes. Heart pounding, she ignored the wind that nearly pushed her off her feet and ran back into the maze of bushes. She reached on her tiptoes to pluck the long silk scarf from the topiary bush. Suzy's favorite color—green. She held it to her face and inhaled the perfume. Looking closer, she saw an ugly, dark stain on the corner of the scarf.

Swallowing past her fear, she forced herself to pick her way through the churchyard instead of giving in to her instincts and running. The back of her neck prickled and chills raced up and down her spine as her heart thudded in earnest. Was someone watching her? Every bush seemed to catch her jacket, making her escape slower, longer. Each tree, each shrub was large enough for an intruder to hide behind.

The rain started to fall, slowly at first and then in earnest. The urge to turn away from her investigation, to run toward the town and its sanctuary of lights, was at its zenith, but some force out of her control dragged her onward.

Thunder crashed loudly with the blinding flash of lightning. Shivering and shaking so badly it was hard to move her feet, Flynn swallowed her overwhelming fear and continued with her search. When she reached the grove of trees at the end and saw nobody, she turned tail and fled. Did something frighten Suzy enough to cause her to run away and lose her scarf in the process or had something bad happened to her?

The arcade was lit brightly, and as Flynn ran in, she spotted Junior playing games. She stopped in her tracks and took a long, deep breath. *Should I tell the police? What would I tell them?* Suzy had angered everyone surrounding her. There was no doubt several people would like to see her cousin gone. Permanently. Most likely

Damon, for one. Had Suzy begun to be a problem for him? If she was telling the truth, it was obvious he was using her. And then there was Marshall. He'd threatened Suzy the last time she called.

She walked up to Ralph Junior, soaking up his quiet normalcy as she went. "I'd like to go home now. I think I caught a chill in the rain." *Go home now.* The words reverberated in her aching head, mocking her.

On the ride home Junior was his normal, taciturn self, something for which Flynn was thankful. She had seen Marshall angry. Would he be capable of doing away with Suzy? Both he and Damon would know places to hide a body where no one would ever find it. That idea was more than enough to send her imagination into fearful places. Closing her eyes, she pictured Marshall's big hands clenched, his jaw tight. He could be capable of extreme wrath—he had a temper.

She stopped her morose thoughts from cluttering her mind. Nothing good would ever come from them. Suzy could have heard a noise in the bushes and had a fright. Anything could have set her in a panic.

Was Marshall capable of killing? Where did that leave her? They were engaged to be married. He had virtual control of her here. If he wanted, he could monitor her every move. She would be a prisoner.

Unless she just packed up and left.

Chapter 23

The rain had finally drizzled off into a kind of fog over the countryside by the time Flynn arrived home. Lights shone on the bottom floor of the house, making it look like soft glows of warmth nestled in cotton. Timmy ran out to greet her, prattling on about the new foals. Mrs. Hopkins stayed in the background for a moment, watching.

What if all this was real? Rainbow's End felt like home to her. She had been living in a fantasy world that was slowly becoming tangible. Tears threatened, her eyes burning in the effort to not give in to the emotion.

"If you don't mind, I'm going to bed. It has been a rather tiring day."

Mrs. Hopkins reached for her wet jacket and she jerked back for fear the housekeeper would discover the hidden secret. "No! I mean, I'll take it upstairs to my room and hang it over the tub."

"Surely you'll want a bite to eat?"

"Where've you been?" Marshall's voice hit her broadside.

Where did he think I was? Where had he been? His hair was damp, his muddied boots were on the rubber mat by the door.

Mrs. Hopkins disappeared inside, mumbling about bringing out some hot tea. Timmy followed her close behind.

Marshall strode across the room and grabbed hold of her elbow.

Flynn tried to pull away, but was hampered by her heavy, wet coat, which she clutched to her chest. She expected the scarf to fall out of her pocket at any moment. He might think it hers, but then again he might remember the scent of Suzy's perfume.

Even though she tried to resist, he didn't relax his grip on her arm. "Come. Sit down and warm yourself by the fire. You look like you've seen a ghost. An' for God's sake, lay the damn coat on the rug if you can't force yourself to part with it."

How she wanted to have this man hold her close. "There's something I need to tell you."

His look was speculative as he waited for her to continue.

An innate caution stopped her confession. "Have you heard from Suzy since the last time she called?"

"No, I haven't." The muscle in his jaw clenched as anger lit his brown eyes, turning them obsidian. "I hope never to hear her voice again."

Any last doubts of him still loving her cousin were demolished by his expression and clenched fists. "What do you mean?"

"It's not important. What did you want to tell me? We got off track."

"Never mind. It will keep."

It definitely wasn't the time to confess her involvement. If she did and he told her to leave, she might never get to the bottom of Suzy's disappearance. The diary had become more than an annoying obsession now. It could be truly a matter of life and death.

The tension dissipated somewhat when Mrs. Hopkins brought in a tray for them and then left.

Flynn poured and handed him a cup and saucer. Their fingers briefly touched as he reached for it. A shiver of electricity zapped through her hand and up her arm. She carefully poured herself a cup, not wanting to look at Marshall to see if he'd felt it, too.

"I'm leaving for Melbourne tonight, and I didn't want to go without seeing you were home safe and sound."

His concern touched her heart, and then she remembered the brooding look he'd given her when she returned from the village.

"How long will you be gone?" She struggled to keep her tone polite and even.

"A few days. I need to talk to the stables who are interested in the bloodlines I'm establishing with the fillies. I've already told Hoppy, and she'll tell Timothy."

You couldn't tell him yourself? Although Timmy and Marshall had made great strides at getting closer, it was clear it wasn't perfect yet.

"I'm tired, it's been a long day." She rose to leave.

Marshall got to his feet and stood in front of her. Their eyes locked as he tilted his head slightly, raw desire in his gaze, before he kissed her. Engulfed in his arms, she absorbed his sweet, tender kiss, which had none of the usual demanding passion behind it.

When he released her, he grinned. "Just wanted to give you a goodbye kiss."

Will there be a hello kiss when you return? She certainly hoped so.

✁✂✁

When she was finally back in her room, Flynn removed the contents of her coat pocket and hung the jacket over the bathtub as she'd promised to do. She found a plastic bag to stash the silken scarf.

Suzy's scent still clung to the damp bit of cloth as she held it close to her cheek. Tears coursed, unchecked, down her cheeks. Tears for the cousin who had vanished a long time ago. Tears for the stranger who had messed up her own life and that of her husband and son.

She tried hard not to think of what might have happened to Suzy in the churchyard. The dark stain on the scarf could have been something other than blood. How would she find out? She didn't even know where Suzy could be reached.

Flynn stashed the scarf with the letter and photo inside a zippered pocket of her backpack. She lay in bed, awake for a long time, a myriad of thoughts whirling about in her head.

The next morning, after a fitful sleep, she awoke late. While she showered and dressed, she thought about the entire situation with Marshall, Timmy, Suzy and the role she had fabricated for herself. It was clear she couldn't stay here forever, waiting for word from her cousin.

Her feelings toward Marshall were as confused as ever. While they were in Hobart, she was certain she loved him. But the nagging idea he was capable of great violence toward Suzy was impossible to overlook.

Downstairs was quiet, the dining room empty. She pushed open the kitchen door. Hoppy and Timmy were eating breakfast with Thelma. They abruptly stopped talking when they saw her.

"Come. Have something to eat." Mrs. Hopkins smiled as Timmy scraped back his chair and ran to take Flynn's hand.

"Sit here with us, please?"

Flynn looked down at the boy and her heart constricted. How could Suzy not want to be with him?

"Thanks, but I don't want to intrude."

Thelma pushed up out of her chair. "Don't talk rubbish. I'll fix you a bite."

"Please don't. Hoppy, I'd like to talk to you in the breakfast nook—that is, if you've got the time."

"Of course."

Timmy left to go look at the fillies, and Thelma fixed them two trays, which they carried through the house and out to the little room facing the garden. Timmy called it the Sunshine Room. He loved to do his homework there and play with his toys on the window seats.

"There's something you need to know." She just hoped Mrs. Hopkins wouldn't say anything until it was the right time to let Marshall know.

She cleared her throat. This wasn't going to be easy. "Suzy and I are cousins. We were raised together like sisters." *Just get it out and go from there.*

Mrs. Hopkins looked shocked, so she hurried on before the housekeeper could have a chance to interrupt. She detailed her relationship with Suzy and how her cousin insisted she check on Timmy. She left out the diary.

"Does Mr. Beckett know?" Mrs. Hopkins' usual friendly look was replaced by wary skepticism.

"No, he doesn't. Suzy assured me my coming here as a nanny was the only way I could get in to see her son."

"Her son, indeed! She couldn't care less about the boy. Hated every moment of being pregnant. How she carried on about stretch marks and being fat." Hoppy's face was pale and stricken, her body fairly vibrating with indignation.

"She must have cared enough about him to take him away." *Why am I still defending her? Out of pity?*

"Timmy adored her, you know. But the woman you

knew as a child growing up apparently isn't the same woman we knew. She was selfish, willful and unfaithful. She only took Timmy away to get back at Mr. Beckett. Even when she had the boy, she was more concerned about her own self and left him with a friend who was too old to look after a young'un properly."

The outpouring of bitterness was expected. Flynn plunged on, again leaving out the diary and treading around Suzy's claim of Damon's participation.

Much to her surprise, the older woman didn't look at all hostile at her confession.

"I know the truth about your engagement." Her words sounded forced. She was clearly uncomfortable with the disclosure.

Flynn understood. It was a betrayal of Marshall's confidence.

"He explained both of you agreed to it in order to get Suzy to relinquish her crazy claims. He thinks Mr. Damon could be a part of her mischief, but I don't want to believe that. The brothers started off on the wrong foot when Mr. Beckett came back to claim Rainbow's End."

If only she and Marshall could be that certain. Suzy without Damon did not pose half the threat as both of them together, plotting and scheming.

"In a short time the engagement could have been for real. Are you so blind as not to know Mr. Beckett is beginning to care for you? He's finally letting his guard down, and now this." Mrs. Hopkins' long, bony fingers folded around the cup, her knuckles white with tension.

"I can't blame you for thinking I might be wanted by Interpol or something just as bad." Flynn described her long history with her violin and the orchestra. "I haven't been to the States in a long time. I—I'm not as fortunate as you and Marshall. No place is home to me."

"I didn't really buy that story about hitchhiking

around the country, but I had no reason to think you were lying, either. It's all a bloody mess. Are there any more surprises?"

"I hope not." How could she tell anyone about the scarf?

"You must have thought Mr. Beckett some kind of tyrant, going to all those lengths to lead us down the garden path. It's how *she* saw him, and none of us could understand why. God knows he tried to give her everything she could possibly want. At first we all loved and worshiped her. But it didn't take long to see her beauty was only skin deep."

"I hadn't seen my cousin for years. She never invited me to her wedding, or told me about her little boy for the longest time."

"She told us she was an orphan."

"Technically that's true, but my mother raised her, as if she were my sister." She sipped her now-cold tea without tasting it.

"She was like a spoiled child, pushing to see how far she could go."

"Is it possible she just needed more of Marshall's time?"

Mrs. Hopkins' mouth twisted in a grimace. "I have to admit he was working long hours. He was away from home quite a bit. But an understanding missus would have realized he had inherited a piece of property that was costing a fortune to run, without any profit whatsoever. He was trying to get it going and pouring all his resources and effort into it, to get it up and running properly again.

"I've no business repeating this, but since she is your cousin, you should know. After Timmy's birth, terrible arguments started between Mr. Beckett and Suzy. The place fairly rang with bitterness and accusations." Mrs.

Hopkins shook her head in remembrance.

"But still, do you think it fair he kicked her out without a place to go?"

The housekeeper shot her a surprised look. "Where did you hear that? It's an outright lie. Mr. Beckett finally put his foot down after Timmy was born. Told her she couldn't leave for days at a time with the poor little nipper needing his mum. Then one day, while Mr. Beckett was away, she packed her bags. When we saw she was taking the boy with her, we tried to stop her. She flew into a temper and said she was only going for a vacation. There wasn't anything we could do. I don't think she even left him a note."

"What did Marshall do when he found out she'd left with Timmy?"

"He was beside himself with worry, he was so afraid she wouldn't take good care of the boy. He wanted to give them financial help, if he could find her. He searched for them a long time afterward, but in the end he hired a private investigator. What a waste of money that was."

"How did he find them?"

"After about a year and a bit, he received divorce papers from an address in Melbourne. He flew there and found her set up in an apartment with some bloke. None of the neighbors had ever seen the boy. Mr. Beckett managed to track the child down. The boy had been palmed off to an elderly mate who worked part-time. Poor mite didn't know who he belonged to or where he belonged. Mr. Beckett brought him home and took out restraining orders against the missus. We never heard another thing from her since then."

Until she called Marshall that night and threatened him.

"There's something not entirely clear to me."

Flynn waited.

"If you only came to report on Timmy, why did you stay?"

"I had no choice. I had to wait until I could get my passport and funds transferred to the bank in the village."

"I can see it must have been hard for you. Stranded in a strange land with a bloke you were supposed to hate and fear. You said you knew nothing about the marriage part of the ad."

"No. That's the truth. Suzy must have thought that a delicious joke on both of us when she left that part out." It had to be a bitter pill to swallow when Suzy found out she and Marshall were now engaged.

"I don't know what to do. It's my duty to tell Mr. Beckett, unless you wish to first. You knew that when you told me, didn't you?"

"I do understand the position I've placed you in by confiding to you. I did try to tell him several times, but I couldn't. I just know he'll ask me to leave."

"You love him, don't you? An' you love the boy."

Tears came to Flynn's eyes and she felt them trickle down her cheeks. She dipped her head and didn't answer.

"I've been with the Becketts since the boys were ankle-biters. If Mr. Beckett would listen to you explain the way you did to me, I don't see how he could help but forgive you for the deception."

"*If* he would listen." Images of the unforgiving look in his eyes when he spoke of Suzy floated through her mind. "He won't ever forgive me."

She leaned across the table and took Mrs. Hopkins' hands in hers. "You asked why I've stayed on after my passport was replaced and funds were cleared. I've grown to love Marshall and Timmy. A lot. They are both so dear to me that I can't bear the thought of leaving Rainbow's

End. I knew someday I would have to tell him everything."

"My dear child, I knew you loved him. An' bless
him, he loves you, too. You might still make the engagement and marriage work, if you give it time."

Time. She didn't have time. Even though she wished
her cousin gone many a time, the stained scarf left behind
couldn't be ignored. If she found the diary, everything
might fall into place. In the meantime, she just had to
hope something or someone had frightened Suzy in the
churchyard enough that she ran away.

A terrible thought—and she immediately felt bad
about it—but what if Suzy planned her disappearance,
subtly putting Marshall under a cloud of suspicion? He
could still lose Rainbow's End.

"Mr. Beckett is stubborn and thickheaded, but fair.
Give him some time to come around. In the meantime,
I'll leave it up to you when to tell him the whole story."
Mrs. Hopkins reached across the table and held Flynn's
hands in hers. "You have got to tell him. There's no other
way around it."

"I know. Thank you for allowing me to do it on my
own."

Too late, a voice echoed in her ear. Too late.

Chapter 24

It was mid-afternoon. Flynn sat in the gazebo with Timmy. Thelma had packed them lunch and they were "camping out," pretending they were alone in the woods.

Rosebushes of every color imaginable surrounded the building, making it appear they were truly isolated from the main house.

"This is fun!" Timmy laughed excitedly. "Dad said I could name the fillies. They can't be mine forever. Dad says we'll have to sell them when they're older."

Poor kid. He was so grown up in some ways and such a baby in others. "There'll be more babies later. You do know that by naming the fillies you'll be a partner with your father in Rainbow's End. In the long run, that's much better than having a filly of your very own, isn't it?"

"I—I guess so. Bloody right, it is! I'm a partner, all bloody right."

"Hey, chum." She gave him a soft clip on his chin with her fist. "Let's leave off the 'bloodies' for now. Okay?"

"What do Yank kids say instead of 'bloody'?"

He didn't really need to know that. Flynn smiled.

"Gosh, it's been such a long time since I've been home, I can't really say."

"How come? Don't you live in America anymore?"

His question shook her a little. She was so close to revealing more than she should. "I was born in New York. But when I grew up, I traveled a lot. I've stayed in France and Germany and…places."

"That's nice." He didn't sound all that impressed.

She had maintained an apartment in Paris for years, but didn't always stay there. Sometimes she stayed at her mother's houses in Spain and France. Dolores may have had more homes, but they didn't get together all that much for Flynn to know.

Suddenly the idea of a nomadic lifestyle seemed so irrational. She missed Dolores. What would her mother think about Rainbow's End, Marshall and Timmy? Putting her slim, still-attractive, cosmopolitan mother in this rural, bucolic setting nearly threw her into a fit of giggles.

"Flynn, Flynn. Are you woolgathering again?" They both laughed at Timmy's mimicry of Marshall.

"I guess I am. I didn't mean to."

"That's okay. Just wait a sec." He leaped off the three gazebo steps and ran around to a rosebush. When he came back, he proudly held a deep-red rose between his finger and thumb. There was a little blood on his palm from the thorns.

"I cut this with the pocketknife Dad gave me for Christmas. It's a special rose. It…it looks like you." Timmy dipped his head, aloof and suddenly shy. "My mum liked the yellow ones."

Flynn wanted to wash the specks of blood from his hand and hug him tight to her. Instead she pressed the bloom to her face and inhaled the heady fragrance. "It's lovely. Thank you." She took a deep breath, not wanting to broach the subject but needing to. No matter who Suzy had become, her son shouldn't forget her. "You said your mother liked the yellow ones?"

Timmy nodded, his dark eyes serious—so much like Marshall's it made her want to cry. "Yep. Mum looked like the yellow ones. But they don't smell as nice like yours."

Why did he pick a deep red rose over the pinks and purples and other colors? She was sure the concept was beyond what he would or could explain. It didn't matter. What was important was that she now had her very own rose. It was as if he'd accepted her into his family.

"You know your mother didn't abandon you, don't you? She'll always love you."

"I guess so. Dad told me that."

Marshall said that? Amazing. "When grownups don't want to live together, they sometimes go different ways."

"He told me that, too. I miss her sometimes, but she…"

Flynn waited patiently and when Timmy didn't show any signs of continuing, she prodded him. "She what?"

"Sometimes she told me she loved me and hugged me a lot. Sometimes she cried and told me I was trouble. I don't remember much."

Poor kid. Suzy had to have deep emotional problems she couldn't handle, unable to talk to anyone about them. She'd never admit to any imperfection.

"I don't know if your mum will ever come home again, Timothy. Grownups have problems they can't share with their children. I know it's tough, but it's true when I say you may understand when you're older."

"Hoppy said that, too."

"Well, then, it appears the people who love you have a lot of good advice. You can talk to any of us about it when you feel sad. Meanwhile, we're supposed to be having fun. Want to play some games before we eat?"

Ralph Junior had come earlier and laid out some pegs for a game of quoits and strung up a badminton net, pounding it lower into the ground so Timmy could hit over it.

"Yay!" Timmy leaped up and tore down the steps. She laughed. His looks and personality had captured the best of both Suzy and Marshall. *This boy is going to be quite a heartbreaker when he grows up.*

They played until she begged for mercy and flopped down on the thick grass. "I'm done! You wore me out."

Timmy grabbed hold of her foot and tugged on it, as if to get her up. Flynn reached for him and they tussled for a moment before their laughter broke it up and they both fell back on the grass, looking up at the sky between the trees.

"Look at that cheeky bird." She pointed upward to a bird sitting in the nearest tree. "He's scolding us for being in his space."

"I'm hungry." In one fluid movement, Timmy leaped to his feet. "Race you."

She rolled over and made a grab for his leg, but he was too fast. They ran to the gazebo, out of breath and laughing when they got there.

They stopped short at the steps.

Marshall sat waiting on the bench that circled inside the gazebo. How long had he sat there, watching? Flynn stared wordlessly at him, her heartbeat pounding in her ears. The tenderness in his expression overwhelmed her.

"I was watching you play together. You remind me of two puppies frolicking."

She pushed Timmy gently ahead of her. The unexpected rush of emotion when their eyes met threw her into confusion. Could Mrs. Hopkins be right? Was Marshall beginning to care for her in the way she'd hoped?

It would only complicate things in the long run.

"Dad!" Timmy started to run over to his father but hesitated at the last minute. Marshall beckoned for him to sit at his side and then put an arm casually around the boy's shoulders.

"Looks like you're having a lot of fun. Hope I'm not intruding." The last of the sentence was directed toward her.

"Oh no, we're glad you're here." She and Timmy came out with almost the same words at the same time. The resultant laughter relaxed the atmosphere.

Flynn busied herself with laying out the picnic provisions, while Timmy told Marshall all about his week.

They sat on cushions on the floor. Their eyes met over Timmy's head and Marshall winked. It was a wonderful moment, with the three of them tucked away on the floor of the gazebo, surrounded by shrubbery and roses. She turned away and closed her eyes, imprinting it on her memory.

Thelma had once again outdone herself in the kitchen, and when they couldn't eat another bite, Timmy started to excuse himself to go out on the lawn to play.

Marshall leaned back with a huge sigh. "Hang on a sec. There's something I want to say."

Timmy plopped back down on his cushion and crossed his legs.

Now what? Whatever it was, it sounded momentous.

"We're taking a vacation. For at least two weeks we are going on a real camping trip. Howzat?"

Flynn watched the interplay between father and son. The present camaraderie was so tenuous, so easily disrupted. She prayed Timmy would agree to go. Marshall must have been planning this for a while. He wasn't exactly what she'd call impulsive—something that wouldn't set well with Suzy.

Suzy. Would any of them ever be rid of her presence in Rainbow's End? Flynn shivered, belatedly thinking that indeed they may be rid of her physical existence, if not the shadow she left behind.

"Are you cold?" Marshall took off his jacket and draped it over her shoulders. The sun had gone behind a cloud.

"Thanks." She wasn't cold, but it was easier to accept the jacket than try to explain the tremor that had rippled over her body.

They both noticed that Timmy hadn't spoken.

"Is Hoppy coming?"

Marshall reached across the space between them and ruffled the boy's hair. "Of course not. She's too…she's getting a little too long in the tooth for this stuff. Besides, this will be a vacation for her, too, without us underfoot. She might visit her sister on the mainland."

"Flynn?" Timmy's thin voice raised an octave with the hopeful question.

Marshall looked at her, his dark eyes penetrating—assessing. "If she'd like to go."

Emotions warred within. It would be a perfect time to search for the diary with everyone out of the house. However, in spite of Marshall starting to show his feelings toward his son, they both still needed a day-to-day buffer. Either she or Mrs. Hopkins had been serving in that capacity. What if he expected too much from a son who had never gone camping in his life? What if Timmy got that mile-wide stubborn streak so much like his father's?

The trip could end in disaster, resulting in a long time to repair.

"We're waiting." Marshall's eyes twinkled. The set of his square jaw showed he was serious.

"I don't know. I'm afraid you'd have more on your

hands than you bargained for, with two inexperienced campers." *Oops, I'm not supposed to be inexperienced at camping.*

"Maybe. But Timothy can pretty much take care of himself. He's a big boy. You should be used to traveling all over the place, if I'm to believe you." It sounded as if he wasn't exactly willing to believe her. That decided her. "I'm willing to give it a go if you are," he added, looking very series.

Not the comforting words she wanted to hear.

Was it safe going off in the boonies with Marshall? What about Suzy? Why had she disappeared? How? Did Marshall have anything to do with it? Surely Flynn posed no threat to Marshall. Especially if Mrs. Hopkins hadn't told him anything about her past. But what if she'd told him and he needed her out of the way too. Now she was being melodramatic.

She looked at Marshall, taking in the set of his wide shoulders, the sun-darkened skin of his neck, the muscled clench of his jaw, his sensuous mouth. She didn't get much farther than his all-too-kissable lips when he cleared his throat, bringing her up short.

"Well?"

"Please come with us, Flynn! We want you to come." Timmy gripped her arm, a surprisingly tight grasp for such a slight boy. She looked into his pleading eyes and saw—*oh, Lord*—she saw fear. He was afraid to be alone with his father.

"Oh, all right. But don't expect me to enjoy it. I'm not a very good sport when it comes to roughing it." Oops, there went her big mouth again, had she said too much? But Marshall was watching Timmy who leaned toward her to give her a hug.

"Of course, being taken care of by two big strong men is a plus any girl would jump at." She hoped to lighten the mood, and her effort was repaid by Timmy's chuckle.

There was no way to know for sure if Marshall had planned for her to come along or was merely tolerating her presence. And there was still his attitude toward marriage to contend with. He never said he had changed his mind. About sex and children without emotional commitment.

Not only did she have a problem trusting Marshall, she wasn't sure she could trust herself. Every day spent with him made it that much harder to imagine that he had anything to do with Suzy's sudden disappearance. Before she was aware of what was happening, he had become a necessary part of her life. She had developed a taste for his voice, his smile, even his frown. But especially his kisses. Could she hold herself in check when they were alone in the bush?

Chapter 25

Mrs. Hopkins was elated that the three of them were going on a trip together. "Maybe this will be a chance for you to work things out between you." The two of them sat in a restaurant after a shopping trip for warm clothes.

"That would be nice." Flynn knew she didn't sound convinced.

"The weather at St. Clair National Park is the strangest in all of Tassie. Maybe in all of Oz, for all I know."

"What do you mean?"

"One day the sun will shine brightly without a cloud in the sky. The next day, or even the same afternoon, a snow might come along in the mountains, chilling everything below. Mr. Hopkins and I spent some time in that area. He loved to camp out and explore."

"Somehow I'd always imagined you lived here forever."

Mrs. Hopkins laughed. "Good Lord, no. We traveled all over the place in our first years together. He was a miner, stayed here long enough to court me and then we moved to Queenstown. He'd already staked a claim there. He never imagined a better life than panning for gold." Her smile was sad, melancholy.

"Wasn't that hard on you? Leaving your family to travel with a man you hardly knew?" Flynn looked at Mrs. Hopkins with a different perspective. She had assumed the housekeeper's entire life had been fairly predictable and dull.

The look on Mrs. Hopkins' face was pensive. "Not for a moment did I ever regret it. I loved him and he loved me. He was in a cave-in with several other blokes once. Thank goodness everyone got outta there alive. But he lost his health after that. He turned from a strong ox of a man to a frail, bent stranger. We didn't have long together, but what time we did have was lovely. Sometimes I think the boating accident wasn't really accidental. He hated the thought of being incapacitated. I wouldn't have minded if he'd chosen to go, but I still hate the idea of him going alone."

The elderly woman's pain was palpable, strong, even after the passing years. "You came back home to live?"

"Yes. Old Mr. Beckett needed help with his boys after his missus passed away, so I came to live at Rainbow's End."

No wonder she thought the world of Timmy. Flynn played with her napkin and looked around the restaurant to give the housekeeper time to regain her composure. It was obvious she hadn't confided her story to many people.

"It must have been hard to come with us on the boat in Hobart."

"I have the utmost faith in Mr. Beckett. He told me it would be all right and I believed him. Didn't mean I had to like it, though."

"You've found your home at Rainbow's End. You'll always be a part of their lives."

"I know. It gives me peace of mind at my age. My biggest wish is to see Timmy grow into a man, and see

Mr. Beckett settled with that big family he wants so badly."

Flynn looked away, a lump in her throat.

Mrs. Hopkins reached across the table and placed work-worn hands gently on top of hers. "I hope your engagement will become real. This trip should do the trick."

Flynn patted her hand and pushed back the chair to get up. "I wish…I wish for a lot of things, but sometimes wishes don't come true."

"We'd better collect Timmy before Lorraine tears her hair out. Even though she's got two ankle-biters of her own, she always offers to keep an eye on him while I shop."

She smiled when she heard Hoppy call children ankle-biters. It was a phrase Marshall used from time to time, also. The Aussies really did have their own language.

Outside the sun shone brightly, the sky cloudless. She turned away from the churchyard, blocks up the street. If she looked in that direction she could see the towering trees and the steeple of the old building.

On the way back to Rainbow's End neither she nor Mrs. Hopkins seemed in the mood to talk until they turned into the driveway.

"I know I'm being a worrywart, but do watch Timmy carefully, dear. He wants so much to please his father, he might do something reckless to gain his attention."

"I promise to keep an eye on him. This trip just might be what they need to bring them closer together, don't you think?" *If Marshall would only allow himself to love again, we could all be together.*

The next morning, just before dawn, they were almost ready to go. Thelma brought out several heavy-looking hampers and set them down in the dining room.

Marshall laughed. "Hang on a minute. We'll only be

gone for a few days, not a year, and during that time I intend to teach these two to fish for their supper."

"Huh! We'll be pretty darn skinny by the time we get home then, if that's your master plan." Flynn loved it when the lines disappeared from around Marshall's mouth and his eyes sparkled when she teased him.

"That's just to tide you over until you get there." Thelma folded her arms over her ample bosom in a no-nonsense manner.

"Okay, then. Thank you for your thoughtfulness." His grin spread as he patted Thelma on her shoulder.

"Oh, get along with you." She flushed at his attention and looked pleased.

Flynn picked up the basket and hovered her nose above the warm towel on top. "Mmm, it smells wonderful. Who wants to eat yucky old fish, anyway?"

Once they were in the car and headed down the driveway, Flynn looked back to see Mrs. Hopkins and Thelma waving.

Timmy started out wide-eyed and alert as they zipped along the highway, but soon fell fast asleep, stretched out on the back seat.

Marshall turned the heater on, fogging up the windows in the back, enclosing them in a makeshift cocoon. "Warm enough?"

"Have you been to the camping place we're going?"

"Lake St. Clair? Many times. There aren't many places on the island I've not explored. Although there are reported to be parts below Queenstown no bloke has ever penetrated, as far as I know." His deep voice resonated in the closeness of the car.

"Are you saying on an island like this there are unexplored areas? That's pretty hard to believe."

"There are forests so thick the sun never shines inside, deep ravines that flow with swollen rivers, and the worst are the Horizontals. We call it being out in the whoop-whoops."

"What? Now I know you're teasing." She enjoyed the feeling of shared intimacy. A gray cotton batting of misty fog trailed by their closed windows, while inside it was toasty warm with the heater going full blast.

"No lie. The dense growth covers acres and acres. You need a machete just to make your way through, and even then it grows back right before your very eyes, or so I'm told."

"Will we be seeing any of this? Will we see a Tasmanian devil, do you suppose?" By now she realized Suzy's silly exaggeration in comparing Marshall to one of the creatures.

"Don't think so. They seldom are seen unless they want to be. I doubt you'd like to run into one, at any rate. We might take a bushwalking trail on Lake St. Clair, if you'd like to try it. It's roughly a one-hundred-kilometer hike—sixty miles or thereabouts for you. I made it in less than four days once. But with you and Timothy...Well, maybe a day out will be more than enough."

He reached across the distance between them and squeezed her hand. "I'm glad you decided to come along."

"Are you kidding? I wouldn't have missed it for the world." She turned away in confusion to look out the window because his look was so affectionate.

By the time Timmy struggled out of his sound sleep, they had made good time and the sun had managed to shine down through a few minor clouds.

"Are we there yet?" He stretched and yawned.

"Not yet, but it's time we took a break, though." Marshall pulled the car over onto the shoulder of the highway. They broke open one of the picnic baskets and ate lunch. The tea from the thermos was hot and strong.

Flynn held her cup tightly to warm her cold fingers.

"Are we in for bad weather?" She pointed to the clouds scooting across the sky faster than before. The wind had picked up, small trees bent against it.

Marshall shrugged. "Who can say? We may run into a heavy rain or, if we're unlucky, a spot of snow."

"Have I ever seen snow?" Timmy said around a mouthful of sandwich.

"I'm sure you haven't." When they finished eating, Marshall took the boy outside into the brush to answer the call of nature.

The road they traveled on meandered through the mountains and down into valleys filled with lush, green ferns. When they finally arrived, she found herself wishing they were still whizzing along the highway. It had been so warm and comfortable.

Once they'd finished hauling stuff out of the vehicle and set up their tents, they sat around the campfire. "We'll just have a bite of something cold and turn in early. Tomorrow Tim and I will catch a bucket load of fish."

The boy smiled, a shy, tentative curl of lip. "Yes!"

A lump rose up in her throat. A month ago he would never have spoken out so.

The wind didn't intrude much into the site Marshall had picked out to peg their tents, yet it was chilly sitting around the campfire. She looked forward to the warmth of her sleeping bag. Timmy must have felt the same, for he said his goodnights and went into his little tent.

Flynn stood up and stretched. "Guess I'll call it a day, too, if you don't mind." As she turned toward her tent, Marshall stepped in front of her, blocking her departure. She looked up in surprise.

"An' here I was, thinking you'd want to bunk with me." His husky voice was pitched just above a whisper. "To keep warm, I mean."

"I don't think so."

His mouth settled on hers with natural ease, his lips moving over hers, his tongue searching. She permitted herself the luxury of enjoying the kiss for a little while before she spread her hands gently against his chest.

He slid his cheek down against hers, pushing away her hair at the nape of her neck, and then began to nibble gently, sending sparks shooting through her body.

"You smell good." His breath was hot against her skin.

He did, too. Back at Rainbow's End, she used to stand with her door slightly ajar in the early morning, to inhale the scent of his early morning aftershave.

"Is this the reason you brought me?" She had to put the brakes on her own emotions, as well as his.

She felt his body stiffen before he dropped his hands and looked at her with dangerous calm. Then he turned on his heel, said "G'night" over his shoulder and entered his tent.

The silence he left behind was more intense than anything he could have said to her.

Chapter 26

Flynn heard voices. Pulling on her jeans and sweat-shirt, she only took time to brush her hair into a loose cloud around her shoulders. The morning was chilly but bearable. It was clear there would be no leisurely bubble baths on this trip, probably not even a shower. Camping out was way beyond anything she'd ever imagined doing.

Is Marshall still upset? She didn't want to ruin their whole trip, but he had no business putting her in that po-sition of refusing his attentions.

After a deep breath, she opened her tent flap, climbed outside and stood still, watching Marshall put-ting things to rights, ordering Timmy about like a five-star general.

Marshall wore a dark-green flannel shirt and jeans. He looked good enough to eat for breakfast. The sunlight penetrating beyond the branches highlighted the planes of his face and touched his hair with fire.

She looked down at her snug-fitting corduroy pants and her comfortable old boots. Her shirt was a flattering deep-wine-colored flannel. What would Dolores say if she could see her daughter this morning?

"G'day, sleepyhead. Ready for brekkie?" Marshall's

voice was friendly enough, in a cool way, his eyes dark and unreadable. He pointed toward the little bucket with paper cups nearby. "You can brush your teeth over there. Up the trail are bathrooms."

"Oh, Flynn! I've been having the bestest time. I met some kids in the next camping ground."

Marshall must have kept his word and got up at dawn. By the looks of it, the trout were biting early. He had them cleaned and ready for the pan after they helped put some more things away to his satisfaction.

"Have you ever been in the army?" Flynn was irritable as she and Timmy continued to do his bidding. She was not at her best early in the morning, not until she'd brushed her teeth and had a cup of coffee or tea.

When Flynn finished and came back from her walk down the trail, Timmy brought her a steaming cup, which was probably at Marshall's instigation if his give-away grin signified anything.

"That feels better. Can I help?"

"You mean like fry the fish?"

They smiled at each other. She was grateful he wasn't angry about last night.

"When was the last time you fried fish over a campfire?" he asked.

"How about never." *Campfire or fish frying.*

Marshall walked across the short distance to take her hands in his. He turned them over and looked down at her palms, rubbing his callused fingers lightly over hers. His touch sent tingles coursing through her body, blending with the early morning chill. She wanted to lean into him to inhale the whiff of outdoors she caught before she backed away. From his thoughtful expression she guessed what he was thinking. Like Suzy, she was practically useless and uselessly impractical.

"In spite of what you think, I can be useful around a

campground. Just point me in the right direction, Sergeant."

His look was amused, but guarded. "Just do anything that suits your talents. I'm not splitting up the chores into man-woman things only to have you declare me a male chauvinist." He dropped to his knees and stirred the coals with a stick.

"What if I don't have any talents?" she challenged. "You must know by now I'm completely out of my element."

He turned his head to look at her, an eyebrow quirked in the way that, for some reason, excited her. "I wish I knew what your element was." His eyes probed hers with an intensity she couldn't mistake.

She wished she could tell him about her talent, but it didn't seem so important any more. It was as if another life had opened up and the other was a fond memory.

Flynn had not been the least bit hungry, but breakfast looked and smelled delicious. Marshall had cooked the fish crispy-golden on the outside, flaky-white inside, and he served it along with thin-sliced potatoes. After the first bite she cleaned her plate in no time. They finished with the usual steaming brew.

"Camping makes you hungry, huh?" Timmy asked.

"You bet, Tiger. You're doing an excellent job, too." She reached to touch his cheek.

"You look good for a novice camper," Marshall commented to Flynn between bites. His eyes held that amused twinkle she enjoyed so much.

"Thanks. You look like the intrepid and fearless leader of all the adventure movies I've ever seen rolled into one." She smiled when Timmy laughed outright without smothering his laughter behind his palm, like he used to do.

"Dad's like Indiana Jones, isn't he?" Timmy laughed at his idea.

Marshall winked at her and saluted his son. "Let's tidy up camp and then Timmy and I'll fly cast up the creek. It's too wet from yesterday's rain to go hiking. The creeks will be full and fast, and we'd have to cross over more than a few of them."

Flynn swallowed with a tight throat and noticed the boy looked up sharply at his father. It was the first time she had heard Marshall call his son Timmy.

"Want to come with us?" Timmy asked.

"Nope. I'm perfectly happy to stay here and get acquainted with the environment. I warn you both, though, you'd better not return without more of those delicious fish."

They were gone all morning and part of the afternoon. Her first thought after they left was how wonderful it would have been to stand in the center of the clearing and play her violin.

She wandered around—not too far, for fear of losing sight of the campground. She always had been terrible with directions. At first the trees and landscape looked the same almost everywhere she looked. Little by little, her awareness sharpened and she saw the differences. Wildflowers dotted the floor of the forest, each little blossom perfect in itself. The sounds of birds singing lent to the magic of the bush. She wished she could draw. She wanted to remember everything about Tasmania.

Settling down to read a paperback she retrieved from her backpack, her mind kept darting away from the words on the page until she drifted into a peaceful doze.

It seemed not long after that when Marshall and Timmy emerged from the woods and into the clearing. Her greeting was quickly choked back when she saw their expressions.

She looked from one face to the other, aware of the strained atmosphere enshrouding them. "Catch anything?" She ventured.

"Nope. Not a bloody thing." He looked at her over Timmy's head. It appeared he was on the verge of saying more, but then changed his mind.

Timmy was subdued, with that stubborn, tight look he'd had when Flynn first came to Rainbow's End.

Either they had quarreled or Marshall had expected too much from his son on the first day. Honesty forced her to admit that, in some instances, Timmy could be considered a bit of a sissy. He was timid, painfully shy with strangers and afraid of his shadow. But he had made so much progress since she'd been working with him. The boy was steadily growing out of his protective shell. Now all that tenuous progress could be destroyed by this trip.

He spent the rest of the afternoon lying on his stomach in his tent, reading or playing his handheld electronic games.

She expected Marshall to chew him out at any moment. Toward evening the sky looked dismal, matching the mood in the camp.

Marshall decided to put off their hike for another day. "Looks like it's gonna pour down. Nothing worse than being on a trek with mud up to your ankles and the rain running down your back."

It was on the tip of her tongue to argue with him, but one look at Timmy warned her he was already worn from the day's events.

That night around the campfire, Marshall tried to break the uncomfortable silence, and then she tried, but both gave up in the face of Timmy's obstinacy.

After supper Marshall yawned and stretched. "Time for me to turn in. I'll go fishing well before daylight. I've been wanting to try out a new place a bit farther up the trail."

"Good night, Marshall." She bent to kiss Timmy's forehead. "'Night, Timmy. Don't forget to say your prayers."

His dark eyes were so unhappy. The urge to tuck him into his bedroll and comfort him was strong, but she sensed Marshall watching her and refrained. Something had happened, and it probably had to do with Timmy not performing to his father's standards.

When Flynn and Timmy awoke the next morning, Marshall was already gone. They ate bread and jam as they sat around the embers of last night's fire, and drank cold coffee to wash it down.

"What happened yesterday, Tim?"

"Don't want to talk about it."

"That's a shame. I can help, you know."

"You can't. He hates me." He swiped at his tears and turned away so she wouldn't see.

She pulled him down beside her on a large tree stump. "Your father certainly doesn't hate you. Did you ever think he might not know how to talk to you?"

"He expects an awful lot from a little kid."

She couldn't help letting out a bark of laughter, but immediately stopped, knowing how serious Timmy was. "Yes, I do believe he expects a lot. But you have to remember his father, your grandfather, was hard on him, too. It's the only way he knows. We have to teach him how to bend a little. He'll learn if you give him a chance. Hasn't he been doing a little better lately?"

He nodded. "He wanted me to wade into the water yesterday, and I was afraid."

"Your father's a strong, powerful man. He would never ask you to do anything if he couldn't protect you."

"Mebbe. Did you know Mr. Hoppy drowned?"

Lordy, where'd he hear that? "I did hear something about that, but it isn't the same thing. Remember when we were in the boat at Hobart? Nothing happened. You know why? 'Cause your dad took care of us. He's real good at that, if you let him."

"He says I'm stubborn."

She laughed without apology. "The two of you are equally as stubborn as the day is long. You'll both have to learn to live with it."

"I guess."

"Okay, then. I'll have a talk with your father later when I get a chance. Meanwhile, let's do some exploring on our own."

"Yay!" Timmy leaped from the stump and picked up the thin limb Marshall used to stir the coals. He danced around the clearing, using the stick as a sword, flinging a make-believe cape back from his shoulders a time or two.

"All right, Zorro. I get the picture. Put your boots on and grab a jacket."

If I can just convince Marshall to listen to reason, this trip might turn out to be a positive experience yet.

They left a note for him and set off on their adventure. The trail wound around, through tall groves of trees and extravagantly-hued wild flowers. Not even the overcast day put a damper on their enjoyment. After walking at least a half mile, they found the trail made an abrupt bend. Just after it, both of them stopped short.

In the middle of the path stood a baby wallaby, with its watchful mother nearby. Marshall had told her to be on the lookout for them. They were a special breed only found in Tasmania, rarely seen.

Timmy knew enough to stay perfectly still. Four human eyes stared into four animal ones. Then with amazing speed and agility, the two wallabies disappeared into the thick brush.

"Omigosh. Dad hoped we'd see one, and we saw two!"

What she would have given for Marshall to have been there. Hopefully, when Timmy told him about it, it might break the ice.

"Let's sit for a minute. Maybe they'll come back." She sat down on a large, flat rock. The uncustomary strain on the muscles of her calves from walking so long, partly on an upgrade, made itself known. The air was crisp, cool and fresh. She hated to admit it, but she was out of breath and needed a rest.

"Can I go a little ahead? I'm not a baby."

"I guess so. But stay where I can see you." This was a big step. He'd stuck to her side like glue since they began their hike.

He grinned. "Can I make noise?"

"Certainly. No one is around to hear us." The boy was so inhibited. Not being around kids his age didn't help. Add to that Marshall, who wanted him to bypass puberty and become an adult. It could have been partly Suzy's fault, too. She was a night owl and would sleep until noon if she could. He probably had to be quiet a lot when he stayed with her.

Timmy wandered farther and farther away as he bent to pick up a special rock or investigate something in the brush. She leaned back on the rock, lulled by the pale rays of the sun that sneaked out from behind a cloud. The sun felt good on her eyelids.

Flashes of her life before she'd come to Tasmania whipped through her mind. How shallow it had been. Her relationship with her mother and fellow musicians was nothing more than superficial. She had shut off every emotion, except when she played her music.

But why? Why had she forced herself to become an empty shell, an unapproachable snow princess? It was no wonder her mother had dubbed her the "vestal virgin." The bitter acrimony between her mother and father, their constant arguments, had nothing to do with her. Yet she'd never faced it, never gotten over it.

Everything had changed now. She wanted to stay with Marshall. She loved him, Timmy and Rainbow's End.

Never in her life had she acknowledged the empty hollowness, the void inside her soul. Ever since she came to Rainbow's End she'd had no choice but to confront it. Marshall Beckett was the only person who could fill that emptiness, make her feel whole, complete. But he didn't love her. He wanted her—that much was clear. His desire for her was obvious almost every time he looked at her. Although it was very flattering, it wasn't enough. He might find her amusing, even think she'd make a good wife and a good mother to that brood of children he wanted, but he didn't love her. In time, when the novelty of sex wore off, would he turn to another? That would tear a hole in her heart she could never fix.

Flynn dug her nails into the knobby rock until she remembered her hands and stopped.

It brought her out of her daydream. "Timmy? Where are you?" She slipped off the rock and began to walk toward the place she last saw him playing.

"Flynn!" Timmy's shrill scream came from up ahead. Pushing through the brush she ran, her pulse racing as brambles tore at her clothing. She stopped midstride when she saw the boy perched on a small ledge above a wide, fast-running stream. Behind him was a sheer wall of rock.

"Hang on, Timmy. Don't look down. I'll help you." She struggled to keep her voice calm, not wanting the boy to see how frightened she really was. The stream looked deep and dark. There was no way she could successfully leap across it. How had Timmy managed to get on the other side? He could slide off that ledge at any moment and be swept away by the swift-moving water.

She nerved herself to try the leap. If she could make it across most of the way, she could then crawl up the bank. What they would do then she had no idea.

Just as she hunched her body to make the leap, she heard a hoarse shout behind her. Too late. She was launched in space.

Landing short, she made a grab for Timmy's hands as she tried to pull her soaked body up the ledge. The frigid water shocked her system, every nerve ending on fire with cold. Timmy's small hand clutched at the shoulder of her jacket. With mounting terror she realized they would never get back across the stream together. Her legs still in the water, she looked down to see if they were still attached, they were so numb.

"Dad!"

Flynn heard Timmy's shout but it didn't make sense to her. She only wanted to let her grip go and slip into the soothing water. Lethargy cocooned her and she closed her eyes, relaxing her grip. Somewhere in the deep recesses of her mind, it registered that she was being scooped up out of the water as rough hands pried her fingers loose from the rock. Marshall's voice sounded so far away, competing with the roaring of the water, and she couldn't understand why she felt his breath warm against her cheek. Opening her eyes to investigate the phenomena was too much trouble.

"Climb on my back, son."

At those words her eyes flew open. She focused on the clenched jaw next to her cheek as he waded through the water, the current buffeting him while he brought them safely to the grassy bank. Timmy had barely gotten the legs of his pants wet. Marshall whipped off his heavy jacket and wrapped it around her.

"You'll be cold," she protested. Her teeth chattered so much she was surprised she could get the words out and still be understood. "You're as wet as we are."

"Quiet, woman. Save your strength. Come on, lad, we're heading back to camp."

Chapter 27

At camp, Marshall ordered Timmy to build up the fire and go put on warm clothes. He took the still-shivering Flynn into his tent and started stripping off her icy, sodden clothing. When he reached for her underwear, she protested. "I can do it." But her hands shook so much she couldn't make them do her bidding. As the numbness wore away, a wave of intense, cutting cold hit without mercy, her thawing body under the onslaught of sharp pinpricks of pain.

Grateful for the seclusion and privacy of Marshall's tent, she closed her eyes, a heated blush staining her cheeks as he finished taking off her soaked underwear and wrapped her in a thick woolen blanket. He held her cradled in his arms while Timmy was busy preparing something warm to drink.

When the boy brought in a cup of steaming brew, Marshall pointed to his backpack. "Be a good lad and get the brandy out of my swag." Timmy did as he was told and poured a liberal dose into the cup Marshall held out.

"Drink this down, Flynn. Every last drop." Over the rim of the cup she looked at their serious faces while they watched her with anxious eyes. Two pairs of solemn, brown eyes mirrored their concern. She drank the hot liq-

uid as fast as she could, keeping her hands wrapped tightly around the mug, grateful for the warmth on her fingers.

"Now, Timmy, I want you to please lay our wet
clothes on that big rock so they'll dry some, and when
you're finished, you are to go into your tent, crawl into
your sleeping bag and get some rest."

"But Dad—" Timmy looked at Flynn, fear in his
eyes.

Marshall's expression softened. "She'll be fine, son.
I promise. If you get hungry, you know where the food's
kept. She needs to sleep now."

Timmy squatted down and tentatively touched her on
the cheek.

"I'm sorry, Flynn. It's all my fault. I hope—"

He looked so miserable, but he had been wrong to go
so far ahead and get himself into that predicament. She
also had to shoulder part of the responsibility for letting
him get away with it. Shakily she held his hand to her
cheek and smiled her forgiveness.

As soon as Timmy left the tent, Marshall opened his
large sleeping bag and gently unwrapped Flynn from the
blanket. There was no light inside except for the shadows
and intermittent sun. The wind blew lightly through the
tree branches.

He helped her slide into the down-filled bag as if she
were a child. She cried out when the cold of the sleeping
bag touched her naked body. Swiftly, he peeled out of his
outer clothing and lay down beside her, zipping up the
bag behind him.

"Wait! You can't do that." The protest, although
heartfelt, sounded drowsy. The brandy was already doing
its job. Her mind felt warm and cozy, even if her body
had not yet caught up.

"Shh…" He touched his finger to her lips and then
softly trailed his fingers over her nose and jaw line, as

gently as a feather tracing her lips with his thumb. Her lips were dry and she wet them with a flick of her tongue, an unconsciously provocative gesture.

He groaned and held her close. "Oh, Flynn." His body heat warmed the length of her chilled form. She stirred restlessly and tried to pull away. "Look at me." He lifted her chin with a hooked finger. "I'm not going to take advantage of the little ice maiden. If you come down with pneumonia, my son will never forgive himself—or me."

She nodded, allowing him to hold her closer, and she started to relax, to enjoy the comfort of this shared heat. An odd warmth suffused her from head to toe—a warmth she didn't understand.

Without being aware she spoke out loud, she said, "It's the brandy." It was the only thing that explained the alien warmth.

"Are you sure?"

A feeling of desire she had never known took possession of her mind and body.

"Don't leave me."

"I won't, sweetheart. I'll be right here. I promise to be good. But I want you to know it wouldn't be such a bad thing to be married to me." His strong hands moved gently over her still-icy body, leaving trails of fire behind in their wake. His kiss was one she wanted never to stop. He nibbled gently at her bottom lip, then made a path of molten kisses down to the pulsing hollow at the base of her throat.

Just as she began to respond, he stopped abruptly, kissed the top of her head and held her close. They didn't move for a long time, and after a while she fell asleep in his arms.

As she dozed fitfully, she felt Marshall holding her hands and felt his lips on her palm. On the threshold of slumber and wakefulness, she couldn't be sure if it had been part of a dream.

၄ၷၷ

Flynn awoke and snuggled more deeply into his embrace. He was still asleep. *What if?*

She wanted so badly to touch him, to run her hands over his body as she vaguely remembered he had done to her before she fell asleep. *What could be the harm? He'd never know.*

Her fingers lightly, tentatively touched his shoulders and moved downward to his chest. She twined her fingers in the curly hair lightly and then moved across to his nipples, rubbing them gently. The urge to kiss each one was almost more than she could bear. An infusion of warmth spread over her body, across her stomach and down her thighs. It was such a new feeling.

She traced her fingers slowly down across his flat, hard stomach, barely touching the hair below his belly. Before she could snatch her hand back, it was covered by his.

He groaned. "My God, Flynn. What are you doing to me?"

"How long have you been awake?"

He didn't let go of her hand. "Long enough." He tilted her chin up and they joined together in a kiss she never wanted to end. His tongue searched for hers, sending shivers of desire all over her, and she responded with a hunger she hadn't known existed within her.

"Marshall. I—I want you to make love to me."

"Are you sure?" He barely moved his mouth from hers as he spoke.

She took his face in her hands and they looked at each other for a long moment. "I'm sure." Just to prove how sure she was, she ran her hands over his chest. She reached behind to massage the muscles in his back before moving down to his waist and lightly touching his taut buttocks.

He inhaled sharply and maneuvered her onto her back. The covers were flung off and he looked at her for a long time. Leaning above her, he touched her hair, bringing a long strand to his lips. He rained kisses over her eyelids, nose and mouth, and then descended down to her throat, lingering a moment at the soft hollow place.

Every nerve ending was alive and on fire. The cold air washing over her exposed body added to the exquisite sensation. He held her swollen breasts in his hands, running his tongue over her hard nipples, blowing gently on them before he captured each one with his warm mouth.

Instinctively she arched her back.

"Not yet, my love. Not yet." He moved his lips over her belly and ever yet downward.

"Wait! What are you doing?" She wound her fingers in his hair but the will to bring him upward vanished under his probing tongue and hot kisses. It was like she was melting into a pool of hot, steaming lava.

When he drew away she felt the loss of his warm mouth and called out to him.

He moved his hands upward to clasp her breasts again, his fingers manipulating her nipples until she couldn't bear it another moment.

Without warning, Marshall rose above her and entered her in one smooth motion. She gasped with shock and pain. He paused and would have stopped if she hadn't raked her fingernails across his back and arched upward, thrusting herself to him. The extension of his body was an intrusion but no longer painful. He moved within her, slow and gently with tender restraint and then with explosive power.

As he whispered love words in her ear, involuntary tremors of pleasure spread across her body. She turned her face and bit into the sleeping bag to avoid crying out, dimly hearing his hoarse groan as the spiral that whirled through her body shattered in a million lights.

They both lay back exhausted and quiet. Then he rose up on his elbow and looked down at her, smoothing the tangled, dark hair from around her face. He kissed her slowly and gently. His hands, possessive and sure, roamed freely over her body. Her breasts still felt tight and swollen, her nipples sensitive to his touch. She reached downward to hold him, his erection slowly hardening. His kiss became stronger and more demanding.

"No, Marshall. Timmy will wake up soon."

He rolled back with a groan, but kept his arms around her. "Flynn. I had no idea, I mean at your age—I swear to you—"

"Shh…It was beautiful. I'm glad you were my first."

He held her away and looked into her eyes searchingly. "Does this mean you'll stay with us? We could have a real marriage, you know, not a pretend one."

No words of love yet, although she recalled she'd spoken of love to him in the throes of passion. She stirred restlessly. "You mean to make an honest woman of me? That's a bit old-fashioned, wouldn't you say?" Her heart surged when she stared into those dark eyes.

"Because I can take care of you, keep you safe. Because we'd make terrific babies."

"That's pretty darn conceited."

Her words were cut off when he gathered her into his arms, almost crushing the breath out of her. His mouth covered hers hungrily, possessively, forcing her lips open with his thrusting tongue. When he stopped kissing her, her lips were bruised, her body weak, but she was filled with tenderness for him. She touched his strong jawline, smoothing the clenched muscles, feeling tension beneath her fingers. It appeared he wasn't as sure of himself as he pretended.

He took hold of her hand and kissed her palm, moving up the inside of her elbow. His lips sought the throbbing softness of her throat once again.

"Flynn."

She felt his breath fanning the valley between her breasts and it created a stirring sensation deep in her middle. His next words melted her heart and erased her doubts forever.

"How I've wanted you for so long. You're the most desirable woman I've ever known. The day you stood in the middle of the road, challenging me and Sultan, you took my heart. A mere slip of a girl with a thick braid of black hair and fire spouting from your eyes. The picture lives inside me always."

Her own heart was near to bursting, but he didn't say the words she needed to hear.

I love you, too, Marshall. I've waited all my life for you.

"You'll stay?"

"Yes," she whispered against his throat, her tongue touching his skin.

"There's so much of this wonderful country to show you. Tomorrow morning I'm going to show you the best sunrise you'll ever see."

She didn't remember falling back asleep until the tantalizing aroma of frying bacon awoke her. She sat up and wrinkled her nose.

"Do I smell coffee?"

When no one answered she looked around and saw a neat pile of clothing at the edge of the sleeping bag. How sweet. Marshall had brought her clean, dry clothing from her backpack. She looked down at her hands, remembering her leap into the water. Some nails were broken and her palms were scratched, but nothing serious.

She tried to straighten her hair with her fingers—her comb and brush were in her tent—but gave up and settled for braiding it into the long plait Marshall was so taken with.

When she pushed back the flap of the tent, Timmy rushed up to greet her. She knelt to hug him.

"Oh, Flynn. I was so scared, but Dad said you would be fine."

She looked around for Marshall. "Where is your dad?"

Timmy shrugged. "Dunno. He said to stay here and watch over you. He didn't even take his fishing stuff."

"Do I smell coffee?"

Timmy took her hand and pulled her toward the campfire, grinning from ear to ear. "Some campers moved in up the trail. Dad asked them if they had any coffee to spare. We only brought tea."

"How sweet of him." She sat on a campstool while Timmy dished up some bacon and scrambled eggs, and poured her coffee.

She tilted her head back and savored the taste of the hot, fragrant liquid on her tongue. The sun filtered through the canopy of trees. She wanted to see Marshall, to touch him, to know that last night hadn't been a dream.

"Let's tidy up around here and we'll go looking for him."

Timmy looked downcast. "He told me to stay here. He sounded kinda mad."

"Mad? Why should he be mad? Okay, let's wait for him." She opened her tent and crawled in to search for her brush in her backpack. Her fingers touched crumpled paper and she pulled out a music program with her name emblazoned across the front as soloist. The last concert she played in Austria. Her heart beat faster as her fingers scrambled to find the zippered pocket. It was open. A picture of her, Suzy and Timmy stared back at her. She turned it over and the incriminating words leapt out at her. *To my favorite and only cousin. Love Suzy.*

Flynn leaned her head down on the backpack and began to sob. She pressed her face into the material so Timmy wouldn't hear. Thoughts of what Marshall was most likely thinking ran through her mind. Betrayal. Trickery. Why hadn't he wakened her to confront her about it?

Drying her eyes, she zipped the backpack up again and threw it in the corner.

"Timmy? Your dad asked you to stay here and wait. Could do that for me, too? I need to talk to him. I think I know where to find him."

He nodded, his dark eyes solemn. So like Marshall's. "If those kids come over from the next camping ground to play with me, is that okay? I forgot to ask Dad."

"Sure. I don't see why not. We'll be back in a jiffy. Let's put the fire out first. That might be safer." Timmy helped her put water over the embers.

"Don't forget your jumper," Timmy cautioned.

She smiled in spite of her trepidation. So like a little man. She tugged on her sweater, then pulled a heavier coat over and retrieved her boots. Marshall had set them near the fire and they were reasonably dry and warm.

She had to get to him. Make him understand. She couldn't lose him now.

Chapter 28

The sun dodged behind dark clouds, as if playing a game of hide-and-seek. A small animal raced across her path in a blur of movement and Flynn stopped, heart thudding, to lean against a tree in support.

Without warning, the trail ended at the rim of a canyon, which dropped off into the mist. The outline of a lake far below looked like a giant, dark eye staring up at her. She sank down on a fallen tree trunk, breathless from the mostly uphill climb. This had to be the place to watch a spectacular sunrise if ever there was one.

She closed her eyes in disappointment. There was no sign of Marshall. A tear slipped free from under closed eyelids.

"That's no way to watch a sunrise." Marshall's voice penetrated her dark thoughts.

Flynn opened her eyes and turned to face him. His gaze was implacable, angry. She wanted to speak but instead put her palms up in a gesture of appeal. *Where to begin? Would he even listen?*

"Why the farce, Flynn? How long were you going to continue on with this deception? Were you ever going to tell me the truth? Did you and Suzy cook this up together? Marry me to help her get Rainbow's End?"

They stood at the edge of the precipice. Marshall moved toward her. It was a good thing she knew in her heart he hadn't done anything to harm Suzy. It would have been very easy to push her over the edge.

She stood her ground. "You're angry and hurt and you have every right to be, but please, don't say anything you can't take back." She rested her hands against his chest and looked up into his eyes. *Only a step away from the precipice.*

Gone were the expressions of tenderness or caring in his face. His jaw muscles were tense, his mouth, so kissable only hours ago, now a straight line of contempt.

He removed her hands from his chest and turned her away from the edge. "I trusted you. So what else were you lying about? For the love of God, you're a concert violinist. How you must have laughed at us all. You called me a country bumpkin once. Now I know why."

"It's not like that, Marshall. I never intended to hurt anyone. Please. Sit. Let me explain."

For an agonizing moment she was certain Marshall would walk away. If he went back to camp without her being able to explain, he was lost to her forever.

A cold, bleak silence grew between them as the tension mounted.

"I'm waiting." His voice was cold, impersonal.

She prayed for the right words. This was her only chance.

Telling him from the beginning about her childhood with Suzy was hard to do. Then she expressed her hurt when, after they'd grown up and moved apart, Suzy never invited her to the wedding or told her about the birth of her son until much later. They sat apart on a large fallen tree. She looked out over the mist in the valley, choosing her words carefully, not wanting to face again the look of cold fury in his eyes.

"She did come to visit me once, when I had a concert in Melbourne. I don't know how she found out about it. That was when the photo was taken. She called me about a month and a half ago and begged me to check on Timmy. To see if he was all right."

"Why the bloody hell wouldn't he be all right?" His voice was dangerously soft.

"You know her. I'm just beginning to. She painted you as an ogre, a jailer, a dominating, inflexible man who terrified her. She said you kicked her out and kept the boy, wouldn't let her see him."

Marshall snorted in derision.

"I know now she was making it up. I knew after I'd been at Rainbow's End a few weeks that something was desperately askew with her thinking. She's sick, Marshall. My cousin is a stranger. Someone I don't know any more."

"Why did you stay with us?"

The same question Mrs. Hopkins asked. She itched to touch him, put her hand on his thigh for a moment, just to feel his strength and warmth. She kept her hands clenched in her lap and took a deep breath. Her instincts told her he had nothing to do with Suzy's disappearance. Marshall could be hard and unforgiving, but he wasn't a killer.

"There was something else. A diary. Suzy wanted me to find it. She claimed it was a matter of life and death. She'd forgotten where she stashed it."

"Is that why you were in the attic and in her room?"

"You knew I was in her room?"

"It didn't seem important enough to challenge you on it. I just figured you were curious. Did you ever find it?"

Flynn shook her head. "It probably wasn't as important as she made it out to be."

"No. I don't suppose it was."

"When she called you that day, I was ready to leave. But I didn't want to leave you and Timmy, not with those wild threats hanging over your head. You brought up the wedding idea and I bought into it, thinking to save Rainbow's End for you."

"Where is she now? I suppose you know that."

"I don't. I'm afraid for her. I found her scarf, stained with what looked like blood, in the churchyard where we were supposed to meet."

"It would be just like her to set that up."

He will never trust me again. His eyes told her that when she dared to look up at him. But her confession wasn't finished. She didn't want to hurt him any more than she already had, but he should know about Damon's involvement.

"There's more."

He looked away, out toward the mist over the canyon. "I don't want to hear any more. You've hidden so much from me. What else? A husband somewhere waiting for you?"

"That's ridiculous. You know better than that—don't you?"

His expression was bleak. "Yes, I do. An' for that I'm sorry. Sorry we played around, sorry you gave up that part of you—the part you'd been saving for someone special."

But you are the special one. Her throat tightened. She had to finish this about Damon.

"Suzy said she was in love with Damon and he was in love with her."

He flinched as if she'd struck him. Flynn wanted him to say he didn't believe it, but his eyes blazed and he smacked his fist into his palm. She jumped at the harsh sound.

"I knew it! I knew she wasn't capable of harassing me on her own. She didn't give a rat's arse about coming back to Rainbow's End, or about Timothy. All she ever wanted was her freedom. Damon set this up, all of it, before she left."

His torment was like her own, but he had to know.

"They were lovers, weren't they?" He took hold of her arms, his grip hard.

"Don't, Marshall. You're hurting me. I don't know if they were lovers. Suzy never said. I doubt it. She just wanted to get back at you, and Damon encouraged it." It wouldn't serve any purpose to drive a bigger wedge between him and his brother. They had to live side by side.

Her gut instinct told her Marshall was right about the scarf. Suzy had disappeared before and always turned up with dramatic flair. Leaving her scarf behind to cause confusion and complications would have been her idea of a delicious joke on all of them.

Marshall moved away from her and leaned against a tree. His eyes were dark and brooding as he looked down on her. "I assume you'll be wanting to leave now. Timmy will be hurt, but he'll get over it. He got over other nannies leaving."

That really cut. She pictured her heart, torn out and lying between them on the ground.

It was so simple for him.

But he was right. She needed to get back to her life. Rainbow's End was make-believe. A fantasy she had created inside her head and heart—without substance. It would be good to rid herself of all the drama and responsibility, to return to reality—to be free and unencumbered. Doing what she was meant to do with her life.

Then why did Marshall look so dejected, and why didn't she feel happy at the idea of moving on?

Silently they walked back up the trail toward camp.

When they got there, Timmy shouted his welcome.

"Hi, Sport. Thanks for staying at camp like I asked." Marshall ruffled his hair. "I think we'll pack it in—go home."

"Aw, I was hoping to stay longer. I just met these kids and—"

Marshall turned away impatiently from Timmy's plea. "Looks like there's a storm brewing. Flynn needs to get back and rest up."

She choked back her protest. It wasn't fair for him to put the blame of leaving on her. She was fine—on the outside.

"You like your new friends, don't you?" Timmy's shirt was buttoned wrong and his knees dirty from sliding on the ground. Mrs. Hopkins would have been delighted. Suzy had liked to keep him neat and clean, like her little doll.

"Yeah!" Timmy jumped from one foot to the other, full of energy. "They let me play soccer with them. The big boys, too." His voice swelled with pride, without a trace of stammer or hesitation.

"That's fine, son. But it doesn't change anything. We have to go."

She couldn't stand the look of disappointment on the boy's face. "I can pack his things away the same time I do mine. What's the big deal? Then Timmy could say goodbye to his new friends."

"The big deal is he needs to learn responsibility. He helped set up camp, and now he needs to help pack up." Marshall's look was identical to his son's, stubborn and inflexible. But this time she didn't feel like laughing about it.

"He's just a boy, a child. You should be glad he's learning to play and get dirty like other kids his age." Her chin jutted out and she gave him glare for glare, ignoring her resolve not to undermine Marshall's authority. He wasn't right this time.

"Flynn had a close call and so did you. Have you already forgotten that?" Marshall looked at the boy.

Timmy ran to take her hand. "It's my fault. I hope you're going to be okay."

She knelt down and took him in her arms.

He broke away and touched her cheek. "Why are you crying?"

She looked deep into his eyes. "It wasn't your fault I fell into the water, Timmy. Don't ever think anything is your fault. Remember that. Children don't cause things to happen. It's the adults who make it happen. Promise me you'll remember that."

He tried to squirm away as something in the camping ground captured his attention, but she held him steady. "Promise?"

Timmy nodded and pecked her cheek with a hurried kiss before he wriggled out of her grip.

Slowly she stood and faced Marshall. How would she bear the next few days being near him, knowing he was lost to her forever? She'd always remember his broad shoulders encased in that forest-green shirt, the sweep of hair on his forehead, the way he made love to her, pleasured her so gently. So many things to remember—and forget.

"All righty, then. Go on, boy, off with you. We'll put things to rights here, and then I'll holler when we're ready to go."

When Timmy ran off shouting and leaping, Marshall turned to look at Flynn. "I've already told you you've done wonders with the boy. I just hope things don't unravel when you leave."

"Nothing has to go backward unless you let it."

"He's been raised by women. I won't have him mol-lycoddled."

"That's nonsense. You want to treat him like a little adult. It will never work. It didn't work between you and your father, did it?"

"No, it didn't. I don't want us to ever be like that, but if he should take over Rainbow's End, he has to learn to be responsible."

"Are you so bitter that you let it color everything that touched your lives when you and Suzy were together?" Her mouth trembled, but she steadfastly fought against her tears.

His mouth hardened, his eyes sparked fire. "What's she got to do with it?"

"Everything! Don't you see, you're punishing Tim-my for having lived with his mother? For having her hair, her build. He'll grow out of some of that, but it's not his fault."

Marshall ran an agitated hand through his hair. His mouth was set in an obstinate line, but his eyes showed bewilderment. "All I know is, she ruined everything she touched. I want to make sure Timothy isn't like her."

She longed to smooth away the frown line between his eyes, to touch his mouth to make it turn up in that wonderful, slow smile she loved—had loved—so much.

"I understand that perfectly. But you have to take it slow with him. He loves you and I know you love him. Just let him develop at his own pace with the knowledge you're there for him."

Marshall came closer and looked searchingly into her eyes. "It's not that I'm without feeling—about you—about us, but the deceptions, the lies, the life you led be-fore you came to Rainbow's End. You are a different per-son to the one who came to us. I can't accept—"

"I know. I understand. It's time for me to get back to my own life."

He was within touching distance, his eyes filled with pain. "I'm deeply sorry that—that we made love. I'd no idea that—what I mean is—"

"You'd no idea you were deflowering a virgin? That's really antiquated thinking, Marshall. Leave it alone. I wanted it to happen with you." Her voice sounded harsh and uncaring, but it was necessary to put distance between them and keep it there, if she was to survive until she left. Right now, she was like a piece of china, broken into a million pieces and held together by only a thin layer of glue, just waiting to fall apart. She would mend in time, but not without submerging herself in her old life. Right now she wanted her old, secure, predictable life back more than anything in the world.

Chapter 29

The trip back home did not resemble anything like their excited journey up to the camping ground. For a while Timmy bounced around in the back seat, full of energy, asking his father dozens of questions about what he'd seen. It didn't take long, though, before he sensed the underlying tension and lost himself in his electronic games.

The silence was so overpowering Flynn wanted to crawl over the seat and sit in the back with Timmy.

They stopped briefly at a small cafe to eat, and when they were back on the road, Flynn dozed off. The next voice she heard was Timmy shouting, "We're home, we're home!"

She awoke to a downpour of rain. Pulling their jackets up over their heads, they ran for the porch, and as they hurried inside, Mrs. Hopkins came to welcome them. Looking down toward the stables, Flynn saw the two Ralphs standing by the building with wide grins on their faces. She knew where Marshall would be going next.

When Marshall went upstairs to change, Mrs. Hopkins drew her aside. "Something's wrong. Do you want to have a natter, or are you too tired from the trip to talk?"

"I'd like to talk." Actually, all she wanted to do was flop down on her bed and sleep until tomorrow or beyond. She was exhausted and empty, but there were things that needed to be said.

"Let's go tell Thelma you're home. She'll give Timmy milk and cookies, and we can take our cuppa into the sun room."

It was all Flynn could do to nod, slowly following Timmy, who ran ahead to greet Thelma. Getting hugs from the ample-bosomed, cookie-smelling woman was nice, and it brought tears to her eyes.

The cook smiled at her tears. "Bless you, child, you must have missed Rainbow's End."

"Yes. We all did." Gratefully, she turned to follow Mrs. Hopkins, who carried the tea tray.

In the sun room she sank down on a soft chair and closed her eyes for a moment. Although it wasn't sunny today, the room with its daffodil-colored walls felt warm and sunny to her. Without opening her eyes, she asked, "How long has it been raining here?"

"It's bloody awful. It started the day you left and hasn't let up since. Ralph had to close the bottom paddock by the creek. It's beginning to rise. Thelma and I had a gander yesterday. It's the first time I've seen whitecaps on a creek."

Without prompting, Flynn told the housekeeper about Timmy's adventures, her fall into the water, how Timmy found new playmates.

"How did it go, outside of nearly drowning yourself? I wasn't sure how you would cope, being from the big-smoke and all. Marshall was testing you, I reckon."

"If he was, I came up well and truly short." She explained how he had found out the truth about her career and Suzy.

Mrs. Hopkins brought the napkin to her lips, dismay evident in her eyes.

"Needless to say, he didn't take it well. I'll be leaving soon."

The elderly woman leaned forward to grasp her hands. "Oh no! It had to come out, but he'll get over it. He loves you, my dear. You've got to believe that."

Flynn shook her head. "No, he doesn't. He wants me out of his life. It's time I got back to my own life, anyway."

"Rubbish! You love Mr. Beckett. An' what about Timmy? Can you just bail out on the child, like his mother did?"

Tears coursed down her cheeks and she had to swallow several times before she could speak. "God knows I hate the thought of leaving Timmy, but as Marshall said, he'll get over it."

Mrs. Hopkins gasped. "Mr. Beckett said that? Men can be so dense at times. He didn't really mean it."

"He meant it, all right. I could see it in his eyes. And, really, he's right. He hasn't any reason to trust me again."

The older woman went silent, dabbing her eyes with the hanky she pulled from inside her sleeve. They sat sipping their tea for a long time, looking out at the rain pelting against the windows.

"It's my fault. I should never have suggested you wait a bit before telling him. He was just starting to open up, to learn to care again."

"Yes, but he was also learning to trust. That's all over now."

"Let me talk to him. Perhaps I can explain—"

Flynn patted her hand affectionately. "Explain what? It would only set him against you."

"But you meant no harm."

"He doesn't think so. He thinks Suzy and I conspired

to take Rainbow's End away. That we were working with Damon."

"Oh no! He can't really believe that."

"Why not? There might be some truth about Damon and Suzy."

"I doubt it. Mr. Damon and Mr. Beckett didn't always get on, but a brother would never touch another brother's wife."

"Regardless. My leaving is the way it has to be. It will make everything right again."

"So you'll go back to your career. Have you missed it much?"

She was almost ashamed to admit she hadn't given it much thought since coming to Rainbow's End. "It will be good getting back in the groove again. I miss my violin. And I miss my mother, believe it or not."

"Well, why wouldn't you? I've wondered about that, but didn't want to stick my nose where it didn't belong."

Flynn smiled. Mrs. Hopkins dearly loved to pry every chance she got. "You'd have to know us both better before I can answer that. But yes, I am anxious to go home."

Home. Why did it have such a hollow ring? Everything in her future was colored by her time spent at Rainbow's End. It was something she'd have to overcome, and only time would allow her to make the adjustment.

"Mr. Beckett will be working at the hydroelectric plant for a little while now. Before you went away on camp, he'd almost finished overseeing the new equipment being installed, but I overheard him tell Ralph he planned to complete the work when he came back."

"Is it dangerous for the valley? Can it be flooded out?"

"Mercy, no. We've lived by the creek forever. Only once, when the boys were mites, we had a bit of a go with the creek flowing over, but nothing happened to Rainbow's End. The rain will stop any day now."

But the rain didn't stop. It was time for her to leave, but the rain wouldn't let her go.

Tuesday came around yet again, the seventh during her stay at Rainbow's End, and Suzy had shown up only once for their scheduled meetings. Two potential meetings were missed due to their stay in Hobart and their camping trip. If her cousin didn't show up today, Flynn was determined to have Ralph Jr. take her directly to Damon's house.

The rain continued to pour down when Junior dropped her off at the church. If he thought it strange, he never mentioned it. "When can I pick you up, miss? 'Tis too bloody wet to walk into town."

"Thanks, that's sweet of you. Give me an hour. I'll wait under the awning by the church rectory." She pointed ahead in the gloom.

Steam from the tail pipes came from behind the truck and blended with the rain as she watched him go.

"What the hell took you so long? Where were you last week?" Suzy hissed in her ear, making Flynn jump away, startled.

They headed toward the overhanging awning she'd mentioned to Ralph Jr.

"Me? I've come here every Tuesday, bar two, and you've only shown up once." Flynn grasped Suzy by the shoulders to peer into her face. "Marshall and I are engaged. You know that of course."

Suzy knocked her hands from her shoulders with an impatient wave of her gloved hand. "What do you mean? How could this be?"

She didn't know. Then her story of being Damon's love interest had to be a lie. He would have told her first off.

Flynn sighed, grateful for Marshall's sake. "It's such a long story." She didn't know how to answer. Suzy didn't have to know Flynn was leaving with her tail between her legs. But her cousin's next words stunned her.

"Well, I hope you're satisfied. You won, you know."

"What?"

"I don't have a snowball's chance in hell of getting Rainbow's End back, but I didn't really want to. I just thought—"

"You thought Marshall should pay for not loving you anymore?"

Flynn was not prepared for Suzy's angry scream. The ugly sound blew away into the rain.

"I stopped caring about him first! I don't know if I ever did care, really. And I just wanted him to pay for thinking he could get rid of me so easily."

"And your son?"

Suzy's expression softened. "He was always better off at Rainbow's End. Even I could see the truth in that. Hoppy spoiled him unmercifully."

"So why'd you leave the scarf behind?"

A look of puzzlement marred the delicate features of her face. "Scarf? Oh, I spilled some wine on it and just tossed it aside."

Just like Suzy. And just like herself to puzzle over something that was not a mystery.

"The diary. Did you at least find the damned diary?" Suzy took hold of her arm in a grip so tight she felt it through her raincoat.

"No. I've looked everywhere. The attic, your room, the library. Been through all the shelves and looked at each book, and behind them, too. Why is it so important?"

Suzy turned away, looking off into the churchyard. "Never mind. It isn't something you'd understand."

They stood for a while in silence. A light came toward them, and Suzy turned back to Flynn and took her hand. "I ordered a cab to pick me up. I guess this is it."

"What? What do you mean, 'this is it'?" Her cousin's words were lacking emotion, flat and desolate. Flynn had never heard her speak like that.

"I mean I'm going to Europe and travel around. I've money from investments Marshall gave me when we parted. I'll meet someone special soon. But, but I don't think I'll be seeing you again."

Flynn gasped, speechless.

"Say goodbye to Aunt Dolores for me, and give Timmy a hug from me. Tell him—tell him his mum wasn't all bad, that she gave him up for his own good." Tears streamed down both of their faces, blending with the cold rain. In an instant Suzy had run to the cab and, in the blink of an eye, was gone.

છાજી

In days to come, Timmy played on the porch when the wind didn't blow the rain in, otherwise everyone except Marshall stayed inside. Several times Flynn had approached Marshall to talk to him about her meeting with Suzy, but he was like a stranger, moving in and out of the house, brushing her away, refusing to talk to her. His expression was remote, unapproachable. Timmy went back into his shell, retreating from his father as he had done before.

Marshall took his meals in the library, for the most part, and then rushed back outside to check the banks of the creek, the orchard, the horses. Was this persistent inspection an indication there was going to be a flood?

Flynn called her agent and Dolores, both of whom were glad to hear from her.

"You've finally come to your senses. You belong here." Dolores spoke with her usual cool restraint. Right at that moment Flynn felt closer to Hoppy than she did her own mother. But there was no getting away from it. She didn't belong at Rainbow's End.

The days dragged by, and each time she went upstairs to pack, she sat on the bed and let her tears fall. It was the only time she dared show her feelings. No one had yet told Timmy she was leaving.

Day and night, fierce storms swept through the valley. Hoppy told her some of the apple trees were uprooted. The feeling of restless anxiety hovered inside the house like a fog, touching everyone. Marshall was coldly polite when they happened to run into each other. She couldn't help but notice the sad look in Mrs. Hopkins' eyes when the housekeeper watched them together.

One morning at breakfast, Mrs. Hopkins waited until Timmy went upstairs before she spoke. "The lowlands in the orchards are flooding, and it's coming up toward the stables."

"Can the men stop it? Will this accursed rain ever go away?"

"'Tis the first time in living memory we've had so much rain. Mr. Beckett's worried sick, though he hasn't said anything."

Mrs. Hopkins' statement verified what Flynn had suspected. At night, when sleep refused to come, she heard his footsteps in the hallway. She longed to comfort him, to draw his dear head to her breast and hold him. But he had distanced himself from everyone, refusing to share the burden of worry.

Both Thelma and Hoppy had boasted time and again that Marshall's entire work crew was like one big family. He was strict and uncompromising at times, but fair. They all loved "His Nibs" as they called him, and would do anything for him. Flynn had been a part of Rainbow's End long enough to know this was true.

When they bundled up and she took Timmy down to see the horses, Ralph greeted them at the entrance to the stables and took their umbrellas. His forehead was folded into a deep frown. He looked worried. Timmy had run off to look at the fillies.

"Is it bad, Ralph?"

"Not good, miss. Not good. The Boss reckons we might have to move the horses up to the village or even beyond."

Sultan allowed her to touch his silken neck, and the memories of a chance meeting on a narrow dirt road seemed eons ago. She'd felt more alive since coming to Rainbow's End than ever before in her life.

Towards evening the rain started to slack off a bit. Restless, Flynn pulled on her coat and boots and headed for the gazebo. One or two stars peeked out shyly from the heavens—stars they hadn't seen in many nights. As she walked through the gardens, night sounds surrounded her. In the distance, the restive stamping and snorts from horses broke the silence.

She picked her way gingerly across the stepping stones before removing her boots to walk barefoot through the grass, sniffing appreciatively the heavy, damp air laced with the sweet scent of roses. The night was cool but not cold, and the grass felt good on the bottoms of her feet.

Reaching the gazebo, she sat inside by the railing, leaning her chin on her arm as she looked out over the garden.

The gazebo was a lovely, old-fashioned bit of architecture with trellised sides and a pointed copper roof with benches all around the inside.

One side of the gazebo was in shadows, the trellis

there covered with thick vines and fragrant flowers. It was one of her favorite places on Rainbow's End.

Marshall spoke quietly. "Good evening."

She jumped, startled. "I'm sorry. I thought I had the place all to myself. I didn't mean to intrude on your privacy."

He didn't answer. The rain began again, slowly, thrumming on the metal roof. Neither made a move to leave.

"This is the first evening I've seen you at home. Is the flooding under control in the north orchard?" It was the first time she'd spoken to him directly since they had returned from camp. For a moment she was afraid he wasn't going to answer. His nearness caused a surge of longing she struggled to control. She clenched her fists until her nails dug into her palms, glad she couldn't see his face in the deep shadow.

Marshall let out a long sigh and finally spoke. The rich timbre of his voice was unusually subdued. "It's not good, but I think we've got it under control. We've lost some good trees, but if that's the worst of it, I'll consider us lucky."

He said "we" and "us" and it was like a stab to her heart. For a while she had been a part of the "we" and "us."

She was thankful he couldn't see her expression any better than she could see his. His aftershave, the horse-and-leather smell of him, brought back memories of their night of lovemaking. She almost cried out in anguish.

"And the horses?" She forced herself to speak through her pain. "Will they be all right?"

She barely saw his nod.

"I hope so. I've done everything I can to drain the creek in that area. The next step would be to move the horses, but two of the mares are in foal, and it's almost their time. I can't risk them losing the foals and possibly dying in the process, too."

"I'm so sorry, Marshall. It can't be easy for you, torn between the needs of Rainbow's End and the work needing to be done at the hydroelectric plant. Mrs. Hopkins said you have to be there, too."

"That's the hard part. If this rain keeps up, the whole valley will flood. Everyone could lose their farms, unless there's a break in the weather. If I can get the extra generator in place in time, we can pump the water away from the valley and direct it down into an area where it doesn't matter."

The floorboards squeaked. He had changed position, was coming closer.

His voice was ragged. "Oh, God, Flynn. I've wanted you for so long, but you've got to understand why it wouldn't work. You once said you wouldn't settle for anything less than total commitment, and love. I can't give you that. I just don't have it in me."

He was close enough to touch now, but neither of them moved closer. The need to reach over and caress his face was sharp and aching inside her.

"I know, and I am deeply sorry for that, Marshall. The least I can do is offer some comfort. Suzy is gone. For good. We met last Tuesday and she said she's going to Europe. I believe her. She will no longer be a threat to you, to Timmy and Rainbow's End. She lied about Damon, they were never together." When he didn't answer, she stared at him, trying to understand the look in his eyes, but his face was still in shadow. "We can't undo what has happened between us, can we?"

His silence spoke volumes. Instead, he brushed the back of his hand lightly under her chin and then drew his fingers lightly over her lips.

She flinched, his touch leaving a trail of fire behind.

Just as she was about to throw caution to the wind and put her arms around him, he pulled back. She longed to snuggle into his chest, to feel the warmth and the security she'd always felt there, but it was too late.

Before she could think of what he was going to do next, he pulled her to her feet and kissed her with bruising force. She struggled in his arms for a moment, startled by the savage intensity of his kiss. And then she began to respond in spite of herself. He released her and bounded down the steps, out into the rain and darkness.

Flynn wept, not holding in her sobs, knowing only the night could hear. She wrapped her arms around her chest, as if to hold her heart together while it was breaking. This was the end. He would never give in. Yet the worst part was he loved her. She knew it with every fiber of her being. What a terrible waste of two lives.

Chapter 30

Marshall and every able-bodied man on the farm worked day and night to protect the bottomland from more flooding. In the entire valley, Rainbow's End was nearest the swollen creek. The sound of its roaring consumed the usual peacefulness. Thelma and her assistants were kept busy preparing hot meals and tea and coffee by the bucket load. Flynn, Mrs. Hopkins, and even Timmy took turns serving the men food and hot drinks in shifts.

Marshall spoke politely to her when they passed—too politely—but he seemed to go out of his way to avoid her. She hoped part of his avoidance was to forestall any discussion of her leaving. She wished she had her violin right now. An ache that wouldn't go away had settled in her chest, and her music might have alleviated some of the pain.

Her curiosity about the diary had her climbing up into the attic again, but she didn't find the missing book. Was this another of her cousin's lies? When she ventured into the library, she saw Timmy sitting there all alone.

The poor kid had been emotionally cut off from his father ever since they returned from St. Clair. She didn't know how to explain what had happened to him. Both she and Mrs. Hopkins told him his father had a lot on his mind.

Flynn knelt to be on eye level with him. "Want to play checkers? You're so smart, bet you've caught up with your homework."

He nodded. "Will Rainbow's End get flooded out?" His forehead crinkled in worry. "If it does, I want to give you something to save."

She pulled him close for a hug. "Your father and the farmhands are working on the north orchard, shoring up the creek banks."

Timmy excused himself and left the room, returning quickly with something in his hands. He handed her a leather-bound book, a sheepish expression on his face. "This was my mum's. She left it behind, so I hid it away. I never peeked inside 'cause it says *private* on the front."

Her heart tripping, she opened Suzy's diary. She barely noticed when Timmy slipped away.

The more she read, the more shocked and appalled she became. Suzy had planned to seduce Damon to get back at Marshall. By taking complete control of Marshall's brother, she was going to convince him to contest the will—to take back Rainbow's End. She didn't want the place, only Marshall's destruction. The admission was all there on paper.

Reading on, Flynn found in one place Suzy wrote:

Damon's a fool. I can have him do my bidding whenever I want and he would always think it was his idea.

In a later entry she wrote:

I must be careful of Damon! Tonight I saw him shoot a man in cold blood. A man who lay meekly in the grass, crying for mercy! If he ever finds out how I plan to use him, he will probably kill me, too.

Flynn very carefully and slowly shut the book, closed her eyes and took a deep, shuddering breath. They were the rantings of a madwoman. Her cousin had to be mentally ill. There was no other explanation for it. No wonder she wanted the diary so badly. Flynn left the room and stashed the diary in her dresser drawer. She couldn't bother Marshall with it now, not with all he was going through.

❦

Flynn awoke to the sound of running in the hallway. She threw on her robe and hurried out to see Thelma and Mrs. Hopkins bringing up armloads of books and smaller furniture to store in the spare bedrooms.

She caught Marshall just as he hurried out of his bedroom, pulling on his jacket.

"What's happening?"

He stopped in his headlong rush and looked deep into her eyes. The moment stretched for what seemed like ages. His voice was quiet and controlled when he finally spoke. "There's trouble with one of the electronic systems at the dam. Seems like I'm the only one left who helped install the equipment. They want me to see if I can repair it. Too much water is escaping."

She put her hand on his sleeve. "Is it dangerous? Do you think the floodwaters could get way up here and come in the house? That seems hard to believe."

"Not likely, but it could happen if the dam cracks under the strain. Hoppy and Thelma are taking some of the books from the lower shelves in the library, just in case. As soon as you're ready, I want you to take Timothy and Mrs. Hopkins and go to the town over by the mountain ridge. It's only an hour's drive from here. I'll have that much less to worry about."

"And the others? Thelma?"

"They all have relatives in the village. I told them to leave before it's too late."

"The horses?"

"The Ralphs will begin loading them up if the water reaches the big eucalyptus trees. The horses in the paddock can find higher ground, but I don't want to take a chance with Sultan and the stable horses."

"What about Rainbow's End?" She touched the walls. She loved the place probably as much as he did.

He shrugged. "If it stays, it stays. There's no reason to lose lives over it. It's just a house, something that can be replaced."

"Oh I know you don't believe that. This place is a part of you. Isn't there anything we can do to help?"

Marshall ran a hand through his hair distractedly. "The way you can help me is to do as you're told and leave." He put his finger to her lips to silence her questions. "There's nothing to be gained by staying here. I don't want to chance something happening to you and the boy at the last minute." He looked as if he wanted to say more, hesitating barely a moment before he pulled her close and whispered, "You both are precious to me. " He turned away to go outdoors.

In spite of her worry, she felt good about Marshall's concern. The hug helped a lot, his words golden.

✧✧✧

Mrs. Hopkins wrung her hands, the long, thin fingers looking pale and bloodless. "We once had a scare years ago, when the boys were small. It was something I never want to live through again. We all thought when Mr. Beckett helped install the new hydroelectric plant it would never happen again."

Usually a pillar of strength in every crisis, the housekeeper seemed undone by the thought of water coming up as high as the house.

Flynn took her hands in hers. They were icy cold. "It won't get this far. I don't see how it can."

"Poor Mr. Beckett." Mrs. Hopkins shuddered. "He poured everything he had into this place."

"It won't happen. The dam will hold."

"You don't know it all. Even if the dam does hold, there are lots of other problems."

Flynn tried to reason with her, but the housekeeper was completely unnerved. "Why don't you take a break and have a cuppa with Thelma? You'll feel a lot better about things when you do."

Without waiting to see if the housekeeper took her advice, she pulled on her *drizabone* and boots and went outside. Marshall had bought her the raincoat for their trip to St. Clair—she kept trying to keep images of their lovemaking out of her mind. It seemed another lifetime ago. The rain had let up a bit again, but it was still gloomy and the sky held the threat of more rain.

She walked down to the stables, slipping and sliding on the slick stepping stones. The Land Rover was missing. Marshall must have taken it up to the hydroelectric plant.

The two Ralphs stood just outside the stable door. They broke off their conversation as she walked up to them, looking like guilty children caught telling a naughty story.

"Morning. I bet you two were discussing the flood situation."

Both men grinned with sheepish expressions. Ralph Sr. spoke first. "Yep. His Nibs said for us not to worry about anything. We was just thinking how soon we should be moving the horses. He left it up to us."

Flynn heard the whinnies and restive stomping of the

horses in their stalls. The animals must sense something, but what it was she couldn't be entirely sure. It was either the danger of the floodwaters or the fear in the humans— or both. "The flood is that close?"

Ralph Jr. shook his head. "Nope. At least me old man doesn't think so. Doesn't hurt to be prepared, though."

"Isn't there anything we can do beyond moving the animals? Marshall said it could be dangerous for the mares."

The men exchanged looks. She sensed they were hiding something.

"What is it? There's something you're not telling me."

Ralph Sr. cleared his throat. He gave a sidelong glance at his son and sighed.

"The Boss said we weren't to do anything but move the horses. After that, me and me boy are to go home. He said you and young Timothy and Mrs. Hopkins would be leaving, too."

She narrowed her eyes and kept her voice coolly assured. "Suppose I told you I was going to march right back into the house, pack up Timmy and Hoppy and send them on their way. After that, I'll come back here and park myself at these stables until you level with me." It was a bluff, one she didn't want to be called on. She had to know what was really going on.

The men looked at her with puzzled, troubled expressions and then Ralph Jr. grinned. "What the heck. Might as well tell her, Dad. You said it probably wouldn't work anyways."

His father shrugged. "I tried to tell the Boss before he left, but he was in too big a hurry to get to the dam. He ordered us to leave, but I got my notions."

His shy hesitation was endearing as well as frustrating. Flynn waited patiently for him to get to the point.

"If we had some sandbags and enough men, we could shore up the creek in the paddock just over there." He jerked his thumb in the general direction. "That's the weakest link. We could divert the flow to run off into the gorge." He took a deep breath, clearly not used to talking so much.

"It would just run its course without harm that way," Ralph Jr. finished. "It's the only way to save the house and stables."

"How many men do we have?"

The Ralphs looked at each other and back at her. "Besides us, there's a handful willing to stay. Some have already gone home to take care of their own families. The Boss gave everyone who wanted it leave to go."

"Can you take the horses out and then come back to try to save the house and stables?" She knew the answer before she even asked the question. They would have done it already if the danger wasn't so imminent.

How furious would Marshall be if his orders were disobeyed? What if the Ralphs were wrong and it was too late for sandbags? He could lose his horses. If she countermanded his orders and they lost the horses—worse still, lives—he would probably believe she'd done it on purpose to get back at him.

But if they didn't do anything, he could lose Rainbow's End. She looked toward the house and thought of the gardens and the huge old trees surrounding it. Irreplaceable. The house was a living, breathing entity to him, to all of them, not a mere inanimate possession like he proclaimed it to be. And with the costs involved in repairs to the property itself—drainage, new fencing, new buildings—he would go bankrupt.

Decision made, she grasped Ralph Sr.'s arm. "I'm going back to the house to send Timmy and Hoppy away.

Meanwhile, you round up all the help you can get. Do you know where we can find gravel or sand?"

Both Ralphs looked indecisive for only a moment and then their eyes lit with enthusiasm. "There's a big pile the Boss stashed down below the stables to repair the smokehouse. We can make use of that."

"Good. I'll bring some sheets and pillow cases, and anything else I can find to make sandbags. You look around for canvas and burlap. I'll meet you at the sand pile." All she had to do now was make Hoppy understand.

Am I doing the right thing? Could this cost Marshall all he held dear? She stepped up on the porch.

Hearing Thelma speaking with Mrs. Hopkins brought her out of her distressing thoughts. They had to get going. She called out to Mrs. Hopkins. "The rain has started again. You and Timmy should go. Thelma too. I'm staying a little while longer so I can move more things upstairs. There's an extra truck I can hitch a ride with when I need to leave."

The housekeeper's ramrod-straight back indicated her disapproval. "I'm not going without you. Mr. Beckett said we all were to go together. I'll not leave you behind." She crossed her arms over her chest, her mouth a thin line. Weeks ago that stance might have intimidated Flynn, but not anymore.

"I'm staying here, too." Timmy stood in the doorway. He'd obviously been listening.

"See what happens when you are stubborn?"

"Me? Stubborn?" Mrs. Hopkins sniffed. "An' I thought we had become friends. Am I just a serf you can order about now?" The hurt in her voice was so real Flynn didn't know how to go on.

"Hoppy, you don't truly believe that. You're not only a friend, you're family. But anyone can see you're nearly at your wits' end with the thought of a flood. And what about the boy?"

"Why can't you come with us? An' don't give me that garbage about moving stuff upstairs. I wasn't born yesterday, y'know. Tell me what you've got planned first, and then I'll decide what's best for Timmy and me."

It had sounded foolproof at the time she countermanded Marshall's orders and gave new ones to the Ralphs, but when she relayed the proposal to the housekeeper in the relative calm of the house, doubts began to surface.

"You don't have enough help for all that work! Most of the hands have gone home to their families. It's up to God now."

Flynn shook her head, her mouth tightening with determination. "Maybe. But you, of all people, know what Marshall stands to lose if the floodwaters sweep across Rainbow's End. It's more than just a place—you and I both know that. It will never be the same for him again if that happens."

"Maybe so. But the property can be replaced and you can't be. Don't you know what it would mean to him if something happened to you?"

The scent of lavender, a smell she would always remember, washed over Flynn as the older woman hugged her tightly.

"I must do this for him." Flynn looked around for Timmy, but he'd disappeared. "You know I have to leave soon. I have to try to make amends before I go. To be honest, I really don't know if this plan will work, but the Ralphs think it will. I trust their judgment."

"Have you thought of the consequences if the hands put all their effort into the sandbags and it doesn't work? It will be too late to move the horses by then."

She had thought of that. Her mouth felt parched and

dry. "He will think I did it on purpose, to ruin him." The look in Mrs. Hopkins' eyes said it all, a wordless affirmation of her belief.

"If we don't take the chance, all of this will become a muddy wasteland. The orchards and the paddocks where he feeds his precious horses will be ruined. What about the new variety of apple trees he just planted?"

Mrs. Hopkins took Flynn's hands in her rough, worn ones and turned up her palms. "An' what of these? How will you protect your hands? Think of your music." When Flynn didn't answer, Mrs. Hopkins sighed with resignation. "Take care, child. We all love you."

Flynn turned away from Mrs. Hopkins, letting her leave the room without more between them. Timmy came in to tell her goodbye and when she knelt, he went willingly into her arms for a big hug.

"You'll be back here in no time, Timmy. Just be a good boy and mind Hoppy." She helped them bring their things out to the waiting car and then went back inside to watch Thelma join them as they left. The rain had started up again. She couldn't tell if it was her tears or rain on the windowpane that blurred her vision when Timmy waved goodbye.

Before they had disappeared down the driveway, she went into the kitchen. The big room was empty and cold now, without Thelma bustling around. Every move she made seemed to echo against the shiny, hanging, copper cookware.

She opened the double-door refrigerator and took out a pot of thick stew Thelma had made just before she left, knowing the men still worked in the stables. There were also a half dozen deep-dish apple pies. "Thank you for your thoughtfulness," she said out loud to break the heavy silence.

Turning on two burners, she put on water for coffee

and the stew to warm. If the men had to work in the mud and rain, the least she could do was keep their bodies warm on the inside. While the stew warmed, she rushed around, gathering up sheets. pillow cases, large table-cloths, any material in the linen closets and spare bed-rooms she could find, piling them high on the kitchen table.

Flynn put on her raincoat and pulled on her boots. Taking one last look around, she shut off the stove. The food would keep warm for quite a while.

Armed with all the sheets she could carry and a big ball of heavy twine, she stood on the porch for a moment, watching the rain pelt down from the dark, gray sky. If things turned out badly and Marshall lost everything, she wouldn't even be able to comfort him. Either way, she'd be leaving Rainbow's End when all of this was over.

Without any more hesitation, she squared her shoulders and walked out into the downpour.

Chapter 31

Flynn hurried toward the stables with her armload of sheets and pillowcases. When she saw the motley group huddled under the shelter of the roof overhang, her heart sank into her boots. A more bedraggled bunch she'd never seen in her life. There were only five additional men besides the two Ralphs. She tried to hide her dismay as she welcomed them.

"There's plenty more material on the kitchen table when we need it." She kept her voice as cheerful as she could. "That's a wonderful start." She pointed to the bales of canvas the men had dragged up.

They all walked down to the paddock, their feet churning the rain-flattened grass. The rain had slacked off again temporarily, but flashes of lightning still slashed the sky above their heads and the rumble of thunder jarred the queasy ground beneath their feet.

As they neared the bank of the creek, the noise of roaring water filled her ears. For the first time since agreeing with the Ralphs, the challenge of saving Rainbow's End seemed insurmountable. Her spirits flagged at what lay ahead of them, but there was no going back now.

She had made the decision, and these men were here

to help. They had passed the point of no return. They had no choice. They had to do it.

When it started again, the rain sluiced down even harder than before. They bent their backs against the downpour and kept working on the sandbags. She stopped and thought about her hands several times, worrying about the possible damage to them. She'd discarded her awkwardly oversized gloves a while ago. It was impossible, with them on, for her to wind the heavy twine around the filled pillow cases and pull up the corners of the sheets when the men shoveled them full of sand. She looked mournfully at her cracked nails and the redness of the skin, all blistered and bleeding, thankful that most of her felt numb and chilled.

Clueless as to how much time had passed, when Ralph Sr. walked over to where she was making the loops around the bags, he reminded her of the passing hours. His back shielded her from the hard drops slanting down into her face.

"Looks to me you could use a break. I know the boys could. Suppose there's a chance of finding a hot toddy somewhere?" His rainwear was splashed with mud and his face grimy.

Straightening her back and stretching felt good. "You bet. Can you spare Ralph Jr. so he can help me bring it down? I've got some stew warming in the kitchen. Tell the men we can take a break over there." She pointed to the old shearing shed with a large overhanging roof and crude tables.

"You're a bit of orright for a Yank. Go on, boy. You heard her."

Flynn and Ralph Jr. loaded up bowls, spoons, cups—everything they could think of—in the large picnic hamper. She found Marshall's liquor cabinet and they piled bottles of whiskey and rum in another hamper, along with the coffee. Looking down at the muddy footprints they left behind, she could picture Thelma and Hoppy having fits over the mess. She managed a grin at the thought.

Several men rushed to help as they staggered down the path with their load. Flynn set up her kitchen while the rain, like a temperamental child, slacked off again. The men gathered around and helped themselves to the steaming stew, tearing off chunks of the bread Thelma had left behind. She noticed the men carefully pouring measured shots of the liquor into their coffee. It was a good idea of Ralph Sr.'s. The warmth of the coffee mugs would prevent their fingers from cramping in the cold, while the alcohol mixed with the brew would keep their insides warm for that little bit longer.

"We've got apple pie, too, but we couldn't bring it down with this load."

"Be fine for celebrating when we finish the job, miss," one man piped up around the piece of bread in his mouth.

She watched with satisfaction as they mopped up the remaining liquid in the bottoms of their bowls with the crusty bread.

"Beaut of a tucker, miss. Mind if we have a smoke?"

It was clear they didn't quite know how to address her. She touched the man on the shoulder. "Please. Call me Flynn. What fine, loyal men you are to do this for us. Marshall will be so proud of what you've accomplished."

"Can't brag yet, miss. There's still plenty of hard yakka waiting to be done." Ralph Sr. sat near his son. She thought they had to be worried about their family, if they lived in the valley. When they finished smoking, she walked back to the edge of the creek with them. They had made some progress where the lowest point was flooding. So far, that was the only break in the bank, but nearby spots looked suspiciously ready to go, as well.

By now the creek was a river, roaring so loudly it was difficult to concentrate on anything but the task at hand. They had to shout to be heard, so they subsided into silence, backs bent, shoveling sand into the makeshift bags and piling them up against each other.

The bags were leaky and crude, but the embankment steadily grew to the point where the water barely splashed over the top. The next problem, according to Ralph, was to try to turn the flow of water toward the canyon below.

Her body cold, wet, and tired beyond belief, she nevertheless forced herself to bend, tie ropes, and help drag the smaller bundles forward. Her legs hardly did her bidding anymore.

She felt a presence behind her and whirled around to face Damon. Behind him stood five new men.

"Hoppy dropped in on their way out and told me you and some men were working to save the farm. I want to help."

A big lump came into her throat as she looked up into his earnest, strong face. "What—what about your own place?"

"It's up the valley, no creek nearby. It'll be fine. What can I do to help?"

She nodded. "Ask Ralph Sr. He's in charge of the men. They seem to be making headway."

He smoothed the strand of hair plastered to her cheek with his thumb. "Marshall sure picked a winner this time."

"If you only knew the half of it," she whispered to his back as he went to speak with Ralph Sr., his men following close.

❧❦❧

When they had done everything possible to stop the

flood and turn the tide, they all stopped to watch, gathered in a close group, waiting. Would it hold? The men smoked and poured some liquor into their cups, squatting down on their heels in the mud.

She would never forget the sight of their strong faces—eyes squinting against the smoke from their cigarettes and pipes, the rain making patterns with the mud on their coats.

Just then the steady sound of water altered and the roar grew louder. The men exchanged looks. Ralph glanced back at the stables, as if judging how much time they would have to dash upward to safety.

They watched the river charging down toward them with the rushing waves slapping wildly at the piled bags.

"Holy shit! They must have let some more water out of the dam." For a long time they just stared, riveted to the spot but ready to dash for higher ground if the waves broke through the barricade.

The sandbags held. The roaring sluice of water swerved past the bags and rushed down toward the lowlands, to drop harmlessly over the cliff and into the gorge below.

The men did crazy jigs, yelling and pummeling each other on the back with excited frenzy, unmindful of the still-pouring rain and the mud they sloshed about in.

It was only then Flynn realized how tired she was. She sagged against the remaining bags, her legs could hardly hold her. Damon put his arm around her shoulder for support. She didn't care anymore.

"Damon? Have you ever killed a man?"

His face showed honest shock and then puzzlement. "What?"

"Suzy left a diary behind. In it she said she saw you shoot a man in cold blood while he was lying on the ground, begging for mercy."

"'Struth, that was her? I had to shoot a wounded sheep that some stray dogs had caught alone in the field. I heard someone running through the bush, after I put a bullet in the poor creature's head. I always thought it was Timmy running away, but I didn't ask him, just in case it wasn't."

One by one, the men slowly wandered away from the spectacle of the water to where she and Damon stood. Damon dropped his arm from her shoulder when they approached, and she immediately felt relieved

"You are heroes, each and every last one of you." She hugged each man in turn. "Do you want to celebrate with some of Thelma's apple pies, or are you too tired?"

Ralph Sr. looked around at the men and then grinned. "Thanks, miss, but we'd better get home to our families. I know they're worried about us. We'll give Mr. Damon's crew a ride home on our way."

"I'm sure Marshall has the hydroelectric equipment in control and none of your homes will be in danger any more, no matter how long this rain lasts."

The men grinned, their demeanor showing how proud they were of their gamble.

"I just want to sit here a moment, get my legs working again." It was obvious by the concerned look on their faces that they didn't want to leave her, but with the gentle urging of Damon, they slowly left.

After they'd gone, she felt awkward with Damon there. There were so many questions she wanted to ask, and yet she didn't want to know the answers. "Damon, there's something else Suzy said in her diary. You don't have to tell me if you don't want to. She said you were lovers and were planning to get Rainbow's End away from Marshall."

The look of astonishment on his face couldn't have been feigned. "Jeezus! Never! Suzy came over several times with some cock-and-bull story about Marshall abusing her. My brother and I don't always see things eye to eye, but I know he treated her like a bloody queen. In the end, I told her to leave me alone. I never as much as laid a hand on her."

Pitiful, demented Suzy. Flynn felt at once relieved and saddened.

The sound of a motor and a car door slamming penetrated her weary mind. Flynn and Damon faced Marshall running down the path toward them.

She looked into his anxious face and before she could utter a word, he lifted her off her feet in a bear hug.

"The men stopped me on the road. They told me what happened, how you made the decision to stay here and fight." He kissed her and then looked at Damon. "Thank you for coming to help." Marshall held out his hand and Damon brushed it aside to pull him into a bear hug.

Tears filled her eyes as she watched the brothers together. Timmy would have his uncle back at last.

When the men stepped apart, each looking embarrassed by their actions, Damon said, "I'm gonna bail. I can see you two have things to talk about." He raised a dark eyebrow in a devilish look of mischief. He tipped his hat to Flynn. "You got a keeper there—make sure you know what to do with her."

When they heard his wheels spin through the mud, Marshall put his arm around her. The rain had started again, and they ran to the gazebo.

Chapter 32

They sat on the cushions, his strong hand on her shoulder pulling her close.

"Bloody nong! I should never have left you here. You might have been washed away." He nuzzled aside the hair that had come loose from her braid. The sound of his deep voice rumbled soothingly in her ears as she lay snuggled against his chest. He held her tight and she wished with all her heart she could stay forever in his arms.

They waited, cuddled together, until the rain slackened again and then, despite her protests, he carried her up the path to the house. Inside, it felt warmer than out, but it didn't take long to realize the heating system had been shut down.

Upstairs, he pushed open the door to his bedroom and deposited her on a large, overstuffed chair by the fireplace. "Stay." He held his palm toward her in a commanding gesture and then knelt to start a roaring fire. He returned to her side and began unbuttoning her blouse, his warm hands touching her skin as he removed her clothing.

She leaned forward to kiss the tip of his nose. "Silly. I can do that."

"No you can't. Is it me or does it seem like I've been spending half my time removing your clothes and drying you off lately?"

She touched his face with her hands in a lingering caress.

After he undressed her, taking his time to explore places on her body that made her breath come in ragged gasps, he pulled out one of his T-shirts from a dresser and slipped it over her head. It came almost down to her knees and hung loosely off her shoulders.

Marshall indulged in a brief chuckle, then held her hands in his and turned her palms upward, despite her struggles to prevent it.

"Darlin' girl! What have you done to your hands?" He brought them to his lips and kissed her fingertips and palms tenderly.

"It's not so bad. Just a few scratches." By now the cold had left, along with the numbness, and she felt each abrasion, bruise and blister. Some fingers were cut deep from pulling on the twine.

"I know how you've always made a point of protecting them, even before I understood why." He brought her hands to his face and held them there in a protective gesture. "Stay put. I'm gonna get some bandages from the bathroom and fix your hands. Then we're going to bed and warm up and stay there all day."

When he returned to her side, he carefully slathered on some soothing emollient. When he finished bandaging her hands, he washed her face with a warm washcloth and put a towel around her head to dry her hair. He lifted her from the chair, cradled snugly in his arms, and deposited her gently into the king-sized bed. The fire had warmed the room comfortably by now, and she almost didn't need the covers. He stood near the bed, raising his hands to pull his shirt over this head. While he was occupied, she reached and ran her hand down the hard erection his trousers hid.

"Cheeky sheila, when did you learn to do that?" He laughed and finishing sliding out of his clothes. He snuggled down against her, pulling her close and the covers up over them.

"You took such a chance, sweetheart. We could have lost everything. The men told me what a trooper you've been, working alongside them." Marshall spoke quietly with his cheek against hers, his warm breath smooth against her skin. His strong arms held her against his body.

The tiredness left her, replaced by wave after wave of desire surging up and down her body where skin touched skin. The need for him was like a heat in her belly that threatened to explode. She cuddled closer, moving against him. Butterfly kisses fluttered lightly over her eyelids, lingering gently on her face, his breath warm in her ear. She pushed a leg brazenly between his, causing him to groan. When she thought she could not bear another moment of his gentle teasing, his mouth descended upon hers in a slow, careful kiss.

Boldly she reached with her bandaged hand and touched his flat stomach, reaching further downward until she felt his arousal. He tensed, a moan escaping his lips.

"I wanted you to rest." His voice was a broken huskiness.

"We will. Later."

"You little vixen. You learn fast, don't you?" He threw the covers off and pushed up the T-shirt until it bared all of her body.

"I love you so much." He leaned on his elbows and held her face between his hands, looking long and steadily into her eyes. "Do you have any idea how much I love you? How much I need you?"

Tears coursed down her cheeks. How she had waited to hear those words.

"I love you, too, Marshall. All my life I've waited for you."

"I know, and I treasure that."

He began to make love to her with tender restraint, and she responded to his lovemaking with every ounce of emotion in her.

The rain pelted against the windows as their loving turned from gentleness to a fierce, all-consuming passion that left them both shaken and speechless.

When the explosions came and she felt his warm seed burst into her womb, Marshall kissed her soft, moist lips and held her tight in his arms, murmuring love words in her ear. She lay, sleepy and warm, snuggled close to the hard length of his body. Reaching up her arms, she twined her hands around his neck, and brought his head down to meet hers as they kissed again and again, unable to get enough of each other.

He pulled her arms away and gently turned her body around so her back was toward him, nestling her close, he pulled his legs up to hold her buttocks and they lay together like spoons. He held her lightly, his chin resting on the top of her head.

"When it dries up a bit, we'll have a proper wedding, love. By the gazebo, with the Ralphs and the hands, Thelma and Hoppy. Damon can be my best man. Howzat sound?"

"Beautiful, darling. Just perfect."

"Try to sleep, my sweet girl. You've had quite a day."

He had barely finished speaking before she dropped into a deep slumber.

Some hours later, when they awoke, he nibbled the back of her neck, sending shivers of delight up and down her spine. She struggled to turn and face him, but he wouldn't permit it.

He held her wrists in one hand while the other roamed where it would, with a gentle persuasion that made the blood sing in her veins. Just when she thought she could stand it no longer, he released his hold and turned her over onto her back, leaning above her and looking down.

"My sweet Flynn. I always thought you so beautiful, even when you turned up at my doorstep all raggle-taggle." He tweaked her nose playfully.

The bandages had come off while she slept, and she was thankful her hands didn't hurt as much as before. She moved her fingers through the thick hair at the nape of his neck. "I thought you hated me." Even as she made the statement, she wondered if it was the wrong time to bring up a touchy subject.

"Hated you? Good grief, I never could have hated you. Sure, I was disappointed to learn you made up all those things about your past, but hate you? Actually, I acted like an arse. I could have lost you with my misplaced pride." When he kissed her, her body awoke like a flower unfurling for the first time. She relished the new hunger that had lain dormant so long inside her, waiting for the right man.

"I had this nagging sensation you needed me, so I left the hydroelectric plant early. I nearly tore apart the village looking for you, until I finally found Hoppy and Timmy. When they told me you had insisted on staying behind, and what you were trying to do with just a handful of men to help you, I nearly went berko." He nuzzled her neck and blew gently in her ear.

"I could have lost all your precious horses."

"To hell with the bloody horses. It was you I wanted safe. I'd already decided I didn't care what you'd done, or how much you'd lied to me. I know you felt you had no choice at the time."

"I did feel that way."

"All I could think of was how much I wanted us to be together, and that you were leaving us." He caught her bottom lip between his teeth and nibbled gently.

"It." Kiss. "All." Kiss. "Turned." Kiss. "Out." Kiss. "Fine." Kiss.

"Thanks to you, love. You risked your life for Rainbow's End, all the while thinking I hated you. Not only that, you may have truly risked your career." He lifted her hands and kissed each finger tenderly, gently pressing her blistered palms to his lips. "I figured, when I found out you'd spun me all those porkies, it was just another Suzy episode in my life. I couldn't stand the thought of that. Not when I loved you from the moment I saw you."

"You sure could have fooled me, you big, overgrown—" His mouth covered hers in playful anger and she clung to him. Someday she would show him the diary, but not before all their wounds had healed and they were a strong family.

"What about your violin? What will you do if your hands don't mend properly? Will you have to leave to play? You can't just walk away from it, can you? We could work something out."

She was touched by his concern.

"Perhaps Timmy's brothers and sisters will want me to teach them to play. That will be enough for me." She knew she spoke the truth.

She kissed the back of his hand and turned it over, kissing the hard calluses on his palm.

"But your life centered around your music."

With a smile she put a finger on his mouth to hush him. "I know. But what I didn't know was that my music filled a void." She brushed a stray lock from his forehead.

"I love you more than life itself, Marshall Beckett. Right now, there's only room for you and Timmy and Rainbow's End in my life."

Marshall ran his hands over her belly. "An' more little Becketts, I hope." He rolled onto his back and put his hands under his head, looking up at the ceiling. "I can see it all now. We'll have kids galore running riot around here, with Timmy the big brother. Can't you see the grandchildren and great-grandchildren all playing about Rainbow's End? At just about that point, we'll let Timmy be the head of the family while we take off for our second honeymoon."

She laughed. "You big ninny! We've not even had a first honeymoon, and here you are going on about our second." She grabbed up a pillow and began pummeling him with it.

Before she could leap off the bed to safety, he reached out with lightning speed and caught her ankle, pulling her to him. He rolled over and pressed her shoulders down. She felt the thud of his heart against her breast.

His lips feathered her face, and when their mouths joined together, she melted away in a blazing spiral of silken warmth.

They made love again, this time slowly and with passionate care, knowing that from this day forward they would have all the time in the world.

About the Author

Born in Phoenix, Arizona, Pinkie Paranya traveled all over the U.S., Alaska, and most of Mexico with her late husband. Ever since she can remember, writing has been her passion. After completing her fifteenth novel, trying to discover the genre she loved most, she still hasn't decided.

Paranya enjoys romances with their intrigue and uplifting happy endings, but she has also published two paranormal psychological suspenses, a cozy mystery, and an Early American Alaskan trilogy.